SILVER MOON

GREAT NOVELS
OF
EROTIC DOMINATION
AND
SUBMISSION

NEW TITLES EVERY MONTH

www.smbooks.co.uk

TO FIND OUT MORE ABOUT OUR READERS' CLUB WRITE
TO;

SILVER MOON READER SERVICES;
Barrington Hall Publishing
Hexgreave Hall
Farnsfield
Nottinghamshire NG22 8LS
Tel; 01157 141616

YOU WILL RECEIVE A FREE MAGAZINE OF EXTRACTS
FROM OUR EXTENSIVE RANGE OF EROTIC FICTION
ABSOLUTELY FREE. YOU WILL ALSO HAVE THE
CHANCE TO PURCHASE BOOKS WHICH ARE
EXCLUSIVE TO OUR READERS' CLUB

***

NEW AUTHORS ARE WELCOME

Please send submissions to;
Barrington Hall Publishing
Hexgreave Hall
Farnsfield N22 8LS

All characters and events depicted are entirely fictitious; any resemblance to anyone living or dead is entirely coincidental

Story based on an original
idea by Master M, with thanks

DUTY BOUND

by

Francine Whittaker

PROLOGUE, AFRICAN REPUBLIC OF BLAWANYA

Hidden away in a desolate part of the country where tourists and foreign dignitaries were nothing more than rumours, an old truck, jam packed with a new shipment of slaves destined for the mine, threw up a thick dust cloud as it rattled past the whitewashed, adobe bungalow. Somewhere close by, a scavenging dog yapped as someone kicked it away from the rubbish dump. And a black girl screamed as the single tail of a guard's whip wrapped around her ankles and brought her down, bringing an abrupt end to her long, barefoot journey and valiant bid for freedom as she sobbed into the dirt.

Inside the low building, the mosquito screens and the lack of air outside combined to produce the oppressive heat of the bare, cement-floored room. The overhead fan turned ineffectually. The young black slave that Dr. Adair Dowling treated as his own kept the room tidy and it was as clean as the dusty conditions allowed. More basic than the other rooms of his fine living quarters, it was the one he preferred to do business in and was similar in size to rooms the poorly paid male mine workers themselves shared, usually nine or ten men to a room in which they had to wash and sleep. But women at the mine had an even worse deal.

In accordance with the Republic's doctrine that declared all women inferior to even the poorest, most lowly of men, the females at the Thomassentown mine were slaves rather than paid workers and owed their existence entirely to the mine owner's generosity to his male workforce in providing on-site and unpaid whores. But with an eye to getting good value from them, once they were considered too old to be desirable, the owner put them to good use in the mine's shanty town as serving women in the bars and cheap eating houses. Treated with less compassion than the scavenging dogs, the slaves were all housed together in a series of cages.

For Blawanya was a major producer of quality diamonds, those of the best quality coming from the Thomassentown mine. The preferred excavation method employed at the mine produced deep and dangerous underground tunnels. In addition, the site also included high security areas where the ore was refined.

There was also a highly profitable – and as yet undetected – smuggling operation.

At first, the two Englishmen who were obliged to do business together, ignored the pretty girl with the close-cropped hair and aubergine-coloured skin as if she were nothing more than a shadow as she entered the room. Wearing the brown collar that marked her out as the property of the mine rather than an individual, she carried a wooden tray on which were placed two iced glasses of beer, the only drink that could satisfy a man's thirst in the exhausting heat. Going directly to the doctor, she bent toward him and proffered the tray.

As always at the regular meetings between the two men, Adair Dowling was seated with his back to the light putting his companion, seated on a similar couch opposite, at a disadvantage, having to squint to look at him. It was an odd relationship between them because although they were not friends, their dependence upon each was clearly evident to both. For it was the pilot's regular flights in the old aeroplane that brought in the medicines and bandages for Dr. Dowling's clinic. But both men knew even greater importance was attached to the illicit cargo that Roy, the blond haired pilot took with him on his return flights, for the world had an insatiable appetite for diamonds.

The world also had an insatiable appetite for cruelty. Adair Dowling was no exception. Before taking the glass from the girl's tray he slipped his hand inside the baggy neckline of her coarse, thin shift and sought out the little screw on the top of the square, medical grade stainless steel, vice-shaped clamp that already held her nipple captive. He tightened it further, forcing the upper bar down harder against the trapped morsel and listening for her sharp intake of breath. Her pain duly registered, he did the same to the other nipple. He smiled as she once again gasped in pain, then still without speaking to her, withdrew his hand and helped himself to one of the glasses.

The slave's big, dark brown eyes widened. Knowing better than to serve her Master's guest without a direct order to do so, she stood awaiting instructions, the darkness of her skin emphasised by the off-white shade of her shift. Officially known by the number tattooed on her upper arm and stencilled onto her brown leather collar, with cruel humour Dowling had named her Freedom, which was clearly designed to emphasise her lack of free will. If she ever had a name of her own, Dowling had never known it and assumed it was probably long forgotten.

Adair glanced across at Roy, a slightly younger man than himself. "You have the stones?"

Roy screwed up his eyes in an attempt to see more clearly. "Safely stowed on the plane and ready for the off first thing in the morning." Laughing, he patted the breast pocket of his thin polo shirt and continued. "Plus my commission!"

Adair was clearly infuriated at the man's lax attitude and poor observance of the security guidelines. His features grew darker as he tried to contain his anger. As usual when displeased, he took it out on Freedom. Addressing her for the first time, he commanded, "Stop snivelling, bitch!"

She dropped her gaze to the tray before her and with a quivering lip she quietened. Nothing but fear of reprisal and obedience to the man who fed, sheltered and abused her, deterred her from loosening the screws. And that was something he cold-heartedly exploited.

"Shut up, or I'll tighten them even more!" Raising his glass of ice cold beer to his lips, he used his free hand to slap the mutely subservient, black girl's tight little arse and send her on her way.

As he watched her pad barefoot across the uncovered cement floor, he could not help smiling at the memory of the fresh, angry welts across her shoulders, partly obscured by the loose-weave of her simple shift. But clearly visible stripes adorning the backs of her thighs were a joy to behold and, swallowing the welcome liquid, he kept his gaze riveted to his own handiwork. As she bent and offered the remaining glass to his guest, he wrinkled his high, sun-tanned forehead. His tone was brusque as he demanded angrily, "You've left them unattended? Suppose someone finds them? What if the guards search the plane?"

"They won't!" Roy answered equally brusquely, adding, "They never do. As an Aid worker, I'm considered trustworthy."

Freedom offered Roy a tempting view down her baggy-necked shift as she leaned forward to serve his drink. Taking it as an invitation to sample her pendulous, dark skinned breasts, he made a grab for them with one hand while reaching for the beer with his other one. Holding his cold glass to his face to cool himself, the fingers of his other hand squeezed her soft, pliable and clamped breast as it dangled invitingly before him.

From England's Home Counties, Roy could have passed as almost anything from a builder to a London cabby or used car salesman, though his passport identified him as an aid worker for NBAF, a small but internationally respected organisation based in the Netherlands. The same charity also provided the clothing, footwear and blankets that were delivered to the mine less frequently on an old truck. But although the Europeans who donated the aid believed it was being used in the poorest regions of Blawanya to treat the sick, like the goods on the trucks most of the medicines Roy flew in for Dr Dowling's clinic were sold on the black market, leaving only the most basic medical supplies for a place where most ailments were caused either by accidents or over-work in the mine. Or from excessive discipline sessions for the slaves. The soothing ointments were a blessing after fifty lashes!

Having received no commands to the contrary, she did not pull away or straighten up but stood patiently as she had been trained to do and allowed Roy to pleasure himself. Still holding the tray's wooden handle with one hand, as she crossed her wrists behind her back to minimise obstruction, she rested it against the back of her legs.

"By all means tighten the screws," Adair offered generously.

"Okay, thanks." As his host had done before him Roy tightened them, first one then the other, pausing to listen for her pained gasp. "Neat little contraptions," he said, admiring the square clamps whose horizontal bars squeezed her nipples almost flat. Then turning his gaze back to his host, silhouetted against the brightness of an African afternoon, as he mauled the girl roughly he addressed Adair's concerns at last. "Relax, Doc. If anyone was going to find the diamonds and discover our real business here, they'd have done so by now." Taking a long slug of imported beer, he squeezed her breast as though trying to liquidise a juicy plum. Holding his beer and squeezing her breast at the same time he angled his head until his mouth was level with its pendulous fullness. Then, moving his hand to cup the clamp with its tortured morsel of flesh in his palm, simultaneously he pressed it back into her breast while closing his teeth on its sweet upper swell.

She had to stifle her gasp of pain-loaded shock in case her master misconstrued it as a protest. But she could not help dropping her tray, and flinched as the wood clattered onto the floor, aware of her Master's displeasure at her clumsiness.

The doctor's rebuke was swift, his tone dripping with scorn. "By God you've earned a lashing this time, you stupid bitch! It's a session on the post in the garden for you!"

CHAPTER ONE

THE KENT COAST, ENGLAND

Before she even saw him, Rusty felt his presence the way you can often register the arrival of charismatic men. Or a dark sense of foreboding warns of some momentous event that will shape your life. So it was with Rusty the day she first met the urbane Charles Hilton.

She was standing beside one of the Cessnas, outside the hangar at the Saxon Hill Airfield, with her back toward the tall stranger when she felt his approach. Despite the prickles of discomfort she felt with his eyes upon her, she resisted the temptation to look over her shoulder as, with a clipboard in her hand, she signed the paperwork concerning the progress of one of the flying school's pupils.

Even from the back and despite the oil-spattered khaki dungarees she was wearing, her impressively feminine curves made it impossible to mistake her for one of the airfield's men. In addition, her long, fiery red hair was barely contained by the baseball cap under which she had piled it and wispy strands fluttered in the breeze.

There was a knot in her stomach as he drew level with her.

He did not turn to look at her as he walked past on his way inside the hangar. His shocking words were directed at her nevertheless and the raw lust in his tone snagged at some primeval longing inside her.

"I'll make a real woman of you. I'll unlock the eroticism inside you that you never knew existed."

While her youthful features still made her look like jail bait, at twenty-four Rusty was very much a woman, with an impressively long list of lovers behind her that proved she was no innocent. She didn't need help from the likes of him, thank you very much! she told herself as, seething, she fought to hold her tongue. The school could ill afford to offend a prospective pupil and so she held her temper under control and made none of her usual cutting remarks. Instead she glared at his impeccably-suited back as he made for the cubby-hole in the corner of the hangar that they used for an office, where Rusty's brother and the other two owners were gathered for a meeting.

Not wanting to appear too interested in the stranger, she slipped her pen in her top pocket and tidied her hair before she ambled inside. Still aiming for an unconcerned attitude, she stopped beside the mechanic they called Gibbo, who was working on one of the planes the Saxon Hill Aerobatics Team used for their displays.

"Who was that?" she asked casually.

Pausing in his work, Gibbo's eyes took in her natural sexiness as he used an oily hand to smooth his black, razor-cut hair. "He's some big bod from Charisma ......a director or something."

"And apparently he's loaded!" one of the other men said as he made his way past them and toward an old biplane on the other side of the cavernous hangar.

Instantly recognising the name of the cosmetics company, she did not know the name of its successful managing director, and tried for a bored tone as she probed Gibbo. "What's a man like him doing here? Does he want flying lessons?"

"I'm surprised your brother didn't mention it, Rust. He's come to discuss a sponsorship deal."

"For the aerobatics team or the wingwalkers?" Being a member of both teams that performed regularly during the summer months at airshows from the south coast to the Midlands, she knew just how important a deal could be.

"Both, I think. You'd better go and talk to your brother and the other guys afterwards."

It was not until he was leaving that she saw the Charisma man again. She was standing outside again, looking at her watch and wondering at three thirty what had happened to her two thirty pupil, when the man came walking toward her as he left the hangar. She looked up when he stopped alongside her, and immediately tagged him as being in his early forties. The intense look in his eyes coupled with the command in his husky voice took her breath away.

"My card," he announced, taking the liberty of popping it inside the open neck of her dungarees where it lodged snugly beside a soft, generous breast in her bra. With a sneer twisting his handsome, moisturiser-and-cologne-treated features, and looking at her with eyes that were the same shade as sticky toffee, he named a pub about two miles further inland. "I have business in the area this afternoon. I'll wait until six thirty at The Will-o'-the-wisp. Be there!"

Without another word he walked away. She opened her mouth to deliver the lippy retort that sprang to mind, but speech evaded her. She swivelled round just as he disappeared around the corner of the hangar. Following quickly, she watched him stride through the car park toward a sleek, four door saloon in Fountain Blue, with blacked out windows. As he approached it, a man walked around from the driver's seat and opened the rear door for him. With an odd, leaden heaviness in the pit of her stomach, she watched the car drive away down the cracked tarmac road that had once been the perimeter track and now led to the airfield's entrance.

With trembling fingers, she withdrew the card. Staring down at it she was surprised by its lack of contract details. Just his name, HILTON printed in black in a bold font, with no indication whether it was his first or last name. She told herself it was intrigue that persuaded her to keep the appointment rather than a rare act of compliance since she was not a girl who took kindly to being ordered around.

After a lesson with her late-arriving pupil, and no further lessons booked that day since the evenings were not yet light, she dashed home and changed into jeans, a white cotton T-shirt and black leather jacket. She pulled on her motorcycle boots and eventually arrived at The Will-o'-the-wisp with minutes to spare.

She drew alongside his car on her black, orange and white Honda Fireblade motorbike and removed her matching helmet and shook her feral red hair loose. With ease which came with routine she dismounted. Not wanting to appear too eager she paced leisurely across the car park, pushing the pub door open with confidence.

Standing inside the doorway and raking her fingers through the impressive length of her hair, she soon spotted him sitting on one of the tapestry upholstered seats behind a table at the back, by the window where he had a good view of the car park. Trying to squash the unfamiliar nervousness gnawing at her insides, she glanced around to see if there was anyone she knew who was present. Although she could not account for it, she was relieved to discover all the customers that evening were strangers to her.

Having composed herself, she pretended she had only just spotted him, flashed him one of her best smiles and made her way toward him. With her handbag in one hand and her helmet in the other, she stopped at his table, standing by the nearest stool on her side of the table.

There was no friendly greeting, and when he spoke his tone was mocking, and left her in no doubt that he had definite views on how a woman should dress. By the end of the evening she also discovered his views extended to how a woman should behave.

"I must commend you on your surprising gracefulness given your masculine attire. Now sit."

Standing her ground, she felt her colour rise as she bristled.

"Bloody cheek! There's nothing wrong with my 'attire,' sunshine!" She saw him grimace at the term but went on regardless. "I can hardly wear a skirt on the bike. Or perhaps you think I should flash my knickers at all and sundry!"

"Flashing your knickers – my point exactly. So I'd prefer that you either wear a flared skirt, or arrive in a more orthodox manner next time. In any case, you'd benefit greatly from obedience training."

Rusty gave an indignant laugh tinged with the sound of real humour as she stood glaring down at him across the table. "Obedience training? What do you think I am, a bloody dog? Listen, mate – "

He cut her off. "Not a dog, my dear, but you are undoubtedly a bitch. You know, I really think we should make a start right away, today – now – here! Firstly, don't ever refer to me in such familiar terms again….." he drank the last of his bourbon and replaced the glass, "or I'll have to take steps."

"Next time?" Her voice rose a couple of octaves, and the other customers turned their heads in her direction. Clearly offended by his ridicule, she nevertheless

wondered briefly if she may have made a mistake.....
perhaps it was just his brand of humour and he was
merely trying to break the ice by teasing her..... she
made an effort to swallow her indignation and gave
a phoney, falsetto laugh as she thumped her helmet
down on the table. "What makes you think this time'll
be so great? And what do you expect me to call you?
Mr Hilton?"

The ridicule was still there in his voice when he
answered, though the terseness with which the words
were delivered left her in no doubt that humour was
the last thing on his mind. "Now you're being silly.
My name is Charles but 'Sir' will do fine." And he was
not laughing as he pointed to the similarly upholstered
stool by which she was standing. "Sit."

Agape at his imperious manner, she sat anyway. As
she slipped off her jacket and laid it across the other
stool, she wondered if he had received a knighthood or
something, and he just preferred to be addressed by his
formal title. Or perhaps, as head of a large company,
he was used to his workforce addressing him that way.
She shrugged. "Bit formal, isn't it? The 'Sir' bit I mean.
Still, if it's what you want, Sir Charles, then......."

"Not want, demand. Other men....." he expanded
impatiently, explaining as if he were speaking to a
child, "men like myself, prefer the weaker sex..... and
by that I mean normal women who don't rush around
the countryside on motorbikes or fly aeroplanes for a
living.......to address them as 'Master.' But I prefer
'Sir.' I'm not Sir Charles, or Sir anything, just 'Sir!'
Surely that's not so difficult for someone with brains
enough to fly planes?"

He did not wait for an answer but rose from the
table. The look he gave her on his way to the bar dared
her to move. When he returned a few moments later

with another bourbon for himself and a fruit juice for her, she opened her mouth to speak. But he shushed her by holding up his finger and retook his seat. He sipped his bourbon, then set it down on the table. As if he were in the boardroom he folded his hands in front of him on the table, then addressed her coolly.

"You may talk when I give you permission. Until then, just sit and listen."

What kept her in her seat when she could have just walked away would continue to puzzle her for some time afterward. As it was, she sat quietly sipping her juice as he went on to tell her with casual arrogance that riding a powerful motorcycle and flying planes for a living were not activities which fitted with his idea of the perfect woman. He followed up with the even more disturbing notion that a woman's main function was as a sop for her man's desires. As if all that was not bad enough he went further, giving her what amounted to a lecture on femininity and a woman's place in society.

The whole diatribe was delivered in darkly sensual, husky tones that, despite her outrage at his words, made her heart beat faster. Her pussy moistened as, ignoring his perverse views to the best of her ability, she imagined instead what he would be like in the sack, telling herself she could put up with even his outlandish attitudes once in a while providing he was a decent fuck!

After a few moments watching her closely, he told her to stand up. When she got to her feet with a vexed sigh, in a tone which sounded very much like a command he told her to stand beside him. The gall of the man! she smouldered as she plonked her juice on the beer mat. She would give him a bloody mouthful in a minute! She sauntered round to the other side of the table and stood at his knee. Now what? she thought, beginning to wish she had stayed at home.

As soon as his hands alighted on her trim waist and turned her around so that her back was toward him, she thought it was probably best not to put up a fight. She realised too that she felt warm, and knew her features were taking on a pink hue as, feeling as if all eyes were on her, she was rooted to the spot. She stayed put even when he ran his hands over her pert backside, assessing its qualities through her tight fitting jeans. It was as if the thick denim were nothing more than flimsy gauze as the firmness of his hands seemed to imprint their shape…..their ownership…. into her flesh. Holding her breath she tried to still her trembling, wanting desperately to pull away from his grasp, while at the same time longing for his exploration to continue.

Having formed an opinion which curved his lips in a satisfied smile, Charles smoothed his hands over her narrow hips and down her legs.

"Good thigh muscle," he commented in a tone that suggested it was a compliment. "Open your legs."

She was not sure when or even why it happened, but somewhere along the line her feelings of attraction to him grew stronger. And illogical it may have been but she felt helpless to fight it, and wanted nothing more than to please him. With her own desire ignited, she no longer gave a damn whether the other customers were looking, or what they might be thinking. All that mattered was doing as he asked. As if she were on auto pilot, she opened her legs.

"Good. Put your hands on your head."

It did not register that she was at risk of being publicly humiliated, for it just seemed right to do as he requested and, planting her palms firmly on her crown, she laced her fingers together in her hair. She drew in a sudden breath when she felt his fingers probing between her legs, and mentally cursed the seams that nestled into her pussy-folds, hampering his inspection.

But Charles was not a man to be held back by anything as inconsequential as seams. Or the public's gaze. Clutching her sheathed vulva in one hand, with the other he reached round in front of her and deftly pulled down the zip of her jeans. As his fingers made contact with the scrap of triangular fabric which passed for a thong, he slipped his hand over the trifling piece of elastic at the top and angled his wrist to better explore her unruly pubes. Without the pretence of finesse, roughly he raked his fingers through them, at the same time tightening his grip on her crotch. She gasped as, in full view of the throng at the bar who openly gawped as they swigged their beer, his fingers delved unerringly through the flourishing, copper-red thicket to the entrance of her quim.

Dazed, she felt as if she were swaying as too late she became aware of the watching men. Why was she letting this happen? Tears pricked her eyes and she tightened the grip of her interlaced fingers in her hair.

Still without seeing for himself the splendour of her pubic mane, his strong digits forced a rough entry that made her cry out. Closing her eyes against the intrusion and a deep sense of shame, she cursed herself for allowing the public molestation. As his fingers continued to agitate her honey-soaked cavern with the harshest of finger-thrusts and jabs, even worse was the knowledge that she was becoming aroused!

Suddenly he withdrew his fingers, and at once she was aware of the terrible emptiness of her vagina. And then her attention was redirected as he held up his fingers so she could see how slick and shiny they were, coated in her sweet secretions. Faced with the evidence of her own wantonness, she stood stock still and watched dazedly and without complaint as he wiped them clean on the bottom of her clean, white T-shirt!

He slapped her bottom with the command, "Return to your seat."

Hurriedly, she zipped herself up again, forcing her soiled T-shirt into the tight waist of her jeans rather than wearing it outside as she had before. Trying for a nonchalant look she went back to her seat. It was not until she had sat down again and he gave her permission to speak that she realised she hadn't said a word since he forbade it. Astounded by her own behaviour more than by his, she answered his battery of questions, some intrusive and some mundane, as succinctly as possible.

"I'm twenty-four, Sir. I love fucking. Not up my bum! Nothing up there! I wouldn't like it, Sir." Her voice took on a slightly bored tone as, hardly paying attention to his questions, she told him everything he wanted to know. "Yes, I give head. I've never swallowed spunk, Sir."

He laughed, sitting back. "Don't kid yourself that you'll ever be anything special in my life, Caroline."

He surprised her by using her given name, especially since she hadn't given it, just her longstanding nickname.

"You're a dirty bitch. Whoever heard of a whore being special?" he sneered.

"I'm not a whore!" she objected, oblivious to other customers' raised eyebrows.

"No? Well, there's nobody special in your life, just a mile long, back-list of lovers. In my book that makes you a whore. Have you any family?"

"You met my brother, Danny Paget, at the airfield. I've no other family."

Again, he fired off questions so quickly that she failed to understand their relevance and answered automatically. "I don't like pain. I've never been flogged. Never been with a woman. I've been flying for years, Sir." Nor did she grasp the change. "I'm in both display teams. In my spare time I like parachuting, abseiling, rock-climbing, and….."

He held up his hand to stop her. When he spoke to her next, although his voice remained level he referred to her in the most derogatory terms, and she noticed it was as if he were talking about her rather than to her. Latching on to her list of activities, he said, "That's very good. So, the shagging little bitch does like pain after all. That's why it's an adrenaline junky. It's not the thrills the bitch's after, it's the pain it feels when the stunts go wrong! But if it's pain the slut's after, I'll give it other outlets for its needs….. I could whip its brains out to save it all the effort. I could get the same bruised effect as when it lands badly by just paddling it from neck to toes, thereby saving it the effort of parachuting from a plane! I'll give it pain like it's never known before. It'll be begging for pain by the time I've finished with it!" He threw back his head and laughed. "Be careful, or you'll get yourself in trouble one of these days."

"But I'm not a whore!" she protested again, indignity causing her to raise her voice more than she intended.

"Be quiet! I know everything I need to know."

He was less forthcoming about himself, though by now she knew he was dangerous. It was clear that the aura of respectability was something he merely projected to the world. It was clearly effective and for a moment she wondered if he was less dangerous than he made out, if it was all just big talk. But whatever dark secrets he may or may not be masking, she knew that this time she really was intrigued. There was no doubt in her mind that she would like to discover the real Charles Hilton. Of course, his outdated, sexist opinions horrified her. Yet at the same time, the promise of danger attracted her, because the stunning redhead was no stranger to danger herself. As a thrill seeker, danger was something she embraced with open arms. He was right about one thing – she was an adrenaline junkie! Danger was something the thrived on and she found herself attracted to the tall, impeccably dressed man in a way she had rarely been attracted to any of her other lovers.

He stood up suddenly and told her, "When I want you, I'll be in touch. You'll be available and come immediately when summoned."

He did not say goodbye or even wait for a reply, just turned his back and walked away. Torn between attraction to him and the voice in her head that warned her to steer clear, she watched from the window as his driver got out and opened the door for him.

Without realising it, the rhythm of her ordered thought patterns.... her feelings.....her life itself.... had already been disrupted. By giving up her will, even briefly, to Charles, she had sealed her own fate, and he would continue to demean her by making her offer herself again and again. For although he was a man who forcibly took what he wanted whether it was on offer or not, he was also a man whose pleasure was best served by making girls like Rusty jump through hoops to offer what he would take anyway.

When she arrived home that evening, after a long soak in the bath to symbolically wash away the stain of humiliation, she made a cup of coffee before switching on her computer.

A quick Google search soon revealed Charles Hilton as forty-two, and one of the country's most eligible bachelors. She already knew, of course, that he was the Mr Big of Charisma Cosmetics, but he also had his corporate fingers in other business pies, including Galandway Chemicals, who were major sponsors of airshows countrywide. She hit the save button of her mental data storage system to keep the information safe, along with another previously unknown fact; he was also the Vice Chairman of a Netherlands-based charity. She followed the link to the charity's website and discovered that although the Netherlands Blawanya Aid Fund, known as NBAF, was not one of the major players as far as charitable organisations were concerned, it was nevertheless supported throughout Europe, mainly by the wealthy. Apparently there were regular flights made by heavily loaded cargo planes that flew into Blawanya, a country located in the southern part of the continent. Once the clothing, shelter and medicines were delivered to the distribution centre, they were loaded into huge trucks and driven into the remotest, poorest parts of the county. There was a photo of one such centre in some place called Thomassentown, where there were also occasional deliveries to the clinic of medicines which were transported in an old, specially converted Mustang.

It was satisfying to know that the man she intended sleeping with was associated with such a noble cause, she thought.

CHAPTER TWO

"What do you think of the new logo?" Rusty's brother asked one evening as she was leaving.

She took in the instantly recognisable logo, the word Charisma inside a gold coloured, five pointed star, that was now applied to the side of the red biplane which they used for the wingwalking team, and which dwarfed the Saxon Angels emblem.

"Okay I suppose, as long as it pays the bills!"

"It'll help!" Danny told her. "Going anywhere special tonight?"

"Nothing planned," she lied, preferring not to tell him that she had seen their sponsor a few times over the past two weeks. Although Charles hid his lascivious nature behind a façade of respectability, it was not only her happiness that was at stake but also the interests of the airfield, and she did not want to run the risk of Danny ruining everything by exposing him as.....as a what? A controlling pervert? "Bye, Danny."

Charles Hilton was a busy man, and theirs was an entirely different relationship to any previous love affair she'd had. He still insisted on being called 'Sir' rather than his name. And it was obvious from the start that he liked to call the shots. They only met at his behest, when he phoned her using an untraceable number, however much she wanted to contact him! He refused to give her his contact details, and although Danny had his genuine business card, unless she went poking around the office or told her brother that she was seeing him, she had no way of contacting him.

He was often abrupt, treating her with contempt rather than affection. And the names he called her were anything but polite. Mostly he spoke quietly and calmly when they were alone, but whenever they were in public, as on that first occasion he enjoyed her humiliation. He always picked her up at her flat, claiming it was easier for him to drive to her place rather than the other way round. That was probably true because, despite her flat being only a mile or so from the airfield, with the arrival of the lighter summer evenings, flying lessons were often booked for later than during the dark, winter months. He was probably right when he said that even with her beloved motorbike she would not have time to go home and get ready if she were to reach his London apartment on time. As it was she barely had time to shower and get ready before he arrived. And because he liked to start the evening with a meal in one of the area's top restaurants, she liked to make at least a bit of an effort.

After showering and washing her hair she would dress again, usually in leggings because she did not own the sort of skirt she thought he would like. Then she removed her duvet and stashed it in the cupboard, replacing it with the spare duvet because he was never too careful about where his spunk ended up…..and she often came so much that she made big, wet patches herself! She hadn't yet been to his London penthouse which, he boasted, occupied the top three floors of a modern building.

His driver, Stratton, would open the rear door of the car and then drive them to Charles' chosen destination. Everything would be fine and they would have a pleasant evening discussing her day or her plans for the summer's airshows, until either another customer was in earshot or a waiter approached their table. Then he would tell her to be quiet, and then raise his own voice deliberately to be overheard.

"Please don't misbehave, my dear – you're embarrassing us both," he had told her once, adding, "if you insist on showing me up, I'll put you over my knee and spank you." Another time he had said accusingly, "how many men does a whore like you shag in day, Caroline?" And once, he had instructed her to play with herself right in front of a clergyman and his party.

Although she knew it was not acceptable behaviour, especially from a highly respected and urbane company director, she could not help the way she felt about him. Despite the warnings in her head and the tremors engendered by her own suppressed rage, she was besotted with him. She looked forward constantly to seeing him again and desperately longed for the day when she would mean something special to him, in spite of his assertion that she never would. Until she met Charles, she had always thought of herself as a free spirit, shunning ties and loathing anything that smacked even slightly of "a relationship."

By now she knew he was a man used to his authority going unquestioned. But whenever they were together his fleeting smiles tempered his arrogance and his domination. It was as if she were under a spell. She found it quite natural to do as he asked without question, speaking only when given permission.

When they were apart and common sense reasserted itself, she analysed everything that happened between them, comforting herself with the thought that there was no harm in him. Alone, she would reflect on whatever had taken place, and convince herself that it was all just part of his playful attitude to sex, just as his roughness was part of it, too. Because sex with Charles was always rough and it was something she was growing accustomed to.

When they returned to her flat, everything would be done at his pace. Having taught her on that first occasion to stand with her legs apart and her hands on her head, it was now becoming second nature to wait in 'the position' until he was ready for her, and she thought it somehow stranger and more binding in her own flat than it had done in the pub. And it hadn't taken him long to introduce her to his other ideas of discipline, which at first she had simply thought of as his "funny little rituals." And although they always made her feel slightly foolish, she knew she would miss them if she were never to see him again.

Making good time, she cut through the traffic easily. Thinking of the new logo as she parked her bike, once inside she shunned the lift and took the stairs. She made herself a quick coffee and sorted out her new leopard print leggings and a black tunic-type top, then dashed into the shower and began getting ready.

When he arrived that evening, he kissed the top of her head as he had taken to doing, then surprised her grabbing her breasts through her top. Smiling at her gasp of discomfort at his rough treatment, he tightened his grip.

As her eyelids fluttered over eyes that were the colour of white wine, he told her, "We're staying in tonight."

"I wish you'd have said! I could have got something in special. Still, I'm sure I can rustle up something to eat," she laughed, at the same time wincing at the pain as his grasp tightened.

"No. I'll have Stratton bring something up later. No more talking. Do as you're told and everything will be fine. Take up the position."

Surprised by the change in plan, she simply stood as directed in her own hallway while he went through to her small lounge and helped himself to the bourbon she had started to buy especially. Then he came out of the lounge, crossed the narrow hallway and went through to her bedroom. When he finally called her, she found him sitting on the edge of her bed, just as he always did when they returned after dinner. Then, again as he always did, he told her to strip while he watched.

With his gaze riveted to her every movement, she peeled off her clothing as sexily as she knew how. But that evening she was miffed that he failed to notice her new, sexy underwear. When she was standing stark naked before him with her muted-coral nipples standing to erection, he pointed at the unruly thatch of fiery copper curls that covered her pubic area.

"Tidy that!"

Dutifully, combed her fingers through it, separating and neatening until he declared himself satisfied with its appearance.

"Position!" When she was standing as directed once more, he undressed himself. When he was stretched out on the bed, propped up on her pillow with one hand behind his head and the other holding his glass of bourbon, he told her, "Fold my clothes and pile them neatly – with yours – on your chair."

Quickly and efficiently she did as he commanded. Although he had made her do it before and despite her joy at obeying his wishes, that evening it seemed to be taking an interminably long time before he showed any signs of actually getting down to it!

Clicking his fingers, as on previous occasions he had her kneel between his legs and take his beautiful, erect phallus in her mouth and suck it awhile. Glad to feel it rigid and throbbing in her mouth, she reached out in her usual way to lovingly caress it.

He slapped her hands away. "No, don't touch my cock, bitch! Never touch it again unless I explicitly tell you to."

Rocking back on her heels, she expelled it and stared at him. "Wh…?"

"Think of it as a holy representation that you're not worthy to touch." With an open palm he slapped her cheek sharply.

"Ooow!" Her hand flew to cradle her cheek but he brushed it away.

"Put your hands behind your back." When she had done as instructed, he said, "Keep them there until I tell you to move them. I don't remember telling you to stop sucking. Get on with it or face the consequences."

With no idea of what consequences he had in mind, she took his cock between her lips once more, gagging as he grabbed the back of her head to force her to take more into her soft mouth.

He removed his hands and she was able to pull back enough to ease her gagging without expelling him again. Delighting in the feel of it, she flicked her tongue over and around it, sucking and dribbling. Putting in more effort than she had ever done before, she hollowed her cheeks. But it seemed that no matter how much effort or noise her exertions engendered that evening, or how much spittle dripped from her mouth, it was not enough. Fearing that he would never reward her by laying as much as a finger on her hot and hungry body let alone fuck her, it seemed an age before his fingers finally clutched her breasts, even more roughly than they had in her hallway. And all the while she sucked, forced to endure such a brutishly-delicious mauling of her breasts until he switched his concentration to her nipples. As he twisted them severely, sending all kinds of thrilling sensations through them, despite the wodge of inflexible flesh in her mouth she cried out in pain.

That seemed to please him, for it was impossible to miss the undeniable delight that shone in her eyes.

It was not the first time she had noticed a flicker of something…..something dark and unrecognisable….. cross his face or caught a glimpse of an emotion that was too scary to dwell on. But she was in no position to think things through as he encouraged her, not with gentle words but simply by force, to take his shaft even deeper, actually ramming it down her throat as he held her head to his groin once more.

With her nose tickled by his cologne-scented pubes, and her vision filled with his spray-tanned flesh above them, it came as a shock to realise that it was not merely the feel of her soft lips around his shaft, nor even her tongue sensuously licking up and down until he was moved to grasp her hair and mesh his fingers that brought him trembling with passion to his peak and spurting his seed into her mouth. It was simply the knowledge that he was toying with her. And she knew then he would stop at nothing to shape her into his preferred form of womanhood. Yet even then she had no real understanding of the dark looks he gave her. He simply withdrew his cock and held her mouth closed so that she had no choice but to swallow hard, at the same time reviling and relishing the taste of his emissions.

"Always remember that it's a privilege to swallow my spunk."

Until that night, after he had come he frigged her to orgasm before getting dressed and leaving her again. But that evening he lay back on her bed.

"Good girl. Now get on the bed."

However, he did not relax his rule of silence, but commanded her to position herself on all fours and turn around. Terrified that he was going to fuck her back passage, she hesitated.

"Behave, Caroline."

Quickly recognising that the innocuous words carried a dark threat, she obeyed at once. Initially she was relieved that he did not move, but nonchalantly reached across to her bedside cabinet and picked up her hairbrush. Then adjusting his position at last, he used it as a paddle to spank her backside.

She tensed and cried out at each of the twelve, hard and well-aimed smacks to her buttocks, six to each side which, had she been able to see them, brought red, hairbrush-shaped blotches to her skin. Although instinct made her want to jump up and rub her bottom, she refrained from moving when he paused. Tensing, she waited for him to reward her by sinking his lovely cock into her wet and waiting pussy.

But before he did so, he had one more affront to her dignity. Instead of his penis it was the hairbrush handle that he thrust into her. And whether it was the fear of his ability to hurt her that stopped her from leaping from the bed and extricating herself forever from his pernicious lust, or her self-destructive urges that hungered for more from him, she could not say, but she endured the cold, brutal handle-fucking with no more than the occasional yelp for half an hour before she began to feel cheated. She put all her efforts into tightening her vaginal muscles in a vain attempt to extract satisfaction from the unresponsive object.

Then suddenly he wrenched it from her. Settling himself more comfortably behind her, he grabbed her shoulders. Then he pulled her shoulders toward him.

"No, don't move, you bitch! Stay exactly as you are. Keep your hands on the bed."

Using her body as leverage to give himself an impetus to aid his punishing rhythm, he began a more personal and brutal violation of her desperately clutching channel. Almost at once he felt her tensing and knew she was about to orgasm. With a pitiless smile, his ragged words came out in time with his thrusts.

"No, you filthy, slut. You're not to come this time."

"Pl....I'm going to c....pl.....Sir...."

"You must learn control. My word is final. You must not come!"

He knew it would take all her efforts to hold back the tide. So much effort, in fact, that she would find little enjoyment in their rutting. And that was just the way he liked things. He wasn't yet convinced that she was ideal material to train fully. If it turned out that she was, then hairbrushes up her cunt would be the least of her worries, he thought delightedly as he framed pictures in his mind.

All the while his powerful pummelling continued, he pulled on her shoulders while unknown to her he reined in his other, more urgent desires for the time being, but which would soon need attending to. Because what Charles really wanted was to see her soft, pale and freckled body strapped naked over a simple stool, a custom-built trestle, or spread tautly in one of the frames he kept in a special room in his apartment. And when he considered her training period had reached the point when she was ready, he would lacerate the delicate skin of her pliable, willing body with no other agenda than his own pleasure. But until then, he would just have to make do with filling her whoring cunt with his spunk.

Before the thought was fully shaped, his spunk erupted in a hot tide that coated her cunt walls. As he relished the feeling, she wailed in despondency at being denied the same pleasure.

Laughing, he pulled out of her. But to his annoyance and despite his wishes to the contrary, she climaxed with a shrill scream of release.

As always, she was left breathless and sore, and knew it would be an uncomfortable ride into work on her motorbike in the morning. But that was a long way off and for now she was content to lie recovering with her lover, luxuriating in the sensually drowsy, afterglow of orgasm.

But it was not to be and he roused her angrily. His tone was brusque as he told her, "I'm disappointed. I'd hoped for so much. Now I find you're nothing but a lazy bitch who can't obey a simple order. You deserve to be punished, but I really don't feel inclined to waste my time." He took his mobile from its resting place on her bedside cabinet, and instructed Stratton to "fetch us something to eat." Then ending the call, he continued as he climbed from her bed, "I'm not often wrong, but this time it seemed I made a mistake. I won't be bothering you again after tonight. Now go through to your lounge, pour me a drink, and set the table for dinner. And, seeing as it's our last meal together – our Last Supper – you may speak freely."

"Please, Charles," she said as she slunk from the bed and across to her wardrobe where she threw on a white bathrobe, "I'm sorry. Why don't you stay the night so that I can make it up to you?" He had never stayed before, but there was always a first time, she told herself hopefully. But what Google had not informed her of was that whenever he left her flat, he went on to a private club, where he would pleasure himself by booking a girl for the remainder of the night and thrashing the daylights out of her until the sadistic lust which his visit to Rusty had ignited was finally sated.

"No, I won't be staying. Now at least do me the service of obeying me this one last time, and set the fucking table!"

Feeling like an early birdman crashing to earth, she did as he asked while berating herself for not exercising more control. She was pouring his drink when she heard him talking to Stratton at the front door.

Re-entering the room with a meal that had obviously been prepared before-hand and somehow kept warm, he gave it to her to dish up. It was while they were eating that she broached the subject.

"I don't really understand what kind of relationship you want from me," adding for good measure, "Sir."

"Master and slave," he said with the slightest curve to his lips.

Admitting that it was a topic she knew something about since it turned up regularly in the "how to spice up your sex life" columns in magazines, she told him that she had never taken it seriously. "My sex life is spicy enough and certainly doesn't need improving!" Smiling coquettishly, in a way that seemed positively filthy she added, "I know I'm hot enough for you..... could be everything you want......so why don't you take a chance?"

He looked at her through narrowed eyes. She did not deserve the terseness of his tone when he spoke, and it shocked her more than his reply itself when he told her,

"Now you're being childish, Caroline." He drained his second glass of bourbon that night and went to her cabinet to help himself to another one. With his back to her as he poured, he said, "I'm a Dominant and I expect all my women to be submissive. You'll recall I mentioned that some men like to be called 'Master.'" He returned to the table. Then throwing her a crumb of hope, he declared that there was a way she could prove herself to him. "If you're serious about making me happy and for this casual affair to develop into something more meaningful, you'll have to learn that my word is law. You'd have to accept my authority in everyday matters. It would mean a huge step up in your training regime, of course. Would you like to give it a go? Think carefully before answering."

She did not need to think. She knew she wanted this dangerous man in her life, and told him that she would do whatever he wanted. "I'll even learn not to come unless you tell me to," she laughed.

"That's what you say now. So, to prove your willingness to learn, you must perform one major task of my choosing. Without knowing all the facts, or being told where or when, you must take my test. Only if you pass will I take you on, and only then can our relationship develop. Do you agree, Caroline?"

Once again she laughed. She loved a challenge and so accepted without giving the matter due thought.

"Now, about that matter of punishment. Go to your room, strip, and wait for me there. And remember the position!"

She got up from the table and did as he asked. Seeing herself reflected in her full-length mirror, she felt rather foolish standing naked with her legs apart and hands on head. And in the lounge, as he finished his bourbon Charles congratulated himself on the expert way in which he had handled her, bringing her round to his way of thinking and setting her up for everything he had wished for.

When he finally came through to the bedroom, he rummaged in one of her drawers.

"What are you look…."

"Quiet!"

Adjusting his position so that she could not see, he extracted two of the fashionable long scarves that all the girls were wearing, a thong and a belt, all of which he stuffed in his pockets. Then closing the drawer again, he crossed the room and commanded her to stand with her knees against her bed, which she did at once.

Standing behind her and without speaking, he uprooted her hands from her head and yanked them behind her back. Forcing herself not to protest, she felt him wrapping something around her wrists as he joined them together, using one of her narrow belts as a strap to bind them. His shirt sleeve brushed her cheek as he reached round in front of her. She did not object when his strong fingers prised apart her lips, and she obligingly opened her mouth wider, only to find it stuffed with her own thong. Then using one of the scarves, he placed it over her mouth and tied it behind her head.

"There, almost ready," he said, and with a flourish produced the second long scarf which he tied over her eyes.

With her senses suddenly denied her, the fingers holding the back of her neck seemed all the more controlling as she was forced to bend over. Still gripping her tightly, they pushed her face down into the duvet. Not daring to move, she steeled herself for whatever indignity was to follow.

The shock of the loud Crack! was as great as the acerbic sting of the rattan cane that struck the soft cushions of her pert bottom. She screamed into the gag, and just heard the swishing noise before the next Crack!

"And so your punishment begins. This is a cane, and if you pass the test I'll set up, then the two of you will become very well acquainted."

Swish! Crack!

Swish! Crack!

"I'll teach you to disobey me!"

The pain was so great that she did not even wonder how he had smuggled it into her flat, did not work out that it had been his plan to cane her all along and that he'd had Stratton deliver it with the food. All her thoughts were centred on her bottom. She could not help but jerk under the impact of each strike. They hurt like hell and each one seemed heavier than the last. Silently screaming her way through another fifteen firebrand strokes, she was forced to absorb the horrendous pain with nothing more than a frantic waggling of her bottom which, of course, he took as encouragement and laughed as he applied the strokes harder.

To her surprise, she found the experience intensely thrilling, and when they were over she wiggled her bottom in what she knew herself was a clearly provocative invitation. Obligingly, and with a smile of satisfaction, Charles laid down one last, agonising strike that had her burying her head further into the duvet.

But when he released her afterward, he did not stay to take advantage of her wet willingness. Instead, he just slipped on his jacket and, holding the cane lightly in his hand, told her to check her marks in the mirror. And as she stood looking over her shoulder with her back to the mirror, gaping at the tramlines that were the recognisable signature of a cane and that crisscrossed her buttocks, he let himself out of her front door without a word of when she would see him again.

CHAPTER THREE

The hangars were all locked up for the night. Tarpaulins covered the windscreens of the planes on the apron. Despite the favourable conditions and the long, summer evenings there were no lessons scheduled that evening, and the Cessnas and Pipers were anchored to the ground by cables.

The flying school's car park was empty, save for the black Peugeot and Rusty's Fireblade that looked as though it belonged on a racing track rather than a normal road. Items of the slim mechanic's clothing and footwear were carelessly strewn between them and were evidence of how hurriedly he had undressed. Rusty's helmet sat atop a pile of her neatly folded biking leathers, with her underwear and biking boots beside the motorbike over which she was uncomfortably and provocatively sprawled, with Gibbo impossibly poised over her.

His frame was surprisingly heavy and, trapped beneath him, reminded her with every breath she took of her own discomfort, and curiously fanned the spark of her lust into a roaring flame rather than extinguishing it. It was a bizarre consequence of her last evening with Charles, and in particular the caning, that she found even a smidgen of suffering enhanced any sexual experience, thrilling her more than pain-free fucking ever had. And illogically she longed for more.

Stark naked with her nipples caressed into erection by lust or maybe the summer breeze, her head rested back on the fairing over the back wheel, somehow adding to her look of vulnerability, and her tousled, flaming red hair hung down over the back in shimmering abundance. Sleekly sensual, she was meticulously arranged in a way that looked casual, with her long legs bent at the knees and draped over the fuel tank, and her feet resting on the handlebars. Her arms were flung down on either side and she clutched at the back wheel to save herself from falling as the tri-coloured bike, standing upright on its main stand, shook and wobbled as Gibbo's cock pounded into her slippery cunt. He gripped her by the shoulders, his oil-stained nails digging into her soft, creamy skin that was prettily dappled with freckles.

With the smell of aviation fuel still strong in her nostrils, and the breeze whispering across her flesh and fanning her moisture-drenched body, she abandoned herself to desire as the mechanic's rhythm threatened to shake the bike from its upright position. With her nipples shot through with throbbing sensations and her pussy wet and juicy, she clung on to the back wheel in fear, not of falling off but of her beloved bike toppling over and scratching the paintwork.

She made a growling sound in her throat and told him coquettishly between ragged breaths, "You're an animal! Nothing but a fucking, rutting animal with a cock that was made in Heaven."

"And you're depraved!" he laughed as he paused for breath. "Utterly depraved! One day you'll meet your match."

"That's what they all say!"

"It won't be pretty," he warned, "when someone takes you in hand! I only hope I'm there to watch when somebody has the guts to tame you."

"Tame me?" For a moment she was taken aback and her eyes filled with sadness as she remembered that Sir had said something similar. But even though she had submitted to his punishment and promised that she would take any test he set up, it seemed he had decided she was not a worthy subject for 'obedience training' after all since it had been three weeks since she had seen him. Nor had she heard from him since.

Willing herself not to dwell on what might have been, she determined to put Charles Hilton behind her and concentrate her efforts on just having a good time with whoever she happened to be with. And so she forced a laugh.

"You make me sound like an unbroken horse. As long as you see a thoroughbred and not some old nag when you look at me!"

A bitch, that was what Sir had called her, though surely she did not deserve the tag. Beginning to realise exactly what he had awoken within her, she wondered if it would be better to let it lie. People already thought of her as flirtatious, taking lovers like other people took showers, and she would hate them to think she was a masochist too.

Everyone knew she was a thrill-seeker. For a woman who exuded so much sexuality, whose every fibre of her being was endowed with extra eroticism and sexual chemistry, it was odd that she always wore dungarees, jeans or trousers of some other description rather than sensuous, satiny creations. But sexy as she was, she was also a competent flying instructor. Whether in the air or on the ground, her pupils were always quick to recognise her intelligence and appreciate her serious, observant nature and leadership. But for Rusty it was all second nature, and the airfield a second home. She had been around planes all her life and, coming from a family of flyers and ground crew, had been taken up in a light aircraft at an early age, so it was not surprising she had become a pilot herself.

As soon as she was old enough she had begun the process of gaining the necessary experience, which included twenty-five hours with an instructor as well as solo flights, along with the other essentials that she now taught, and had finally gained her licence at the earliest possible legal age of sixteen. She loved flying, especially the formation flying she did with the Saxon Hill Aerobatics team, and relished the freedom of her solo aerobatics displays, and always got a high from wingwalking.

She needed someone who could make her feel as alive as when she opened up her bike on the motorway, or performed rolls flat out in a plane; a man whose lust could match her own, someone to thrill her. Except Charles had taught her she needed a man whose lust exceeded her own.

Breaking in on her thoughts, Gibbo demanded, "What would you do, Rust, if someone came along and found us in the middle of a quickie?"

She sighed. A man whose sexual excitement was crushed by the thought of discovery was anathema to the girl whose very first sexual encounter had taken place – when her father had been in charge at this very same airfield – with her father's best friend, a pilot. He had been much older than she, of course, and ever since then she had searched for a man to live up to the one who had taught her to fly in more ways than one!

"They won't. They've all gone home." With slow wilfulness she formed her lips into a sulky pout. "Now do you want to fuck me or not?"

"What if Tony or Tim were to find out? Or worse still your brother? I'd be out on my………"

Her laugh cut him off. "For fuck's sake! Danny won't fire you just because you screw his sister occasionally. And neither Tim nor Tony can give you the boot when they've both had me behind the hangars!"

"What if they got wind of our arrangement……"

"What arrangement?" She trembled with suppressed anger. What was wrong with the bloody man? A few drinks after work followed by a few shags in his Peugeot or her flat, and he thought he bloody owned her! "Look, you don't have any sort of hold over me. We're not joined 'till dismissal us do part!'"

"You know what I mean, Rust."

Still trapped beneath his body on the bike that stayed miraculously upright, she said, "Yeah, I know what you mean! Look, if you've done, then say so now and we can pack up and go home. But if you do want to fuck, for God's sake let's just get on with it!"

Whatever else Gibbo lacked, at least their maker had endowed him with a better-than-average cock, though she reminded herself that Gibbo had been employed for his skill and willingness to work for low pay, not his looks or his blessedly proficient screwing abilities. But he was also a competent pilot himself. He was not bad looking either, with thick, black hair that was soft and cropped so short it put her in mind of an animal pelt.

But the sad fact remained that she had only turned to Gibbo again because she had somehow blotted her log with Charles. It was odd that she felt ready to accept the kind of strange relationship that he had offered, because to a girl who valued her freedom as much as Rusty Paget believed she did, close emotional ties of any sort were an abomination. If it were not for the fact that her brother was one of the three owners of the flying school, she knew she would not go out of her way to even see her only living relative! So why did she want Sir so badly?

"Are you really the kind of girl who enjoys flitting from one man to another, Rust?" Gibbo asked as he his cock began to stiffen again inside her. "Is that what you really want for the rest of your life?"

No, what she wanted was someone to fulfil her needs. Except since meeting Charles she was not entirely sure what those needs were! He had stirred up so many new and wild emotions.....if only he were here! But he wasn't, and Gibbo was. And at that moment, with her body racked with desires that desperately needed satisfaction, Gibbo would have to do.

He began to squirm around on top of her, and all thoughts of keeping the bike upright forgotten as he tried to adjust his position and get more comfortable.

"Oooow!"

He did not seem to notice her pained cry, nor the way her features contorted as his bony limbs dug into her. And she wondered if he knew that in improving his own comfort he turned her discomfort into actual pain. And that pain – insignificant compared to what Sir had put her through – finally brought about a change within her that was like the opening of some as yet undiscovered flower. And instead of taking the chance to wriggle herself into a less painful position, she accepted the hardship not only as a price worth paying but also her duty. And as her eyes watered with pain, and lust tore at her insides, she trembled. Looking up at him again, her mouth broke into a sexy smile. Because it seemed to the panting redhead that Gibbo might be worth the trouble after all! His cock quivered and thrust deliciously, battering her insides for all he was worth and sending ribbons of eroticism fluttering hotly from her belly to her quim.

She sank further into the familiarity of welcome, wild arousal. As he ground his hips against hers, his words kept time with his movements as he mocked her.

"You fucking bitch! Think you're going to treat me like all the rest? Throw me away and wipe your feet all over me? Listen, you'd better remember that you're just the girlie around here…..the big tits and pretty face to impress the punters, no matter how 'brave' you think you are. Flying planes, riding motorbikes…..you weren't born a man, you've got a cunt! That makes you the one that gets screwed! Someone should have taught you how to behave years ago. You're just-a-fucking-cunt, darlin'!"

Her heart pounded excitedly as the bike wobbled. Wide eyed, the tip of her tongue wet her lips. She was going to fall, she knew she was! Never had she known him to fuck like this! His cock hammered away inside her, knocking the wind from her as she remained trapped and painfully uncomfortable. And she was loving every minute of it. He was right about one thing, she thought vaguely, she was a female, and no matter how much she enjoyed the other aspects of her life, as far as sexual desires were concerned she wanted to be treated like one.

This had every chance of turning into a fuck to remember after all, she thought, exhilarated as tremors of arousal shook her and the bike beneath her spread and uncomfortable limbs. Her mind threw up the possibilities of the motorbike finally toppling over and the mechanic dragging her into the grass and fucking the daylights out of her. She licked her lips again in joyful anticipation as their breathing became more ragged. She wondered if he had a cane……..

With her eyes closed she cried out with abandon, not caring if Security were making their rounds or not. Thinking of nothing but her own enjoyment as the sensations of his dominant passion clutched at her insides and brought her need for satisfaction into focus with HD clarity, her feet fidgeted wildly on the handlebars. Her hands clenched and unclenched as she gripped at the back wheel. Awash with lust as her vaginal muscles tightened then relaxed, she gave one final, stifled cry as her orgasm broke. And fast on the breaking of her climax, his hot spunk splashed against her insides. Then with grunts of satisfaction he collapsed over her.

The warmth of calm washed over her and, unable to move as his weight kept her trapped on the Fireblade, for a moment they both lay limp and shattered, their mingled emissions seeping from her quim and leaving sticky patches on the bike. There was no way that she and Gibbo could ever have just a working relationship, she told herself, there had to be more. And as they slid from the bike at last, she wondered if this intensity of feeling was the kind she could have expected if her affair with Sir had developed into something worthwhile ...if she had taken and passed his bloody test!

Moments later, after cleaning herself on the oily rag Gibbo tossed at her, she used clean tissues to wipe every trace of his spunk from the bike that was her pride and joy. He dressed quickly, and while she was still struggling back into her leathers, Gibbo was driving away in his Peugeot without uttering a word. Even as she wondered how she had let a man like the sadly absent Charles slip through her fingers, she was willing to accept Gibbo as a reasonable replacement.

That was why she invited the mechanic to her flat the following evening.

The doorbell was ringing aggressively as Rusty stepped from the shower. Grabbing a towel from the rack, she wrapped up her long, wet hair into a fairly decent turban. She snagged her white cotton bathrobe from the hook, and allowed steam to escape from the room as she opened the door.

"Coming!" she called as she knotted the belt around her trim waist and padded into the hallway.

Oh hell! she thought as she hurried toward the front door, leaving wet footprints on the laminate, Gibbo was early! Despite the fact they would end up naked in bed, she had wanted to start off dressed, with her hair and make-up done. But she supposed his live-in girlfriend had gone out earlier than he had anticipated, so he had come straight round.

They'd had little opportunity at work to talk because, apart from the flying lessons, she and her brother had spent a lot of time with "the brothers" as everyone referred to Tim and Tony, discussing the upcoming airshows, the first of which was in Hampshire that coming weekend. And then there were the rehearsals for the stunts themselves, something she enjoyed and although she had been doing them for years she still put as much time into as possible.

The bell rang again, one quick, sharp and impatient Ring!

"Okay, okay!" She unhooked the door chain, opened the door and, without looking she stepped back to let Gibbo enter. Bending from the waist she began to rub at her hair. "Go through," she said as she pushed the door closed with a click, "make some coffee and I'll be with you in a minute."

There was not even a grunt in reply. Instead, the towel was snatched away and her hair tumbled out. Her head snapped up in surprise.

"Sir!"

He was standing in the hallway with her towel draped over his arm. His deep set, toffee-coloured eyes looked at her grimly and the mouth was set firmly. His air of authority in the narrow space was overwhelming and his temper uncertain.

"I'm ....sorry.... I.... wasn't expecting anyone......" she flustered.

"Don't lie to me, Caroline," he censured her icily while his eyes were full of disdain. "You were expecting someone."

"Only my brother," she lied stupidly, listening bleakly to her words falling of their own volition from her lips as they compounded the falsehood. "He's popping round this evening to talk about the airshow......this weekend....." her words ebbed away to nothing. Knowing instinctively that he was not fooled for a moment, she lifted her gaze warily to his. Feeling insignificant in his presence, for several seconds she just stared, her pale eyes wide as she tried to work out what was wrong with her. She should have been thrilled to see him, so why did she feel like a kid a caught behind the bike sheds by a teacher? It wasn't as if she was unfaithful.... how could she be when there was nothing of any substance between them? Of course, there was Gibbo, but he was the only one, she excused herself. And besides, Charles probably had beautiful women buzzing around him all the while and surely a man like him would not hold back! So how dare he show up and look down on her with contempt?

And yet, she reminded herself, to have him here again was exactly what she had wanted for weeks, and the treacherous way her pussy quivered made it impossible to deny that it was still what she wanted. But something was different.... she could feel it... something had changed between them. Unable to bear the silence as he stood and looked her over, and simply for something to break the icy chill settling over her flat, she told him, "It's okay. Danny doesn't know about us, Sir. I haven't told him."

"As you won't be here to see him this evening, the whole thing is irrelevant." He seemed to come suddenly to a decision and flashing her a dangerous smile he said, "Look, we don't have time for this nonsense, Caroline." He reached for the end of her belt, gave it a gentle tug and watched it unravel and her robe fall open. "Take it off."

Now that he was here, handsome, broad shouldered and filling her narrow hallway with his presence as well as the spicily-musky aroma of his cologne, as she stood before him it seemed the most natural thing in the world to do as he asked. She shrugged off the robe and he took it from her, draping it with the towel across his arm. She made to move away, but he checked her with nothing more than a look.

At five foot ten he was hardly a giant, and yet he had a way of making her, at five foot six, feel small and fragile. All at once she could not wait to put on her heels to level things up a bit. Even as a kid she had always been sure of herself and had matured into a confident young woman. Illogically, she felt even more vulnerable now than she had when she had been caned. Because up until now, low self-esteem was something that afflicted other people. But an attack of nerves rendered her unable to meet his eyes a moment longer and bowing her head slightly she lowered her gaze to the floor. She was caught completely by surprise as an unfamiliar feeling of .... not shyness exactly, more like inferiority swept over her as she stood naked before him while he, fully and impeccably clothed as always and wearing a tailored dark suit and shirt, let his imperious gaze run over her.

Men had always found her curves sexy and she had always looked upon her generous breasts as an asset rather than a hindrance, but she was sure that at any moment he would list her shortcomings. Whether or not he even liked what he saw was beyond her, for never had he turned such a critical eye in her direction.

And so she grew more apprehensive as the seconds ticked by.

The first thing Charles noted was that she was almost standing correctly. Her feet were spaced a foot or so apart, though he would prefer them wider for easy access to her deliciously plump cunt. Of course, if she were to become his slave, he would have to have that pubic bush shaved off, though he supposed it was amusing to see a veritable conflagration between her creamy thighs. But really it was just too thick and straggly to be thought of as anything other than a hindrance.

He smiled. It was interesting that, even without being told to she had crossed her hands behind her, as if she were waiting for him to tie them. Although he had taught her to stand with them on her head, he could not be angry because he saw it as an indication of her inner, latent desire to become the perfect submissive, something that was reinforced by the almost perfect placing of her head which was bowed toward the floor with her eyes downcast. Although he rather suspected it was not to show the respect he would soon be demanding, but because the silly bitch was sulking. Still, a few slight adjustments and she would be pose-perfect.

Her crinkled, long hair was still wet and looked darker than its normal fiery copper. With its natural parting on the right it fell diagonally across her forehead. And he realised it was the first time he had seen her without make-up. She was beautiful, there was no doubt about that, he thought as he took in the features of a face that tapered to a sharp, pointed chin. Her pale, creamy skin was enhanced rather than cursed by a muted sprinkling of freckles which spread from her forehead down to her narrow ankles, with the densest cluster across her long, finely chiselled nose. Her lips were rather fleshy and gave her a natural pout, though he was not the first man to notice that she had a knack of exaggerating it when she was disappointed or merely trying to get her own way. And getting her own way was something he would put a stop to, as long as she passed his little test, of course.

And then there were her unsettling eyes, almost unnatural, a sort of pale, ghostly colour that was either very pale green or some other, lighter shade.... with a yellowish tint.....like wine or champagne. It all depended, he thought, on either the light or her mood, and was usually made all the more spectral by the dusky smudging of the eye make-up she usually favoured above and below them. With lust warming his loins he wondered what colour they would appear when she was finally at his mercy, crying and screaming in his playroom.

As she stood stock still and naked, while his imagination was centred on her body stretched to its limit on one of the punishment frames in his playroom, he continued his appraisal. Although from their first meeting he had intended to make her suffer the ignominy of actually trying out for the opportunity to be maltreated and subjugated for his amusement, until that moment he hadn't realised quite how much of a delightful plaything she would be. Considering her breasts with a barbarous regard, he relished the thought of whiling away his time abusing them, and, dropping her robe and towel to the floor, he reached out with both hands. Slipping a palm beneath each breast to weigh them against his ideal, he handled them as casually as if they were steaks to throw on the barbecue. He satisfied himself that they were perfect specimens for the kind of treatment he hoped to administer regularly, heavy and delightfully malleable, with small areolae and big, coral nipples which, on every occasion he had been with her, hardened appetisingly and remained erect for some considerable time. They were, quite simply, tits that were made for maltreatment.

Despite her charming curves, he was gratified that her high level of fitness in no way camouflaged her sleek sensuality. Releasing her breasts, he ran his hands down to her slim waist and toned belly. There was certainly no need of a corset..... but when had "need" ever been a consideration in matters of his slave's suffering or his preferred dress code? Her hips flared charmingly, too, giving her an almost perfect figure for a man of his tastes.

Withdrawing his hands, he took a pace backward.

"Turn around."

Slowly, she turned around, and he was given a perfect view of her hollow back and slightly plump behind with its peach-like split that divided it into two soft, malleable halves. Failing to understand how that glorious arse had gone unpunished for so long before he came along, he wondered how he had himself refrained for so long from taking the cane to its soft cushions, and why he hadn't yet repeated the exercise. And he found himself at a loss as to why such a tasty specimen of wanton womanhood hadn't been snapped up by some dominant and turned into the perfect submissive long before now. He laughed inwardly, promising himself as his eyes raked downward over her long, shapely legs, that he would enjoy putting the matter right. He would make a slave of the slut yet.

But before that could happen, she must prove herself worthy of his time and effort. After all he was a busy man! With his business activities with Charisma, and Galandway Chemicals, his time was limited. Then there was his club, his charity work for NBAF of which he was Vice Chairman, and social life, all of which tended to interfere with his keeping of a 24/7 slave, involving the trouble of feeding, exercising, and disciplining her while he was busy. What he really needed, he thought as Rusty kept on turning since she hadn't been told to stop, was another submissive bitch to replace his last one. And the slut rotating before him would be ideal. But until he could curtail her activities without attracting unwelcome attention, he would have to tread slowly. Her brother, Charles told himself, should not be a problem.....like all men, Danny Paget had his price.

Everything depended on the slut herself.....would she have what it took?

Rusty was beginning to feel dizzy. She could hardly believe her own stupidity. Just when she was trying to pick up her life again, he had turned up without as much as a phone call, and here she was, nude, and twirling round and round like a dervish in her own tiny hallway. Shivering, and bored with being stared at, she was losing her patience. Well, enough! She would tell him exactly what she thought of him.

Stopping without permission, she sighed and swivelled round to face him. Without thinking, she snapped, "You could have warned me you were coming over!"

Almost before she had finished speaking, she received a slap to her shoulder that almost knocked her off balance. "You agreed to take a test, an evaluation of your willingness to do what I ask, when I ask.....I use the term 'ask' loosely, you understand. And if I remember correctly the whole point was that you wouldn't know in advance. So, either you come with me now, Caroline, or not at all."

Pouting at the futility of making a point when she had lost the argument anyway, she snatched the towel from his arm and began to rub her hair again, putting all her energy into unnecessarily vigorous rubbing since it was almost dry.

"Okay, Sir," she relented. "If you'd just like to make coffee while I dry my hair properly and put on my make-up, I'll be with you in a few minutes. We'll have the coffee, then I'll get dressed." She turned to go into her bedroom, but he caught her by the arm.

"No make-up, no messing with your hair, just get dressed. I'll wait in the car. If you're not there in seven minutes precisely, I'll drive away and you won't see or hear from me again." With that, he let himself out and closed the door behind him.

Damn the man! She rushed into the bedroom, put her long hair in a ponytail, then yanked open her underwear drawer and made a quick selection. Pushing Gibbo to the back of her mind, she wiggled her breasts into the pink and black spotted bra that showed a decent amount of cleavage, then dug out the matching thong which she stepped into. She hooked her finger beneath the narrow piece of elastic at the back and pulled it to set it comfortably up the crack of her bottom. Next, she wriggled into a pair of hipster, brown leather trousers. There was no time to close the drawer! She took her pseudo leopard-skin jacket with the deep neckline and lapels from the hanger which she tossed onto the bed, and pulled the stretchy jacket closed at her narrow waist and fastened the one, oversized button.

She checked her reflection to see if she looked sexy enough; the trousers were so tight they looked as if she had poured herself into them and revealed a fair amount of pale, bare flesh between their top and the hem of the short jacket. Making no attempt to cover the bra which was almost fully visible, she grabbed a pair of knee high, brown leather boots from the bottom of the wardrobe and leaving the door open, sank down on the bed to pull them on. Then, running her hair through her fingers and giving it a rather attractive, tousled look as it continued to dry naturally, she ran from the room. On her way to the front door she collected her shoulder bag and made her way down to the car, out of habit choosing the stairs rather than summoning the lift. Her heels clattered and echoed around the bleak stairwell of the four storey block as she hurtled downward, frantic that she was not going to make it.

Bursting through the fire escape door and out into the street, she recognised the quickening of her breath and the rapid beating of her heart as the precursors of stunt flying or one of her other extreme activities, and there was always the huge adrenaline surge that saw her through to the end. Gladly she admitted that she lived for the twin highs of adrenaline surge and orgasm, and in the time she had known Charles she had discovered that he was an excellent source for the latter. And in her heart there was no doubt that he would turn out to be a good source of both. A good enough reason, she thought as she took a steadying breath and looked for his car, to go ahead with whatever he had planned, even though it would not be dangerous and would probably turn out to be quite bland.

Spotting Charles' sleek classic car with its blacked out windows parked just beyond The Chivalrous

Huntsman pub, she headed toward it at a more sedate pace, determined not to appear flustered in case he mistook it for fear. Except she was afraid, scared witless that he would drive away just before she reached it. Breathless and with her heart thumping again, she increased her pace.

It was not until she was within touching distance that Stratton got out and walked round to the pavement side where, ogling the cleavage that spilt temptingly from her bra, he opened the rear door for her.

Charles had removed his jacket and was sitting on the driver's side of the backseat with a glass of bourbon in his hand. He leaned across to help her in. "At last! With only half a minute to spare."

"Sorry! I was as quick as …….."

"No, you weren't. Still, you're here now." He flashed her a heart-stopping smile, then took her hand to help her into the roomy interior.

As she bent her head, as always she was struck simultaneously by its old fashioned opulence, the magnolia leather upholstery and walnut trim, and the smell of polish that spoke as much about its maintenance as it did its worth. She was just turning to sit beside him when he stayed her arm.

"Not there." Without letting go, he straightened in his seat and used his other hand to pull down a little seat opposite him that was positioned on one side of the old fashioned, centrally set walnut drinks cabinet. "Sit there."

"Yes, Sir." She moved across to the seat, while Stratton still stood on the pavement holding the door open, watching. Almost stumbling over Charles' outstretched legs, she said chirpily, "you'll have to move your feet."

"No, I won't," he said, his tone maddeningly even. "You'll just have to be less clumsy. Hurry up and sit, there's a good girl."

With a mulish sigh, she took her seat.

"That's better. Now, my dear, are you sure you want to go through with this?"

"Not if we're going to sit here all night! Please, Sir, can we just get it over with?"

As his toffee-coloured gaze adhered to her breasts, he reminded her, "You're supposed to do it without question or complaint."

Oh, for God's sake! she thought irritably, wondering if they were going anywhere at all or were just going to sit outside the pub all night. Then hoping to fool him with her bright smile, she said, "Yes, Sir, sorry Sir. I said I would, even without knowing what you've planned, Sir."

"And I have no intention of enlightening you. You already know all you need to know. Do your give your consent for me to carry out my intentions? Are you prepared to do whatever I say without question?"

Exasperated by the formality of something she had expected to be fun, she nodded.

"Say it, bitch!"

Flinching at his sudden outburst, she pressed back against the seat. Thoroughly sick of the whole thing and beginning to wish she hadn't bothered, she had a good mind to get up and tell him where to stick his bloody games. But it was as if a buzzer went off inside her head, reminding her that he was about to introduce her to the kind of sexual satisfaction that no one else had ever come close to offering, and warning her that it was she who was supposed to please him and not the other way round. She smiled weakly, and heard herself not just giving her consent but repeating his own words back to him.

"Yes, I'm prepared to do whatever you say, without question, Sir."

"Lean towards me."

The last thing she saw before she leaned forward and he bound the black velvet strip tightly across her eyes, was a glimpse out of the corner of her eye of Gibbo's Peugeot driving past.

She heard the soft click as Stratton at last closed the door. As she sat up straight again, she thought it better not to point out that Charles had caught her hair in the knot and that it was pulling like hell. But still Charles was not satisfied.

"You'll stay blindfolded until we reach our destination. Now, pull down your trousers as far as possible without removing your boots, then do the same with your panties."

It was an awkward struggle that necessitated her lifting her bottom from the seat. When she had done as he commanded, he told her to open her legs as wide as possible and put her hands on her head.

"Good girl. No matter what happens, you're to keep your hands there until I tell you otherwise."

She felt him reach past her and knock on the glass partition to alert Stratton. Almost at once, she felt rather than heard the quiet engine start and the car wafted easily away from the pavement. With her heart thumping once more, she listened to Charles' voice, low and husky over the smoothness of the car's engine as he spelled out the kind of life she would have if, by the end of the evening, he considered her worthy.

"I've no intention of making you give up your flying. After all, we've both got our own lives to lead, things we must do and people we must see. But I will require you to move into my apartment. I demand obedience at all times, even when we're apart. Whether the commands – and make no mistake that they will be commands – are given orally or simply by a gesture or look, you must obey instantly. Providing you meet my requirements this evening, we'll go into more detail later. For now, just sit back, don't move and don't speak until I give permission."

CHAPTER FOUR

BLAWANYA

The air was filled with the sound of baboon chatter. Adair Dowling sat in the shade on the veranda at the back of his bungalow on the edge of the savannah, situated about an hour's drive outside Thomassentown, the dusty shanty town where the mine workers' social hall, cafés and accommodation complex were situated, along with the medical facility. It was two hours' drive away from the vast Thomassentown mine itself, where the male workers toiled in the worst conditions for a mere pittance.

Enjoying an ice cold beer, every once in a while he looked up from his paperback and turned his gaze instead to the sight of Freedom, whose naked body was perfectly displayed on the whipping post for his delectation. With her back toward him she was suspended upside down, the back of her head, covered in tiny, tight curls hung about ten inches from the ground. She must have one hell of a headache by now, he mused.

He had already reduced her to tears by giving her backside and shoulders a good going-over, and he was taking a well-earned rest. It was unfortunate that there was no escape for the slavegirl from the afternoon sun that scorched the earth, but it would be a shame to move her inside and spoil the view. The only other, more permanent alternative was to relocate the post from its current position to one farther down the garden where there was shade from the mighty Baobab tree. But he could not face the upheaval, and it meant getting men from the mine to do the job for him. Besides, he thought it an amusing picture – against the backdrop of the tree's strange, root-like branches that made the Baobab look as if it had been planted upside-down, which accounted for one of its many other names, upside-down tree – it looked as if the branches were growing out of her feet!

The legend that Yonas Nsambu, the mine's wealthy, black owner, had told him, claimed the tree's incessant talking had offended the inhabitants of paradise who had uprooted it and thrown it out of the garden. Apparently it had landed upside-down and taken root. Dowling himself was quite happy to have it in his garden, because its leaves and fruits – those that the baboons didn't eat – were a handy supplement to his slave's diet, the leaves especially when they were boiled. And Jacob, the servant he employed and who cooked and maintained the garden for him, knew several methods for serving the apparently delicious fruit that was known locally as "monkey bread" and that was rich in vitamin C, and which could even be brewed into a refreshing drink. And the leaves could be ground to make a coffee substitute. Adair had sampled it once and did not care for it, but it proved useful for cutting costs at the clinic where he gave it to patients instead of real coffee.

He took another slug of beer, then focussed his attention on the post again. As the baboons in the Baobab finished gorging on the fruits and left the sanctuary of his garden, he listened for her groans which always blended so well, he thought, with the birdsong and sounds of the small, scurrying African wildlife that inhabited the place. But to his disappointment it appeared that either she had fallen asleep or had grown used to the torment, neither of which he was prepared to accept. Letting his book drop slowly to the ground, he eased himself out of his wicker chair, snatched up his single-tailed whip and crossed the distance between them like a man bent on vengeance.

He did not bother to walk around to check if her eyes were closed as he gave her the once over. Nor did he give her well-being any consideration, though he noticed in passing that she was trembling. And so she should! He drew back his arm and mentally selected his target.

"Go to sleep and deny me, would you? Well, I'll not have it, you selfish bitch. Wake up!"

Whizz!

Crack!

"Aaaarghh!"

That was more like it! Delighted at the reaction from the whip's burning sting across her dark-skinned torso, when he spoke his voice was thick with the tone ridicule.

"Ha! You weren't expecting it there. Perhaps..... here?"

Her screams as the lash fell neatly into the crease where her thighs joined her buttocks was even louder, and so he struck another nine times in the same place before moving his target once more. And so it went on, each fall of the lash producing a scream to drive away the wildlife for miles around.

He did not hear the soft footfalls of old, open-backed shoes as they approached, and was about to aim for the back of her thighs when his endeavours were interrupted.

"I'm sorry, Doctor, Sir, but you have a visitor."

Adair swung round to face the intruder.

"Who is it, Jacob?" he demanded impatiently.

"Mr Roy, the pilot, Sir. He says he must see you, Sir."

Irritated, he wondered what he wanted since Roy was not due to pick up the stones for another week yet. He hoped it was not the man's attempt at a social call. After all, it had been a long, tedious morning at the clinic, seeing to the men's medical needs and checking the status of the women whose cycle rendered them unclean in Blawanyan eyes. Surely a man was entitled to a bit of relaxation?

"Show him into the front sitting room," he growled, glaring at the servant as if it were his fault that Roy had turned up unannounced and that his own malevolent sport was necessarily curtailed. "Then come and cut the whore down. We'll need beers."

The square room in which the meeting took place was the one in which he always saw Roy, the man he considered spent too much time with the locals. He could understand why he hung around the cages, molesting the women through the bars since Adair did the same thing often enough himself. But what he could not understand was why Roy spent so much time loitering around the black men's accommodation complex, sometimes with one or other of the slaves in tow, or drinking with the black men in the bars.

Although the two men drank beers together at their regular meetings, and shared Freedom too, Adair had never considered the man a friend or even someone to impress. After almost two years he still hadn't invited him through to the more comfortable part of the sizeable bungalow, nor even to the garden where on the shady veranda at least, at this time of day the heat was just bearable.

Curiously, the pilot was holding a length of blue rope, at the end of which was one of the mine's slaves. Wearing a slave's brown collar and a permitted cotton shift, like all the slaves she had nothing on her feet.

When pressed, Roy said he had simply taken the woman for his own use.

"Do me the courtesy of having her naked in my house!" Adair told him, making reference to the accepted, local tradition that held that no woman should be brought clothed into another's man's dwelling. Still annoyed to have his leisure time broken into, while Roy untied the rope to enable the girl to pull the shift off over her head and reveal her beautiful, black velvet skin, Adair pointed to a hook the that he'd had inserted into the wall at about shoulder height, located at the end of the couch on which Roy now sat down. "Make sure she's properly tethered, at least while we discuss whichever burning issue you think too important to hold over until you're summoned in the usual way!"

Adair's lips were tightly pursed as, seething quietly, he went through to another room to fetch from his safe the goods he had received only hours earlier. As he dropped them one by one into the special leather pouches that Jacob's friend made, the doctor lifted each unpolished stone to his nose and inhaled the essence of womanhood that he liked to imagine was still on them, having been removed so recently from their warm and moist hiding places.

Meanwhile, out of sight Freedom went silently about her duties. Released at last from her cruel bondage, with her tears dried on her face and the imprints in her soft flesh of the rough, baobab rope, she slipped on her own shift. Then she hurried to fetch the imported beers and poured them into the ready-chilled glasses. At last she entered the room with her tray, upon which stood the two glasses of beer, both glasses with droplets of condensation running down them that mirrored the droplets of sweat running down between her breasts. Ready to offer herself, as well as the beer, she stood in the doorway until her master summoned her as, without a word passing between them, Adair re-entered and dropped two leather pouches into Roy's open palm.

"They're light this time. If you'd waited until I sent for you – "

Roy cut him off. "Okay, so there's not so many this trip." Seated in his usual place, the pilot slipped the pouches into the side pocket of his baggy trousers and continued. "Sorry, but I can't wait. See, I'm leaving this shit hole for good!"

Without revealing his surprise, Adair crossed the room to take up his customary seat on the dusty couch beneath the window, and flung Freedom a contemptuous glance. He knew he maltreated her, but the worse he treated her the more the stupid bitch loved him for it. He supposed she considered herself fortunate because, whereas slaves were not permitted to move around freely and were kept locked up unless working, tagged as his personal slave by a disc hanging from her clitoris, she was able to move around the shanty town unhindered as she ran errands for him. Sometimes she walked for several hours into the nearest big town for his special supplies that could not be bought locally, and it always amused him to see her trudging along the roadside loaded with bags of the special groceries, alcohol and other goods, carrying some on her head in the traditional manner. He could never resist speeding past in his car and blasting sand up at her. And he wondered if she realised what the little device he had fixed on the inside of her collar actually was; although it rubbed her sore, he doubted she knew that with the aid of his laptop he could track her movements, find out exactly where she was, making it quite impossible for her to escape.

Sitting with his legs crossed, he fixed his younger countryman with a piercing blue gaze. At the same time he snapped his fingers to summon Freedom. Obeying as quickly as she could without spilling any of the precious liquid, she went across to stand before the couch on which he was sprawled. He pulled himself upright. Helping himself first to her nether-charms and then his beer, he rummaged around inside her pussy while he addressed Roy in his usual, brusque tones.

"I'm surprised at your decision." He nodded toward the other black girl who crouched obediently on all fours. Now stark naked apart from the brown leather collar with her crumpled shift heaped close by, she was an attractive specimen. "What will you do about her?"

"Take her, of course!"

"I'm not convinced you'll make it, not with her in tow. They'll come looking for her," Adair told him matter-of-factly. He placed his glass on a table and, pulling his fingers free of Freedom's cunt, he addressed her angrily. "Who said you could get dressed?" Without allowing her time to either answer or put down her tray, with both hands he gripped the neck of her shift and rent the garment to her waist, exposing her pendulous, dark skinned breasts. Taking out his displeasure on the poor girl he callously squeezed and mauled them, before swinging her round to stand with her back toward him so that he could admire his handiwork from the garden. Then with his customary slap to her backside he sent her off toward the pilot. And as she crossed the room, he nodded his head toward the crouching girl, continuing the conversation as if he hadn't been distracted. "After all, she is the mine's property."

"They have hundreds of them! They won't miss one."

For the first time, Adair laughed. "That's probably true. What's her history? Any brands or other identification?"

"Only her mine number, and I'll get that altered….. get someone to do a design to mark her out as belonging to me, bought and paid for."

A slave's history was important insofar as proving ownership was concerned in a country where demand was high. Apart from the rich merchants and businessmen who kept attractive slaves for sexual use and older women to do the work, the country depended on female slave labour. Although any woman deemed suitable to be sold to a wealthy individual could find her status elevated to one of a man's four permitted wives and dressed accordingly, her enslaved condition was still mandatory. But under the guise of freedom to placate the watching, free world, she could be coached in the niceties and accompany her "husband" to official functions at home and even abroad.

As far as the general population was concerned, there was nothing wrong or outrageous about female slavery and the practice was commonplace, often serving as a form of international currency. Although the Thomassentown mine, in common with the other mines usually bought the females for mine use legally, it was not alone in periodically sending its guards on raiding parties into the countryside to abduct suitable girls. And once a mine slave was considered too old, she would find herself put up for sale at auction, eventually winding up confined to the laundries, kitchens or anywhere else where she was kept out of sight working in one of the cities or larger towns. The hotels especially needed such women.

But the demand for slaves who were astute and pleasing to the eye was also high and were used as frontline workers in restaurants, shops and hotels, where they were known as "free" women and where, to appease the foreigners' sensibilities they were paid meagre salaries, though each female "employee" was marked with her owner's brand on her belly.

Although Adair treated the sick at his clinic, he did not associate with the black workers themselves, on the whole he confined his socialising to the Europeans he actively sought out on his regular visits to the city, and the European nurses who worked for him. Although under normal circumstances he would not actively seek Roy's company, their mutual feelings regarding slaves made their meetings more entertaining. But there was no one in Blawanya he would actually call friend.

Aware of his good looks, Adair knew people thought he looked more like a secret agent in a movie than he did a doctor. Always smart even when dressed casually as he was now, with his short, sandy hair and blue eyes, his rugged good looks made his European nurses' hearts flutter. At forty, having left his London practice far behind, he had done well for himself in the African republic, as the deceptively sprawling bungalow with its own neat gardens front and back testified. With no one to question his diagnosis or authority, only the mine owner himself had superior accommodation, and that was at least three hours away on the road in the other direction, on the outskirts of the nearest, sizeable town.

In an attempt to avoid Adair's imperious eyes that were once again trained on him, the pilot switched his own gaze to Freedom as she leaned over him. Slender and so obviously yielding, her big eyes shone with both the joy and fear of serving her master. She wore only the torn and baggy shift that had been allocated her, enabling Roy to take in the delights of her breasts which hung loosely, like two dark, exotic fruits toward gravity as she leaned forward to serve him his beer.

At the back her shift was short enough to ride up her backside, giving Adair a view of her developing welts, setting his heart racing with the need to discipline her further. As he leaned back beneath the window and used an ivory handled fan to cool himself, the doctor feasted his eyes greedily on the blatant view of her cunt.

Leering at her, Roy did not thank her as he took the proffered glass, then knowing what was required of her without being told, she set the tray aside.

Without consideration for the crouching girl at the end of the sofa who panted like a dog as she waited for him to provide water, Roy placed his glass on the table and reached for Freedom's breasts with both hands. As she obediently crossed her hands behind her, with a soft, squidgy mammary clutched tightly in each palm he used them as purchase to adjust his position to sit more comfortably. Then he squashed and wrung them harshly until she finally gave little cries of discomfort. Sniggering, he persisted with his brutal manipulation. Releasing one breast to grab his glass, while he swigged thirstily he forsook her other breast and turned his attention instead to her long nipple which he twisted and pinched until she cried out.

"Aid in and diamonds out! Our paymasters knew exactly what they were doing when they got involved with Blawanya's needy," he said at last.

Freedom leant over him as he harried her long nipple with one hand and held his half-empty glass in the other, while she kept her eyes obediently lowered, having no choice but to endure his rough treatment. It would not have made any difference, of course, even if he had known that she hadn't always been a slave, but came from across the border where she had lived as a free woman, an elegantly and expensively dressed princess – the daughter of a tribal king who had thought he was offering his beloved daughter to the church rather than a lifetime of slavery in Blawanya.

And it was Freedom's secret shame that that was how she knew the truth concerning the Aid that arrived on the big trucks, because much of it was sold to the people of her own country. And although some of it did eventually find its way to Blawanya, and the men of Thomassentown were the recipients of some of the clothing and footwear, it tended to be the items that hadn't been sold off at the kraals on the way. But without the blankets that arrived from time to time, the caged mine slaves would be completely exposed to the elements at night, forced to huddle together for warmth. Whatever else she was forced to endure, Freedom knew she was fortunate because she enjoyed the relative comfort of a mattress from the clinic, a pillow and a blanket. And, most of all, she had shelter, even though it was not in the bungalow with her master but down at the end of the garden.

"Slut!" Dowling addressed his slave suddenly.

Obligingly Roy released his grasp. Still with her hands behind her back, smilingly she turned to face her master.

"Fetch my cart," Adair ordered.

Trembling, she scurried obediently from the room, returning moments later pushing a stainless steel medical trolley. Its three shelves were laden with all kinds of frightening-looking, stainless steel implements, most of which she had experienced at some time. At Adair's command she dropped onto her hands and knees beside it with her torn shift falling off her shoulders, she silently awaited his pleasure as he deposited his empty glass on a small table and rose from his seat.

Slowly and deliberately he moved around behind her, then ripped the remnants of her shift from her back, revealing for the first time the extent of the welts he had laid down earlier.

"My God! Did you do that?" the awe-struck pilot asked as the excitement caught huskily in his throat.

"Just before you arrived," Adair told him proudly, adding mockingly, "That's one good thing about the whore. She might not burn as the brightest candle, but she loves abuse. I'd go so far as to say she was made for it. I've had others before her, and I use the caged sluts too, but she's the only able to take anything like I can give!"

Jacob entered the room with two additional, ice cold cans of beer, while behind her and out of her sight, with great ceremony Adair, more for show than for health and hygiene, donned a pair of latex gloves. He selected one of the implements from the trolley and held it up for Roy to see. Using the thumb-operated ratchet he demonstrated its scissors-like action.

"In the medical profession it's known as speculum," he said as he closed the implement once more. He placed his gloved hand heavily on her back and felt her flinch as the latex touched her skin, then flinch again as he inserted the closed three-and-a-half inches long business-end of the tool into her rectum. Laughing as she screamed in pain as he pushed it further in, he had taught her to acknowledge the sound as a soothing balm and to relish the pleasure her pain brought him. When it was in as far as it would go, he announced matter-of-factly, "one uses a jelly, of course, to ease its way for one's patients….at least, one does when practising back home." He felt her tense as she listened for the operation of the ratchet that would open her anus. About now, he thought, she would feel sick with humiliation as she felt her secret hole being stretched wide….and wider….. "Most amusing, don't you think?" he said when she was stretched a good three inches.

Getting to his feet and without putting down the remainder of his beer, the pilot hunkered down to peer inside the opened anus, assisted by the light Adair shone into the gaping hole. Taking up Adair's invitation to choose something from the trolley, they paid no attention to her trembling as he selected a long, steel dildo from the bottom shelf, he angled the dildo around the handle section of the speculum and shunning the tube of medical jelly as Adair had done, with a nasty smirk he shoved it inside the beckoning cavity.

"Uhhh!"

Wincing with pain, the poor slave failed to concentrate her thoughts elsewhere, feeling nothing but shame as the men continued their conversation about the security measures and the way the guards were always searching for evidence of smuggled diamonds.

"I'll miss watching them search the sluts," Roy confessed. "I've even seen them stop yours while she's been running your errands." He did not see, however, the way her face contorted with pain at the brutal violation of her behind, though it would have made no difference if he had. "Strange that they never catch anyone. You'd think they had other things on their mind!" Thrusting the dildo in and out, and stopping every now and then to guzzle beer noisily and wipe his mouth on his arm, the men laughed about the building on the edge of Thomassentown where the guards sat watching banks of computer screens, for there were electronic surveillance cameras everywhere, especially around the slaves' cages.

Freedom had spent time in the cages, too, and knew that sometimes the guards went right into the cages and examined slaves at random, making them bend over and submit to a humiliating probing of their arses or cunts. But like the other slaves, she did not realise they did it for the cameras, sometimes even poking their fingers down a slave's throat until she gagged. And they had no knowledge either of the footage that appeared on the Internet, and so naturally they assumed that the guards were always on the look-out for diamonds, either in their raw or polished state since the mine had facilities for both. And the two men could not help but laugh at how the guards exploited their victims for pleasure….. and money too since the films they sold brought them money from abroad.

Freedom cried out at the violation of her back passage. But that only increased their lust as they continued to subject her to the twin horrors of pain and shame. While Adair held her open with the speculum and Roy continued to torment her with the dildo, the subject of their conversation shifted as they talked and drank over her defiled body as if the circumstances were the most natural in the world.

"So this really will be your last trip?" Adair probed as he watched the molestation of his property without concern.

"The very last!"

"You fly out tomorrow – "

"And back with the medicines and stuff in a couple of days. Then it's just a case of walking away from the plane and I'm out of here for good."

As he spoke, Roy plunged the full length of the dildo in and out with renewed vigour that made her scream.

And the force of his thrusting was so strong that her hands and knees would no longer hold her and she collapsed onto her stomach. But Adair merely slipped one latex-sheathed hand beneath her and, with the other gloved hand still spread out on her back, lifted her back into position so that his companion could continue.

"Then make sure you're well out of it by the time the Dutchman gets here!" Adair warned. "He's due to pay us a visit sometime soon. It's a publicity stunt to promote the charity's good works – building the clinic and donating aid – so he can show it off and tap the rich for a few bob at some gala dinner– " he broke off, laughing at the thought.

"He's one mean-arsed bastard I don't want to run into," the blond man replied as, tiring of the dildo but leaving it sticking out from her rectum which was still held open by the speculum, he reached beneath her and let his fingers find Freedom's long, pliant nipple which he twisted as sharply as before.

"He'll have your balls rather than risk you exposing the operation," Adair told him brusquely, then added, "I can understand your decision if you feel the risk is too great. But it's always been a risky business. You knew that at the start. And you can't deny that the rewards are great."

"It's the dust I can't stand," with undisguised malevolence Roy's eyes loitered over the other instruments on the shelves and spotted the clamps he had seen before. "The risk I can cope with! Most officials can be bought if you know their price, and I soon got to know the going rate of the ones I dealt with." Gesturing toward the stainless steel, vice-shaped clamps he indicated his interest, and then watched with awe as the doctor fitted them, one at a time.

Holding a clamp with one hand and using the finger and thumb of the other Adair poked the slave's delightfully long and helpfully erect nipple through the square device before tightening the screw on top that forced a little steel bar down against the imprisoned nipple.

"But eighteen months is long enough. I'll miss the flying, of course, any flyer would! And the excitement. But most of all I'll miss the constant supply of sluts. You're a lucky man, doctor, to have a specimen that seems to thrive on little more than maltreatment," he observed, his tone admiring as the second nipple was finally imprisoned.

Naked, on all fours, with her skin marred by welts, her speculum-stretched anus penetrated by the stainless steel dildo and her nipples agonised by the clamps, her heart swelled with pride as the two men laughed at her plight. With her nipples throbbing fit to burst and her rectum ravaged by fire as its cruel defilement continued, she knew they would never understand. As always when things got this bad, the strangest desire to have the pain increased and to be fucked into the bargain overtook her to such an extent that her insides quivered with need; somehow her pain transmuted into longing, and then longing transmuted into peaceful and joyous acceptance. And she wondered as the men talked of the other slave, if she felt the same way.

"Still, like I said, I'm taking this one back with me," Roy jabbed his thumb at the other girl, still panting and on all fours. "But it's time to pack it in, see if I can't find something as lucrative back home."

"Is there much call for your line of business 'back home? You don't want to change your mind?"

Standing behind her with his legs pressed up against her dark-skinned arse, Adair suddenly wrenched out the dildo.

"Aaaarghh!"

Not caring that it was more painful than when it had been inserted, while his slave whimpered and shook, the doctor unzipped his trousers and extracted his penis. Then, crouching down he shuffled into a more comfortable position, closed and withdrew the speculum and then plunged his iron hard cock straight into the vacant hole. While his poor slave squirmed beneath him, he pressed his latex-covered hands down onto her welted back to steady himself and began a fast a furious fucking of her backside that sent alternating waves of shame and pain through her entire being.

Extracting his phallus suddenly, he stood up and used his hands to raise her rear. With her hands still flat on the cement floor and her legs almost straightened, it offered better access to her vagina. Adjusting his own position, gripping her hips tightly and bending his knees, he sank his cock deep into her belly, rocking her violently he fucked her while the blond man retook his seat, drank his beer and watched.

With a grunt, Adair discharged copious amounts of his hot, sticky liquor, laughing as he filled her to overflowing. He pulled out of her and, as spunk dribbled down her legs, he wiped his cock clean on her whip-scored backside, then waved his hand vaguely to indicate the diamonds in the other man's breast pocket. "Just think of all the extra commission you could make." He walked slowly to the table where he had placed his own beer, took a couple of swigs as he stood beside her again and ran his forefinger along her backbone just to see her flinch. Like the other slut whose thirst had weakened her to the extent that she was close to collapse, Freedom was panting loudly. But his concerns were centred on his own predicament…... Without a pilot there was no way to get the illicit diamonds to Amsterdam, where the craftsman at Van de Velde's factory turned the insignificant stones into gems that were sought after the world over.

The legal route and the one which the legal Thomassentown stones made, and where the Dutchman – as Van de Velde's associates called him – conducted his legitimate business, was to the Central Selling Organisation in London, from where the stones were distributed throughout the world. Without a pilot here in Blawanya and the cover of the charity that was also based in the Netherlands and fronted by Pik Van de Velde himself, the whole operation would collapse and cost the Dutchman millions in lost revenue.

"You're a good man," Adair flattered as he placed his foot on Freedom's hand as a warning not to move. "Why don't you stay? Say the word and it'll be business as usual. No one need ever know that you considered quitting. We'll forget this conversation ever took place. On the other hand, I hope the Dutchman doesn't know where 'home' is. I wouldn't want to be in your shoes if he ever tracks you down. I'm surprised you don't just take the diamonds and run." At least then, Adair's own conscience would be clear when he warned the Dutchman to send his men after him.

"As you pointed out, he's not a man to cross."

"Then why bother coming back?" Adair said as a plan took shape in his brain. "Surely not out of some misplaced sense of duty in bringing in aid?"

Roy laughed and jerked his head in the direction of his tethered slave. "To get the bitch, of course."

Making no further comment, casually Adair gestured an invitation toward the sperm-filled cunt he had just vacated.

The pilot was quick to respond. Within moments he had sunk his own shaft up to the hilt inside her and was thrusting fiercely. And as he pounded into her, he told his host raggedly, "Don't worry about me. I've got a bit tucked away for a rainy day. Besides, there's always work to be had for a man of my talents. I might try my luck over the border…….."

"Which border? I wouldn't bother with Botswana, because most of the mines there are Government owned these days."

"I wasn't thinking of Botswana, or diamonds! I'll lie low for a bit before eventually moving on to South Africa, where we…" again he jerked his head in the girl's direction, "can get a flight home easily enough. Back on British soil, as a pilot I can always find something. There are plenty of rich guys around with their own jets, if not in the UK there's the rest of Europe. Besides, I haven't exactly been idle. Whenever I've gone into the only decent town this side of the city, I've been asking around. And I've been checking the web regularly. There's a lot of wealthy folk out there looking for a pilot to double as their bodyguard." He laughed. "I may even end up flying the Dutchman himself around and protecting the bastard from his enemies!" With that he climaxed, his own hot fountain of spunk mingling with the doctor's inside the girl.

"I wouldn't count on it," Adair told him as Roy withdrew, and he handed him some surgical wadding to clean himself, before summoning Jacob and ordering him to bring two bowls of water for the slaves. He was surprised by his own enjoyment in sharing the girl and almost wished he hadn't decided to have Roy picked up and arrested. He could not be one hundred per cent sure whether it was his suggestion that had put the idea into Roy's head, but he knew without a doubt that he had changed his mind, he would make this last delivery but would abscond with the diamonds within hours of leaving, taking the slave with him. And he knew where he was heading, so just had to bide his time until the stupid bastard made his move. It was a pity, but there it was. To take his mind off the inconvenience and give himself time to alert the authorities, he suggested, "Then let's make your last evening special. My bitch needs punishing …..look at her, pathetic creature! We'll take yours as well and mount them face to face on the whipping post….."

"Tit to tit!" The pilot added excitedly, heat and titillation flushing his face.

"We'll have some more beers, and give them both a flogging they'll never forget!" Adair nudged Freedom with the toe of his Italian shoe. "Well, get the beers, you lazy, good for fuck-all, slut!"

CHAPTER FIVE

KENT

As the car glided along, in her darkened world it seemed to Rusty that her other senses became more acute. The various ingredients that made up the fragrance of his cologne seemed to separate; she could definitely smell ginger, and there was a waft of citrus as well as musk. As a whole it seemed to overpower her in the sealed interior of his classic car. And then there were the other smells, too, like the lavender of the polish Stratton used on the interior, and spunk.....yes, it must be spunk.... She knew it was ridiculous, it was impossible to pick out the individual smells. It was all Charles' doing, she mused, he was somehow playing mind games, controlling her thoughts.... emotions too. That was the function of the blindfold, she realised, that and the fact that he simply didn't want her to know where they were going, of course!

The low hum of the car's engine entered into her senses as well, and seemed to combine with the excited throb in her clitoris. And that grew worse as she realised that he was watching her.....hadn't taken his eyes off her since they set out. The intensity of his toffee-coloured gaze engendered a warmth that she felt rise across her flesh. From the pinkening of her face down to the apex of her flushed thighs, where wanton desires burned ravenously. She was a hotbed of desire.

With her back toward the driver and separated by the closed, sliding glass panel that reminded her of a cab, Rusty remained perched on the pull-down seat with her leather trousers and panties around her knees and her hands clasped together on top her head throughout the entire journey. Although Charles hadn't tied her hands, she did not attempt to remove the blindfold. She was determined to see this thing through to its conclusion. Besides, he was watching her.

Unable to suppress a shiver of excitement as his hand made contact with the soft flesh between her thighs where her ginger pubes frizzed with abandon, she held her breath as his fingers burrowed through them. He was always rough, but she was not prepared for the increased harshness with which they delved into her ravenous cunt and drew in a startled breath.

"Quiet!"

She could not help fidgeting on the seat as his skilful fingers stirred her insides into a frenzy.

"Keep still. If I want you to move, I'll tell you."

Sitting rigidly to try and keep from moving as he began to plunge his fingers in and out with a tenacity that edged closer by the second to persecution, her insides responded by squelching noisily. She teetered on the brink of orgasm time and again without being permitted to reach the apex.

"I'm going to come, Sir," she breathed huskily.

"No, you're not. We've been through this before. For your own sake, you must learn to control it."

As if she had no understanding at all of the reason they were there, she came back with a cheeky retort. "Charles! Don't be such a bully," she compounded her sin with a sexy laugh before adding, "I want to come!"

When he spoke again, there was a real note of anger in his voice. "You must understand, Caroline, that I don't want you to. Now be a good girl and shut up!"

But he was not going to make it easy for her and renewed his efforts. Almost instantly she was hovering on the brink once more as his fingers grew even more aggressive. This time she had to admit that it was

painful. Painful yes, but ooh…..it was so…..ooh…..
she was going crazy with a need to come! And although
she guessed correctly that he had a drink in his other
hand……..perhaps it wasn't bourbon after all but
champagne of which he drank copious amounts……
his scant regard for her enjoyment seemed to add to
her own arousal, causing ripples of torrid warmth to
ebb and flow with such regularity that she thought she
would die.

Her muscles were about to go into spasm when he
withdrew his fingers altogether and he sat back in his
seat. "If you come, Caroline, I'll have to punish you
and you won't get to take the test. Sit quietly until we
stop and I tell you to get out."

Rusty felt his arm brush against hers as he opened
the drinks cabinet again and heard more liquid flowing
into the glass. She licked her lips, realising that she
hadn't had anything to drink since lunchtime, apart
from a mouthful of water when she first got in from
work. Now her throat was parched, due as much to a
slowly developing panic on her part as much as thirst.
She realised her stupidity in getting in the car with a
relative stranger, to let him blindfold her and to take
her God knew where to take some bloody unknown
test! But she also recognised the excitement that was
always present when she accepted a new challenge,
like parachuting for the first time. As excitement
overrode caution, she ignored his instructions and
dared to ask for a sip.

"Don't you understand 'no talking'? And no Dutch
courage allowed either!"

She could hear him laughing. Not with general
good humour or the absurdity of the situation, but
mockingly…..at her, sitting in his car blindfolded,
with her hands on her head and her trousers round her

knees, being ordered about and laughed at. No one ever laughed at Rusty Paget and it was too much to ask of her when she was in such a heightened state of arousal. "Then do you have any water?"

"Yes."

"Then I'll have some of that."

"No, you won't."

Finally it was too much. Letting her nerves get the better of her she set aside the civility and obedience he demanded and pressed the issue.

"You bastard! I'm thirsty!"

His reaction was swift and he raised his hand to strike her. But then, deciding not to waste his time and without her ever knowing how close she had come to feeling the full extent of his wrath, he lowered his arm and laughed instead. When he spoke again, it was with such polite authority that it maddened her even more.

"My dear girl, you've so much to learn. Firstly, I told you to keep quiet and I really would prefer it if you did as I request. Secondly, you may not have a drink because I said 'no.' And thirdly, I really don't care that much whether you're thirsty or not. You may have a drink later. So please, no more of this silliness. This is a momentous occasion, Caroline. You must appreciate how significant a part it will play in your life. If you fail to impress me, then I'll have to consider our short and charming affair at an end. And I'm afraid I'll have to renege on the sponsorship deal and tear up the contract before the ink dries."

Why was she antagonising him? she wailed silently. For the sake of her own sexual desires she wanted to be here, wanted to go through with it, wanted to really get to know this man and learn everything he was willing to teach her. Besides, the sponsorship money would make all the difference in the world to the teams. She had no idea whether or not he knew of her own accomplishments as a member of both, but it made no difference.....she could not risk their future.

"I've been tolerant so far this evening, but don't push me," he warned. "And at this stage you really should not need reminding that you must address me as 'Sir.' You won't find me so magnanimous on this matter in particular from now on."

Sighing plaintively and not daring to speak, she settled down.

She could not gauge how long they had been travelling and wished they would reach their destination soon. Sitting in the quiet with only the sound of his breathing and the engine's low hum, it was not long before her mind began wandering again, recalling things he had told her about women screaming with pain simply for a man's pleasure as they were flogged to orgasm, and her clitoris tingled the more she thought about it.

Any alarm she had initially felt had given way to pleasurable tingles of double-strength excitement. Charles was giving her exactly what she craved, she realised, the chance to be tested, pushed to the very limits of her ability and endurance. And no matter how much she tried to fight against it or dismiss it from her mind, what she wanted more than anything that evening was to make him proud of her so that they could get down to the real business of a relationship, whatever kind it was that he was offering. And with the realisation came a change within her, a change so subtle that she hardly noticed it herself. For something intangible had touched her soul, a thing that dug deep to the very core of her being and unearthed an as yet unrecognised masochism that in time would bring about a totally new, and complete, acquiescence.

The luscious redhead was determined to do whatever he required of her, for the fear of losing the opportunity to stretch herself, or more importantly lose the man who would make her stretch herself, was greater than her fear of the unknown. She had agreed to perform any feat he selected from a list of her favourite pastimes and could foresee no problems, because whichever he had chosen, she had probably done it so many times that it would be a piece of cake. But there was still the matter of the conditions and restrictions he was imposing and that he hadn't yet revealed.

The blindfold made a farce of her sense of direction and she had no idea where they were or even where they were heading, even though she knew the local roads intimately. Nor could she tell how long they had been travelling, though in reality it was not long at all. And then, despite the smoothness of the ride and the low hum of the engine, she felt the change when they began travelling up a steep incline.

The car crested the incline and coasted to a halt in the deserted car park. Sliding the panel open, Charles instructed Stratton to wait in the car, closed it again, then told her to tidy herself. As she reached to untie the blindfold, he slapped her hands away.

"No, Caroline," he said, "Pull up your knickers and trousers first. I decide when it comes off, not you."

Awkwardly, she did as he asked, giggling as she half-stood and wriggled herself back into her tight-fitting trousers. Then misjudging the position of the seat, she plonked herself down too hard.

"Now what, Sir?" she asked quite naturally as, still unseen, he reached for the jacket of his suit.

"That's better. I'm just putting on my jacket," he said simply, smirking at the thought that she would not be needing hers as he shrugged it on. Then leaning toward her, he pulled her head down toward him and reached to untie the blindfold.

The sudden brightness as it was removed made her screw up her eyes as Charles got out of the car. Slowly, as she became accustomed to the light, he extended his hand and helped her from the car into the light of early evening, under a sky that was perfect for flying. For a moment she stood her ground, puzzled. Although she recognised her surroundings instantly and knew exactly where she was, Pilgrim's Leap was the last place she had expected. And they were only a few miles from the Saxon Hill Airfield.

"So, you're ready to prove yourself worthy of my attention?" Charles asked scornfully.

Rusty's heart leapt as she repeated the word in her mind, attention. He had already made it clear that whatever else developed between them, it would never be love, there would never be a place in their relationship for that particular four letter word. Somehow that made the whole prospect even more exciting. Besides, she had never been particularly sentimental regarding her lovers. Sentimentality was an emotion she kept exclusively for old aeroplanes!

"I'm waiting for an answer, Caroline!" he chided as they walked side by side from the car.

Walking at a brisk pace they soon covered the three hundred yards to the unassuming but aptly named Clifftop Café that crouched close to the ground for fear of being blown by the upland winds closer to where the land had eroded into formidable cliffs. And she smiled as she recognised the Harley parked outside the building that, having been open since seven thirty am to serve the needs of walkers, sightseers and birdwatchers, at almost seven pm was just closing for the night. Guessing that the bike's owner, a man she had known for many years and whose group she had ridden with several times on their charity runs, was having a coffee after a late session with a novice rock climber, she briefly wondered at the wisdom of bringing a novice to such a testing location even on such a still, windless evening. But then, Jake was the expert and always knew exactly what he was doing.

At least her hair had dried on the way, she thought stupidly as they reached the café door, which opened to discharge the impressive bulk of Jake Morgan, the biker and activity centre owner who came out to greet them. His curt, nodded acknowledgement to Charles was followed up with a cheerful, "Hi, Rusty."

Powerfully built and genial, he was wearing a wet, purple polo shirt with the words 'INSTRUCTOR, Zenith Sports' emblazoned across the back. Carrying a rucksack, he did not seem surprised to see them as he fell into step beside them, drawing her to conclude that he and Charles had been in touch previously. So whatever kind of surprise the test was to her, Jake was in on it.

"Jake. Good to see you," she smiled, genuinely pleased to see him.

With a small, greying beard, a moustache and almost bald head, his tattoos stretched over muscles which bulged from the short sleeves of his polo shirt.

Charles returned the greeting with a nod of his own head, then turned his attention to Rusty. When he spoke, there was a note of irritation underscoring his patronising tone as without looking at her, he raised his voice as they all headed for the cliff's edge.

"My dear girl. I'm a busy man and I really don't have time to keep a constant watch on you, and so I'm of a mind to allow you to follow your own career, though I shall have to curtail your leisure pursuits. However, if you're to have even a hope of becoming my occasional plaything, you must respond immediately when an answer is required. Seeing as you've chosen not grace my question with an answer, it seems I must yet again repeat myself. But be warned, this is the last time I shall do so. Are you ready to prove yourself worthy of my attention, Caroline?"

Feeling belittled in front of Jake, her answer was surprisingly buoyant when she answered. "Yes, I'm ready."

This time Charles did not falter and that back of his hand made contact with her check with a resounding whack!

"I will have respect, Caroline!"

As her hand flew to her burning cheek, she caught Jake's eye as he lifted his own hand in her defence. Although he was puzzled, it was enough to make him back down. He raised his eyebrows questioningly as with a soft voice she enunciated the words clearly.

"I'm sorry, it won't happen again, Sir. And yes, I'm ready, Sir."

As if unaware of the glorious weather, it was an ill-humoured English Channel which battered the small, rocky cove into submission. From somewhere above, another rock broke away and fell to its doom, shattering into so many shards on the shingle. With limited accessibility from the next beach further along the coast, Beggars Cove was frequented only by occasional, foolhardy holidaymakers in search of "the perfect" place for a picnic and so ignored the flags and notices that warned of hazardous conditions, or experienced rock climbers in search of a thrill. It was a lonely, inhospitable and utterly beautiful inlet that was best viewed from Pilgrim's Leap three hundred feet or so above, where the view across to France was slightly hazy.

Having learned the nature of her test at last, Rusty was standing apart from Charles, who stood looking down at the cove. Bending from the waist, she hopped unsteadily as she tried to remove her boot without toppling over. When she had done so, she put her bare foot down in the grass, took a moment to recover herself as she laid the boot aside, then repeated the procedure with the other leg. Focussing on the excitement of the challenge, she put aside her surprise and tried to smother the embarrassment she had suffered in front of Jake, revelling instead in her luck that Charles had chosen abseiling …. something she had done many times from this very location, and at which she excelled. Although he had made provisos, she reminded herself, to make it more of an ordeal.

She unfastened the sole button of her flimsy jacket and laid it down across her boots. Standing barefoot in her bra and trousers and looking like an innocent that knew she was about to lose her virginity, she reflected that there had never been so much at stake before. For she realised it was not just her obedience regarding the abseiling he demanded because he was well aware that she would relish the chance to impress him with her skill, it was her total compliance with anything else he commanded that he sought. It was strange, she mused as her heart began thumping fit to burst, she wanted to be obedient……wanted discipline….. more than anything. Although in some ways discipline was very much part of her life since you could not fly or participate in any other risky or daredevil activity without it, in the shape of personal discipline, obedience was something she had never really experienced, having pretty much had her own way all her life.

And yet still she could not fully eradicate the lurking fear of failing. She couldn't fail! she told herself adamantly, thinking of the contract that meant so much to the teams. They were giving their first public appearance of the year shortly, and then there were airshows at various locations throughout the summer, culminating in annual Saxon Hill Airshow when for two whole days the airfield would be open to the public.

But failure would also mean losing Charles, and that was something she could not contemplate. Any yet she knew he had chosen this feat to be her test with a selfish knowledge on his part that even if it was something she was adept at and knowing that she would not pass up the chance, it would be the most humiliating thing she had ever tackled. And humiliation was not something she coped well with.

She cast her gaze to where Charles was standing, looking down at the bleak reality that was Beggars Cove, and seeing for himself how treacherous the descent could be, and she wondered if he had any idea previously of the risks. Although she had descended from greater heights in the past, few were as testing as the three hundred feet descent to Beggars Cove. There was a deeply disturbing side to Charles that was being revealed to her for the first time, and yet it was a side of him she had the unhealthy desire …. yes, she had no doubts now that it was an unhealthy desire, she acknowledged wryly….. to become acquainted with. Because in her heart she knew that she would do anything he asked of her, no matter how painful or humiliating. But, of course, he would not ask her to do anything ever again if she did not pass this blasted test.

She tried to stem the tide of her wandering mind as she turned to see Jake approaching, treating him to an appetising view of her heaving, melon-like breasts as they struggled to remain inside the low-cut, black-spotted pink bra. Despite the lustful glint in his eyes and the slight bulge she detected in his trousers, his smile was grim as he joined her and began to empty the contents of his rucksack onto the ground.

"These are the only things he's sanctioned. I don't know what's going on here, Rusty, but you're way out of your league with this guy. And where's all this 'Sir' nonsense come from?"

Contrary to her mishmash emotions, she tried for a casual tone as she told him fallaciously, "Oh, that's nothing to worry about, it's just a handle, that's all. And the rest.....well, it's okay too. We've discussed it.....been through it a couple of times and I'm happy to do it, if that's what he wants." As if to prove a point, she unzipped her leather trousers and began to peel them off, revealing the tiny pink triangle with black spots that barely contained her wild thicket of fiery pubes. As she hooked her thumbs beneath the elastic at her waist to pull down the thong, it was more with anxiety than modesty that she said meekly, "Why don't you go and talk to Charles.....please?"

"Listen, Babe. You and me go way back, and even I wouldn't ask you to do it without the proper kit! How well do you know this guy?"

"We're lovers."

She flashed him a radiant smile and although it set her palest of wine coloured eyes sparkling and gave them an uncannily silver cast, it did not match the quiet, almost submissive way she was speaking. As both biker and instructor, he had known the knock-your-eyes out gorgeous girl for several years, and had even fucked her a few times. Yet this was a Rusty he barely recognised. Gone was the chirpy banter between them, and gone also was her usual sprightly way of moving. There was something about her bearing that he could not quite put his finger on

Again, she favoured him with the smile that at any other time would have had him inviting her to his bed.

"We've been seeing each other for a while, Jake. He simply asked me if I was interested in doing a special challenge…..to raise money for the charity he's involved with. Don't worry. It's okay….I'm okay…..honest." .

"Well, okay, if you're sure, Babe. But I'm registering my professional displeasure!"

"That's your prerogative, Jake. Now, p…..please go. I…..I….. don't want to keep him waiting."

Although Jake thought he detected fear, in fact the goosebumps that chilled her pale skin were engendered by the very different emotion of sexual excitement. Though quite why she should experience such bizarre tingles and shivers now was quite beyond her. With her nipples throbbing and her pussy quivering, she could only conclude that, once again, the need to orgasm was as great as her need for that heady adrenaline rush.

Jake turned and made his way over to where the man who had given his name as Charles Hilton was standing. He reflected as he came alongside him that the Rusty he knew had always believed she was as good as a man and never allowed female frailty to hold her back. Yet that evening it was as if she had become…..he searched his mind for a word….. somehow subservient. It was in no way obvious or outlandish, except for the 'Sir' nonsense, though the proposal that she could ever be subservient was itself outlandish, of course. He could only conclude that it was just something in her demeanour that this arrogant stranger seemed to give rise to.

Rusty continued taking her clothes off as the two men stood facing each other at the cliff's edge. Slowly and without a word passing between them, as if their movements were orchestrated they turned their heads in her direction. With differing agendas their eyes loitered over her while she prepared for her descent.

Jake shook his head slowly as the shapely, by now totally nude redhead tucked her hair up beneath the Zenith Sports helmet. She was in way over her head with this guy! he thought. She knew the dangers and the myths surrounding the location, of course, because she had made the descent many times. But certainly never like this!

He watched as, once again hopping first on one leg then the other, she slipped on a pair of thick red socks from the permitted gear, then laced up a pair of sturdy boots, before reaching for the rope which she began to wind around her waist. He was convinced that she must be feeling as stupid as she looked, starkers except for the socks and bloody boots. And the helmet, of course. But there was no getting away from the fact, as she continued to coil the rope around her narrow waist, that she also looked incredibly horny. Though that, he reminded himself sternly, was not the real issue.

Why she was doing it at all was beyond him. Naturally he understood the thrill seeking side of it, but he was surprised by her irresponsibility at doing it naked. But what he could not even begin to understand was why she agreed to do it just because Charles Hilton told her to! It could be a risky sport at the best of times, that was why it was such a thrill; the rope which would carry her weight was controlled by a friction mechanism which checked the rate of descent. Braking devices could easily get snagged on rocks or sliced right through on the jagged cliff face, which in this location was subject to frequent rock falls. But at Charles Hilton's insistence, she would be doing it naked!

Unaware that both men were watching her with similar bulges in their trousers, Rusty felt anything but sexy as she stood with her hands behind her back, trembling with excitement and unaccountably perspiring, waiting for permission to start. Wearing only the helmet, socks, shoes and the rope coils that bulged from her waist, she stood on the fine summer's evening with perspiration dripping from her fiery-copper, pubic bush. Her bare skin burned and took on a silky pink sheen as the men discussed her in hushed tones.

Something that Jake was only now, at this late stage, aware of was the fact that to make it more difficult for a girl who was accomplished at the sport, Hilton had brought a little toy along with him that he demonstrated slyly.

"I'm sorry, Mr Hilton, but I really can't allow it!" Jake informed the wealthy businessman as he examined the device Charles handed him.

"Don't be absurd, man. It's only a butt plug."

"Well, not unless she's properly kitted-out," he qualified as he turned the thing over in his hands, imagining with more relish than he cared to admit where it would lodge.

Although Charles did not raise his voice and was polite throughout, there was a contempt underlining his words when he replied, though Jake was not altogether sure whether the scorn was aimed at Rusty or Jake himself.

"She's got the clips......"

"Carabiners," Jake corrected.

Charles sneered as he continued. "A helmet. And boots. The bitch won't need anything else, Mr Morgan."

"Yeah, yeah, and the rope. But apart from that she's stark fucking naked!"

"I don't see your objection. She's a fine specimen, don't you think?'

Jake had always considered her to be eye candy in the extreme. But it was the first time he had ever seen her like this.

"Besides, you agreed readily enough to my conditions when I first made the request."

"But I didn't know about the fucking plug!" Jake looked over to where Rusty stood patiently waiting, her helmeted head bowed, her booted feet apart and her hands.....without gloves......behind her back. It was true that when the man in the suit had first made contact with the instructor, he had been intrigued by the idea of her abseiling naked. To find out who he was dealing with, while Jake had initially had him on the phone, he had stalled for time before committing fully to do his own quick Google search and, once he had discovered that the man was the wealthy, womanising director of some mega company, he had stopped reading. After all, if he was wealthy and was prepared to pay over the odds, it was good enough for Jake who reasoned that it could only benefit his strapped-for-cash activity centre. But now that the moment was upon them, Jake was having misgivings. Rusty's concentration was bound to be hampered by the two inch long plug. Especially if she was not used to it as Hilton maintained smugly. And to cap it all, he was not happy at the way the bastard referred to her!

Charles nodded his head in Rusty's direction and again, there was the derision. "When I rang and explained what I had in mind for the little tart, you couldn't have been more helpful. I made no secret of her identity, Mr Morgan. Don't forget that it was you who chose the location! 'Nice and blowy up there,' you said, 'give her something to think about,' though it seems you rather let me down on that point. And you were not shy in pointing mentioning the rock falls and hostility of the cove."

"But it's a long way down. Look, it's getting late, and you seem to forget she's got to climb all the way back up again, bearing in mind that it's a long, arduous climb in the very best conditions and it could well be hours from now…. and pitch dark…..before she makes it back to the top. So how do you propose we get her back up?"

"No problem. I've come prepared." Slipping his hand in a jacket pocket, Charles took out his mobile and made a call. "Stratton. Bring the winch."

Registering Jake's dismay as he ended the call, Charles replaced his mobile and continued. "While we're waiting for my driver, perhaps we should give her something to occupy her." For the first time, he raised his voice as he summoned her, his voice cutting through the still evening air. "Get over here now, Bitch!"

Jake was stunned by her immediate response as she hurried over to where they were standing. But he was even more stunned by the meek way she presented herself, as if she were waiting for some kind of permission to move. With the rope coiled ready for use, she stood directly in front of Charles, with her hands crossed behind her. Then with a slow, sexy and slightly mischievous smile, she addressed him.

"Yes, Sir?"

The instructor shook his head, still unwilling to accept her explanation for why she addressed the man she claimed was her lover in such deferential terms. More unbelievable still was what happened next.

"Open your legs, Caroline. I want to explore your cunt before your descent."

As directed and without hesitation she opened her legs.

"Wider."

Her face was flaming as she moved them further apart.

"Before I touch you, I want you to frig yourself. Make you're wet for me."

As Jake's unease grew, he could not help his own smugness when something inside her seem to snap and she reacted in the way he would have expected her to.

"No way! Get lost!"

"And you were doing so well," Charles sighed. "I warn you, don't make me angry, Caroline. Just do it, and I'll overlook your disobedience."

A pleading tone that crept into her voice when she answered him.

"Please! N…..not here, Sir. I…..I….I'll do anything…….anything you ask, Sir….."

"That's what we're here to determine. I won't tell you again."

Jake looked on with a combination of amazement and disgust, though he could not deny his own arousal. He told himself that he should land a couple of punches on the mad sleazeball, yet the stirrings of his cock in his pants as he watched her slavishly obey the command and slip her slender finger down to her quim was enough to check him. Reviling himself for not putting a stop to her humiliation as her finger parted her glorious pubes then disappeared inside, his gaze was riveted to the apex of her thighs. The light glinted on her helmet as she lowered her head and with deep concentration, she frigged herself furiously with one hand while keeping the other one behind her back.

Of course, everything sleaze-in-a-suit said was true, he thought as his own hand strayed to the front of his jeans. Cupping it over the hardened bulge, he could not deny that in a secret corner of his mind, he had fantasised many times about the lovely, innocent faced but racy Rusty yielding obediently to his secret desires. Enchanted by this new side to the girl he considered his friend, Jake found himself unable to do anything but watch and wait and the scene unfolded.

The change within him was a gradual one. Forming the opinion that only a slut would allow herself to be so humiliated, he, with a developing, secret admiration for Charles, saw her as he did; shame beautified her, and suited her, too. As his own lust increased and he frantically rubbed his bulge through his trousers, he lost all sense of time as he watched her lewdly obeying her Master's commands.

But it was not until another man approached carrying a heavy duty winch that Charles issued his next command.

"Stop!"

She stopped immediately and withdrew her finger. Without being told to she held it up for him to see . He made her show Jake, as the man called Stratton set down the winch, then while keeping a respectful distance Charles slipped his own finger inside her.

"Let me test how wet you are." After an exploratory stir that clearly aroused her and satisfied him, Charles said affably in a tone and volume that was clearly meant to shame her as he continued to stir up her woman sap, "Listen to that squelching, gentlemen. It really doesn't take much at all to get this slut wet! It would be quite amusing if it were not so filthy. Still, it would be a shame to waste such juiciness, so would you mind assisting me in a little experiment?"

"Anything I can do to help," Jake said huskily as he stepped forward.

"Stratton, tie her hands, please."

Jake watched him withdraw his finger and when Charles also held it up for him to see, he smiled at how shiny it was. He did not object when Stratton stepped up behind her and bound her hands but found himself hoping he would tie them tight enough to prevent her pulling free. When Stratton took a step back to show that his task was completed, Jake noticed how it made her already prominent breasts stick out even more. He delighted in how stiff and dark her nipples had grown despite the shame which coloured her features so sweetly. Charles placed his hand on her helmet and pushed her down to her knees on the wet grass. He placed a firm finger beneath her chin and tilted it upward.

"Open your mouth, Caroline. Mr Morgan?"

Jake did not wait for a formal invitation. Hastily he unfastened his fly, withdrew his cock from his pants, and holding the back of her helmet in one hand he roughly drew her head toward him and at the same time thrust his throbbing phallus into her sweetly compliant mouth. As her lips closed around its engorged hardness, he did not concern himself with whether or not she was doing it through choice just as he did not care that she was unable to push him away. If anything, the limitations forced on her by her restricted condition both added to her charm and increased his lust as he drove his shaft toward the back of her throat.

Although she had always considered herself something of an expert since she had given head more times than she could remember, her throat was sadly unconditioned to such rough treatment. It was the last thing she had expected from a man she considered her friend and had trusted with her life on more than one occasion, and with the added shame of Stratton's lustful gaze turned upon her, with her skin turning an even deeper shade she gagged hopelessly on Jake's rigid shaft as she was forced to perform public fellatio. At the same time she had no choice but to yield to the brutal handling with which Charles attended to her breasts, her nipples in particular coming under painful attack as they were twisted so viciously that it brought tears to her eyes.

But Jake was too far gone down the road to climax to object to Charles' orchestration as he said, "Don't let her swallow it! That's a reward she doesn't deserve. Let her have it between the eyes!"

She was taken aback that Jake, taking him quite literally, withdrew and she just had time to close her eyes as hot fountains of spunk hit her forehead and eyelids. It cooled almost instantly on her hot skin and squeezed into the corners of her eyes, making them sting. Rivers of the gloopy liquid ran down her nose and cheeks.

"You see, she really is nothing but a filthy bitch after all," Charles announced contemptuously as, still holding onto her nipples, he pulled her up to her feet.

She felt fingers touch her hand as Stratton released her from her bondage. With nothing to wipe away the spunk she used the backs of her hands, she saw Jake take a few steps back to reflect on his own lewd behaviour. She could only start to guess at how much his complicity in her maltreatment sickened him.

Ashamed, he gave her a furtive look. She was trembling and she knew that he misconstrued her need to orgasm as fear.

"One more thing, Caroline. Turn around and bend over."

Sure that Charles was about to penetrate her from behind and finally fuck her to climax, without question she did as he asked. Adjusting her stance to steady herself, she thrust her backside up and toward him.

He took a tube from his pocket and as he unscrewed the cap he told her matter-of-factly, "It's time you learnt something new, my dear." With that, he squeezed out some gel.

She flinched and gave a little squeal as he smeared something cold over her anus. Too late she realised its purpose was to facilitate the breaching of her back entrance. Panicking, she made to get up, but Charles was ready for that.

"Stratton, hold her still."

She felt two heavy hands on her back. And then there was the most god-awful discomfort she had ever known as something hard was pushed with megawatt pain into her nervously clenching, secret entrance.

"Aaaarghh!"

"Quiet! For God's sake relax, and it will go in easier." Again he pushed, smirking with delight to discover that he had finally found she had one hole that was still virgin. He gave one final push.

"Aaaarghh!" It felt as if her insides were being rent beyond repair.

It was only the flared base that stopped it disappearing completely. "Too much fuss! It's only a small plug."

It might be a small plug to him, she thought as the dreadful object lodged inside her made her feel uncomfortably full, but it felt like a broom handle to her! Never had she felt so dirty. The shame of having anything up there was bad enough, but the fact that she had been so publicly defiled made her realise for the very first time in her entire life that she was not bullet proof after all. Her vulnerability came as a shock to her and, overcome by a desire to expel the object, she bit her lip to stop herself from sobbing. After all, she had said she would do anything......but his next words filled her cold dread.

"It's the best thing for you, will open you a bit before you take my cock up there. Now all we have to do is find some way of keeping it in because I'd hate to have to put your panties on. Stratton, did you bring the tape?" Looking up, he took the proffered reel of bondage tape from his driver and, wound it around her waist, then through her legs and stuck the end to itself at her stomach.

"Thank you, Stratton." As Stratton removed his hands, Charles helped her upright. "Good girl Caroline. I know that was a trial for you, painful too, but for me it was a moment of pure joy. If you want to continue making me happy, you must appreciate that it's only by your suffering that I'll find pleasure and you want me to be happy, don't you? Now, check your equipment again because it's time for your descent, to prove once and for all that you will obey me in everything I ask. To earn my respect and the opportunity to serve me without question or complaint."

Jake felt uneasy. Now that the moment was upon them and Rusty meekly checked her equipment one last time, he shook himself back to reality. Realising the full import of his hastily-made decision in agreeing to the nude descent with a butt plug up her arse, he wished there were some way to distance himself from the evening's events and put his own despicable behaviour behind him. The thought of anything happening to the girl he had known for so long filled him with horror. He had to help her, defend herself against a man that would bring about her complete degradation.

"I'm sorry, but I can't allow it!" he repeated at last.

For the first time, Charles glowered toward him. "I've paid handsomely for this event to take place, Mr Morgan. It will go ahead."

With shame, Jake realised that the thought of anything happening to his extreme sports business filled him with an even greater horror. He jabbed his thumb over his shoulder toward the low-level building. "Look, it's a bit late now. I've got the keys to the café so why don't we all go back inside and discuss it?"

Seeing as there was no way to expel the plug without removing the tape, Rusty shifted her weight from one leg to the other as she tried in vain to settle the object more comfortably. She looked from one man to the other, with blood pounding in her veins and butterflies fluttering around her stomach. It was not entirely unpleasant and certainly was not unfamiliar given the frequency of her leisure pursuits, but usually she had a choice in the matter. Of course, in theory she still did; she could say she had changed her mind and just walk away. Except she did not want to because…. because to have to give up and walk away now would be a failure for which she could never forgive herself.

Waiting for permission was the worst part. She refused to dwell on what had just taken place, and wished the matter was settled once and for all. She found herself smiling at the thought of winning Charles' praise and attention. The way he had congratulated her filled her pride. For a girl who was usually at ease with herself and confident in familiar surroundings, she was gripped by the altogether new feeling of existing entirely for the pleasure of someone other than herself which overrode the more normal exhilaration that accompanied her extreme sports.

As Stratton walked up behind her and attached the final rope that would allow him to electronically winch her back up, Charles took a roll of bank notes from his pocket. Addressing the instructor, he said, "Where's the harm? We both know that she's done this sort of thing many times before."

"And so she has," Jake eyed the bank notes with a glimmer in his eye, "but never naked. It's not me, you understand. Personally, I love to see her naked. And the butt plug doesn't seem to be too distracting for her. But it's Health and Safety, see. They'd crucify me if she had an accident, close the activity centre down for good. I mean, what if she were to scrape herself on the rock-face?"

"Then she'd have remarkably scratched tits, my friend, and save me the trouble of flogging them." Charles counted off a few notes, reached across and poked them in Jake's breast pocket. When he did not refuse them, Charles told him unnecessarily to take as much care fastening the rope as he would under normal circumstances.

As Jake made the essential adjustments, Charles took the few steps across to where Rusty was peering down at the waves that crashed into the cove now that the tide was in. He slid his finger beneath her chin to tilt her head upward. Then he addressed her coldly. "Okay, bitch, remember that you're doing this for me, not you. It's my pleasure that counts, not yours. When you reach the bottom I'll have Stratton operate the winch to haul you back up again."

To her surprise, he kissed her full and brutal on the lips.

Rusty's descent was more thrilling than she could have imagined. Somehow her nudity, coupled with the plug stuffed inside her that filled her to capacity and seemed to become part of her, added a whole new dimension to her endeavours by sending bolts of red hot arousal scudding through her, stimulating every fibre of her being to the extent that if anyone had touched her as her feet entered the waves at last, she would have exploded with pure joy.

Standing for a moment with the water crashing around her knees, she looked around Beggars Cove and revelled in its cruel beauty as she revelled in Charles' maltreatment. For she finally accepted that he was a cruel and depraved individual. And she realised she loved him for it. She wished he were here now, in the late twilight of a summer's evening, so he could take what was rightfully his and they could enjoy her shame together. But he was some three hundred feet above her, and she was a seething heap of filthy, wanton womanhood that begged for the promised glory of sexual abuse.

Having no alternative to satisfy her desires, she leaned her front against the rock face, folding her arms to shield her face and thrusting her breasts against its roughness to ease the throbbing in her nipples by grinding them against the roughness. Then freeing one hand she slid it downward to her cunt, only to find it taped and inaccessible. Screaming loudly and emptying her lungs in frustration she discovered a new, strange kind of joy, as she realised he controlled her even with such a distance between them. She closed her eyes..... and melted, welcoming the dark that closed over her. It was only the rope being anchored above her that stopped her from falling.

And up on top of the cliff, where unbeknownst to Rusty a mobile floodlight was trained upon her, with his fist tight around his cock, Charles finally spouted his seed over the edge.

"That's it. She's out cold," he laughed. Then noting the looks of concern and puzzled delight that crossed Jake's face, he assured him that everything was as it should be. "She can't come to any harm, my friend. The rope's so taut it's holding her upright, though I think she's beginning to sag a bit. Okay Stratton, bring her up."

It was an exhausted and limp Rusty who was electronically hauled up from Beggars Cove. She was laid out on the grass in the near darkness. Covered with sweat that dried on her body and left her flesh cold, she was unconscious after her ordeal. Her breasts were attractively scratched from where she had ground them against the cliff, and Charles could not resist running her fingers across them. Then while Jake removed her helmet, Charles removed the waterlogged boots and laughing, with an exaggerated display of satisfaction he stood up and upturned them to empty out the sea water.

Kneeling down beside her once more, he stripped off the socks and threw them aside. "I'll keep the rope," he announced. Gathering it up, he rolled her over onto her belly and tied her hands behind her back. Then he pulled it down her back and wound it round her feet to secure them.

"What about the butt plug?" Jake asked as he looked down lustfully at the girl who had done them all proud and whose new and unsuspected frailty thrilled him.

"I was planning on leaving it in, but...."

She stirred as Charles ripped off the tape. She jerked as her subconscious registered the pain of the plug's hasty withdrawal, but she settled down again and slept.

"There's a girl who's happy in her bondage," Charles said. When the men's laughter had died down, Charles proffered the still-warm butt plug. "Keep it as a souvenir," he smiled as Jake took it from him.

CHAPTER SIX

LONDON

When she awoke in Charles' guest room that night – still bound hand and foot – it was to find herself in a spacious, almost completely open-plan living space whose few interior walls were glass, the apartment being spread over three floors, with floor to ceiling windows in every room and with a full 360 degrees view of the skyline.

Strangely she was frightened as she lay in bed taking in her surroundings, but was puzzled to see two six inch triangles, made of chrome, hanging from the high ceiling of the guest room. Spaced about five feet apart, they dangled from two chain links just beyond the end of the bed. Then she noticed similar triangles, spaced the same distance apart, at the head end of the bed, with a third one, placed between the two and hanging right above her head. With a mental shrug of her shoulders and an irritation that she had already been awake over half an hour and there was still no sign of Charles, she was beginning to wonder if the events of the previous evening had ever taken place when he finally came into the room, smiling.

"Lie still and be quiet. There's something important I must attend to."

Her gaze followed him as he went across to the open bathroom, she saw him going to a cupboard then drawing water. He returned carrying a bowl of water, ropes draped over his arm and a collection of other items that left her mystified. Setting everything down on a stool with a square padded seat covered in white leather and with chrome legs, he told her to stretch her arms above her head. When she had complied he bound them together and, with an expertise that made her gasp in admiration, he threw the rope up and through the triangle directly overhead. Catching the end, he pulled it to raise her arms and, when he was satisfied that they were tautly stretched, he hitched the end around the rope to hold it. He freed her ankles, only to bind them again one at a time. He drew her legs wide and secured the ropes in the same way through the two triangles at the other end. It was not until both legs were stretched widely and painfully in the air that she discovered the purpose of the other items. Working quickly he covered her pubic area in shaving foam and then held up a razor.

With widened eyes, she pleaded. "No! Please Sir!"

Whether she was afraid or simply objected to being shaved was no concern of Charles's as he proceeded to remove her unruly, fiery pubes, then rinsed her afterward to reveal for the first time the smooth, pale skin that had lain unseen beneath them.

"There, much better," he said when he was finished. "Now I can see your cunt in all its aroused, pink and puffy glory. This is how I want you, totally naked and accessible. And this is how you will remain. In your bathroom," he jerked his head toward the disturbingly doorless glass partitioned, en suite to indicate he was referring to that room rather than the bathroom at her flat, "you'll find everything you need to keep it that way. If I ever catch sight of even one unsightly red cunt-hair again, it will be the worse for you. Don't test me, bitch, or you'll be sorry."

With that, he gathered up the things, took them back to the bathroom and then told her on his return, "you can clear them away before you go to work in the morning. "Well, that's it for now. I'll see you tomorrow."

"What? No! Don't leave me, Sir. Please, not like this! Please, Sir, I beg…"

"You'll be doing a lot of begging from now on, my little slut. But this time, it falls on deaf ears because….. how remiss of me not to tell you….. I prefer to sleep alone. This will be your room, where you'll spend all your nights. Unless, of course, I restrain you in the playroom or perhaps in my bedroom. It's been an awfully long day. I'll turn off the light as I go. Goodnight."

With her arms and legs stretched tautly, her first night under her Master's roof produced a fitful sleep and hours of misery for the poor girl, while Charles slept soundly in his bed at the other end of the open-plan top floor.

A spindle-legged woman whose too-dark-for-her-age hair was gathered in an unflattering bun on top of her head set Rusty free early the next morning. Wearing a dated blouse and sober, knee-length skirt she turned out to be McBain, Charles' housekeeper.

Speaking in a harsh whisper she told Rusty, "he wants you showered, dressed and out of here within the hour. Your clothes are in your bathroom. Come down to the kitchen and there'll be coffee and toast waiting."

As well as a voice that grated on Rusty's nerves, McBain also had an annoying habit of finishing her sentences. It all began innocuously enough when Rusty, rubbing her wrists and ankles to get the blood flowing again, first opened her mouth.

"Where's…?"

"Your Master? Mr Hilton doesn't get up this early."

She repeated the word in her mind….Master. Yes, she supposed he was, now. "Then I'd better go and….."

"Say goodbye? No. He said you're not to disturb him. You'll find yourself in real trouble if you do! You're to come back here after work and he'll see you then."

"Okay, thanks. But where's…..?"

"The kitchen? Two floors down." McBain gave her directions, adding, "Hurry, or you'll never get through the traffic!"

It was only then that Rusty realised she had no transport, and no money on her for the train not even a handbag, because Charles had picked her up from her flat the evening before. And the revealing outfit she had worn then was hardly suitable for an early morning commuter. But she need not have worried because when she eventually found the kitchen, she also found Stratton waiting to take her home.

When Charles had left her instructions to return that evening, he hadn't considered for a moment that she would disobey. And in that he was proved correct. He was in the apartment already when she finally arrived at the barrier of the underground car park.

Having paid the security officers at the luxury apartment block to inform him immediately of her arrival and then detain her in the car park to give him time to come down and see her, although he was displeased that she arrived in her leathers on her Fireblade, he was nevertheless delighted to meet her and show her to her designated parking bay.

"You know I disapprove of your riding that motorcycle!" he told her as she removed her helmet and they entered the lift.

"So how else am I supposed to get here?" she snapped, running her fingers through her hair then quickly added, "Sir."

"I really must sort you out with a car."

"Why? I can't drive one! I've got a licence for bikes, Sir."

All this coming and going would surely be nothing but a barrier between them that would hinder his total command and allow her more freedom than he had anticipated.

"Then I shall have to provide you with new leathers. Your current set is far too masculine for my taste."

Ideally he needed a slave that he could keep permanently at his apartment, not just before and after work but who would be on hand 24/7. His initial plans were to put Rusty under the supervision of McBain during his absence and forbid her to leave the apartment without his express permission. Of course, he would have to find some way of keeping tabs on her when she did. But at the moment the chance of implementing his plan appeared slight, because these were modern times, and Rusty still had too much of a life of her own. He could only hope that time would be on his side, and that once he had her fully trained, no one else would snap her up. After all, he was a man with an eye to a good business proposition, and if the opportunity were to arise to make money from his hard work, then he might be tempted to sell her. But he would have to be offered a considerable sum.

When he opened the door to his apartment, he sent her straight to the same bedroom which he informed her was now her own room, and ordered her to strip naked. And that set the pattern of her life for the foreseeable future. From that point onward, it was as if she was leading a double life. And so successful was she that whenever she was away from Charles she reverted back to her old self, burying the submissiveness sufficiently well so that it went unnoticed by her brother and work colleagues. Nobody yet knew of their involvement, except for Jake, who she hadn't seen since the evening of her test. Because, sadly, Charles forbade all activities that were not connected with flying and the airfield.

She spent little time at her own flat, the majority of her things having been moved to Charles' penthouse apartment. There was a communal roof terrace, and numerous balconies, with the master bedroom, the guest bedroom and the playroom located on the twenty-ninth floor of the landmark building. There was another bedroom located two floors down, on the same floor as the kitchen. McBain and Stratton had their own flats in the service area of the building. With its magnificent views over the Thames and the Canary Wharf development, the building was taller than any of the others in the immediate vicinity, with none of them high enough to overlook it. Rusty knew she would never feel comfortable living there for although it was luxurious and airy, she felt as though she were living in a goldfish bowl because there were no curtains or blinds at any of the huge windows not even the bathroom. Luckily, only the occasional helicopter came close enough to see inside the white and chrome furnished apartment whose floors were real wood throughout because, McBain informed her, it was easier to mop up spunk and other bodily secretions from them than from a carpet.

Over the next few weeks, Charles made surprising headway in turning a thrill-seeking, fuck-hungry girl who had always thought of herself as bit of a tomboy into a stunning, pain-seeking submissive. Although Rusty's natural sexiness had always turned heads, and Charles admitted it had certainly turned his, wherever they went together she now attracted glances that were a mixture of envy and mistrust from women, and clearly desirous glances from men. She seemed to glow from within, and her new docility gave her added allure.

If it were not for his back-tracking on his intention to buy her a car and make her sell the powerful bike, she would never have managed to make it through the traffic from the Kent airfield to his apartment in time to see to his needs after a busy day at the office. And from the beginning he made it clear that after work, a man needs a little relaxation; when he needed to let off steam, if she were not on hand to flog – something she took to with gratifying enthusiasm – then he would have to go to the bother of hiring in a bitch for the evening.

Although she was subject to discipline from the start and received regular floggings, the first occasion when he had subjected his copper-headed slut to physical chastisement in the playroom, was a joy they would both remember for a long time to come. It was on one of their first evenings together and, after a quick, light meal prepared in advance by his housekeeper, he allowed her to enter the playroom for the first time.

He bound her hands behind her back, then ordered her to climb the spiral staircase that led upward from the lounge where the plasma screen TV was located. Telling herself that she was like a doomed man heading for the scaffold, with her heart racing she did as she was commanded.

Like all the other rooms, it was open-plan, although it could only be reached from Charles' own bedroom which, up until then was, quite ludicrously and unbelievably frustrating as far as the slave was concerned, strictly off limits. Insisting he preferred to sleep alone, just in case she had been tempted to disobey his "no entry" policy, he had concealed the playroom by hanging a long, black curtain from one side of his bedroom to the other which now he yanked down to finally reveal it in all its fiendish glory.

She had no opportunity to survey his bedroom in any detail as he ushered her ahead of him and, glimpsing the playroom for the first time, with the widened eyes of horror, she stared and drew in a terrified breath.

Like all the other rooms in the penthouse, it was fully glazed from floor to ceiling without any means of screening it from the outside world. The difference was that instead of furniture, there was a range of free-standing frames and structures that both alarmed and thrilled her. Instead of everything being made of chrome, in this room wood was also very much in evidence, the two mediums working surprisingly well together. She was not surprised to see the wooden X-shaped St Andrew's cross since on one occasion he'd mentioned it before, saying that he had a good mind to have Stratton remove it and set it up in his study so that she could be mounted tautly while he worked. But what really set flutters of alarm in her belly were the leather restraints and chains attached to it.

She gaped in wonder at what seemed to be a chrome trapeze hanging on a short chain from the ceiling.

"Awfully good for suspension," he told her.

At once she had an awful feeling that she understood exactly what suspension was, and saw herself hanging by her hands. But what she did not understand was that her hands would be tied or, if he was in a particularly frivolous mood, he might decide to suspend her from her ankles instead! Also hanging from the ceiling in various locations were triangles, about the same size as those in her bedroom and that she assumed were used for much the same purpose. And another, much larger one that was suspended on a longer chain than the trapeze so that the bottom was about two feet off the floor. There were various designs of what turned out to be whipping frames, some with padding like the stool in her room, and some without.

There was a free standing cupboard that reminded her of a kitchen cabinet, and a tall, narrow locker that was also free standing. There was a wooden table four feet wide and seven feet long.

"You'll notice it has a white, easy-wipe surface," he said, adding, "nice and clinical, sturdy too."

She could not miss the restraints at each corner.

"You've done well so far. But prepare yourself because the next bit will be painful," he said kindly, almost regretfully, she thought as he smoothed her hair with one hand and ran the back of the other one down her already perspiring cheek.

There was a softness in his eyes that moved her and led her to believe there was affection there after all.

But she should have recognised already that his heart could be as cold as a blast of wintry air that freezes where it falls, and hard as an anvil on which iron is shaped. This one moment was nothing but a lapse because he would rarely show any real tenderness toward her. And when he turned his toffee-coloured gaze to her again, gone was all trace of kindness, and in its place was a frightening coldness that while filling her with dread, had the strange effect of making the fire of lust burn in her loins.

Tying her hands together in front of her, he made her step into the large triangular frame, holding it still for her as it began to swing. Then he raised her hands and attached them to the apex. Next, he had her spread her legs, placing her feet in the lower corners and attaching them.

She could not help noticing that outside it was a clear night. The moon was bright and showering the playroom in ghostly silver, making it almost bright enough to see without the added light source when Charles threw the switch of the spots on the overhead tracks. She gasped raggedly as she realised that if there were any helicopters around that night, their pilots would have a clear view of a room lit up like a stage.

"I'm just going downstairs to my study. I've a conference call coming through in about half an hour, and I find I'm rather in need of a bourbon first. I'll keep the call as short as possible, then when I come back we can get down to the real business of a decent flogging. Up until now, I'm afraid you've had to put up with a rather second rate service!" Laughing, he turned his back and left her.

She had so wanted him to watch and enjoy her shame before taking her to the next level.

With no way of gauging the time, she thought she had been forgotten and that she had been there for hours. In reality, he returned just over an hour later. And the sight of the whip he carried brought a cry of alarm to her lips. With a red handle of seven inches long, the sixteen suede tails were twice that length. He did not speak to her at all as for several, unending minutes that aroused and terrified her as she anticipated the impact from the whip, he considered what he would do next.

And then he began and she had no choice but to endure an absolute blizzard of strikes. Sometimes the spiteful tails caught her belly too as they switched between the meat of her breasts....her arms..... thighs..... breasts again..... then cunt..... breasts. In some strange way that she could not explain, agony was flecked with pleasure ...... still he went on......agony.....lights on the back of her eyelids.....agony...... pleasure blended with agony…….it was not that the agony lessened it just sort of…..grew warmer…..more pleasurable….. more……pleasurable.

"Aaaa ….ooooohhh….."

He adjusted his position for the best possible shots at her lithe, sweat-sheened body, then braced himself. Barely had she time to form the thought that the pain he was wringing from her body was exquisite before he struck again. On and on it went.

It was clear, he realised after another twenty lashes or so, not only by the aching in his own arm but also by the way her head lolled, her vocal chords failed to do their job and she hung in a stupor that could have been pleasure or agony induced Charles did not really care which. All that mattered as he finally laid the whip aside to lower her so that he could release her and wishing he had called for Stratton or McBain to help with the insensible slut, was that she was perfectly and exquisitely striped as the welts continued to develop. He untied her ankles and then her hands, catching her as she limply fell backward.

He carried her through to her room and laid her on the bed, turning her over onto her belly so that he could examine her back. She had taken the ordeal admirably, he thought proudly as he turned her onto her back once more. There was a stirring in his chest as well as his pants as he took in the look of her, defiled by the rope marks around her ankles and wrists. She would be one mass of pain when she awoke, he mused, and only then would they discover whether she had passed out because she could not stand the pain, or whether it was the pleasure she couldn't handle! He supposed it would be amusing to discover whether or not whipping agreed with her, but of course, he would continue whipping her anyway, either as discipline or simply for his pleasure. Mostly, he smiled, it would be the latter.

She was stirring.

Still standing beside the bed, he waited a few more moments until she opened her eyes.

"Welcome back." He taunted her with a few names before he informed her, "well, that's well over forty lashes you received before you passed out. I'm afraid I lost count. But you did quite well for a beginner. We'll build them up gradually. I'm afraid you'll feel the effects for some days to come, depending on your level of fitness, which we both know is pretty high as is your tolerance level. Now, I really think you should thank me."

Her strange, wine-coloured eyes sparkled as she smiled weakly. And her voice was a hoarse whisper when she answered. "Thank you, Sir. I'll look forward to the next time."

Taken aback at her apparent enthusiasm, he said, "I'll make it a regular occurrence. As soon as your skin has recovered enough for a decent tally, we'll get down to work. Probably try some wrist suspension. Until then…." he unfastened his flies and, as she lay there barely moving, he stepped out of his trousers and removed his silk underpants to release his rigid shaft. "I find I'm in need of relief." He climbed onto the bed and settled himself.

She cried out hoarsely as his helm made contact with her sore, flogged labia, then cried out again as his cock drove straight inside, penetrating deeply. Pounding into her as if he were trying to get value for money from a whore he had picked up on the street, he battered her insides painfully. Yet after everything she had been through, she could not have moved even had she wanted to. Docile and virtually mute beneath him, she cooed sweetly as he fucked her with a ferocity she hadn't seen before.

She wanted to tell him she was coming, tried to tell him, but such was her weakened condition that it was impossible to give any prior indication. Instead, she went into wild spasms and managed only a feeble, "Oooohhhh" as she orgasmed with him still inside her.

"You filthy slut!"

Whether or not he was truly angry she could not tell, but in any event his body went rigid as his own climax exploded inside her, splashing her insides hotly. Then when every drop had been expelled, he slowly withdrew. Leaving her with spunk spilling from her sore cunt, he moved to the top of the bed and, grabbing up a hank of her shining, fiery long tresses he cleaned his cock in their sweetly fragranced softness.

And for the first time, her overriding emotion after her ordeal was one of unmitigated joy.

CHAPTER SEVEN

The rule that her nether regions were to remain hairless was something she fastidiously complied with rather than make him cross with her, for despite their life together she was still fearful of losing him.

Although she still kept a few things at her flat, it was as much for the sake of appearances as convenience. As far as work and her rehearsals, life seemed to go on as before, though on his insistence she had cut back on all her leisure pursuits. She went to work each morning and, since the airshow season had begun he allowed her to continue as normal, she took part as in previous years in the aerobatic displays and wingwalking. It saddened her that he never came to watch, because she wanted to thrill him the way she thrilled the crowds so that he would be proud of her. If she meant nothing to him as a lover, she wanted to mean something to him as a flyer! When she dared to raise the subject with him, he threatened that if she ever mentioned it again he would disallow her participation completely. And that was something she could not bear to live without, despite everything she felt she had gained by becoming submissive. Or, as he preferred to call her, his slave. And that is what she truly became every time she crossed his threshold.

Unbeknown to Rusty, in fact he attended every major event. Whether it was simply as an observer or in his official role as a sponsor. But in whichever capacity Charles attended, he took great pride in her talents and achievements, refusing to admit the truth, excusing himself with the thought that she had no right to question his movements, no matter how submissive she had become!

One of the things he insisted upon was the wearing of a collar. Although he never made her wear it for work, she found it waiting for her on the glass-topped table by the door every time she entered his apartment. Made of black leather with a metal ring embedded at the front, she always snatched it up eagerly and fastened it promptly around her neck. As if it were a parachute or life vest, she felt safer when wearing it, and so did not object to not being permitted to remove it, not even for sleeping, until she left him again in the mornings. So if they went out to dinner or to some other function it remained in place, though sometimes he told her to cover it with a silk scarf and at other times made her display it brazenly in public. More than anything ,she wished he would let her wear it for work!

Another thing he demanded, despite the lack of blinds or curtains anywhere in the place, was her complete nudity whenever she was in the apartment, unless he gave her some special garment to wear. He liked to see her wearing a figure-shaping basque or corset, and she often wondered whether he'd had another slave before her because there seemed to be several in different colours and fabrics, though only some were in her size. Never having worn anything like it before, at first she had viewed the pretty, lilac and white silk garment he laced her into as if it were some archaic method of torture. Especially when he drew it in so tightly she could hardly breathe. Nevertheless, when she saw her reflection in the mirror, with her fiery copper hair hanging loose over her shoulders and wearing the ensemble of American tan coloured sheer stockings held up by suspenders, she had to admit that the effect was amazing. And when she had slipped on a pair of stiletto shoes that were a perfect match, she looked again, and felt so incredibly sexy that it was all she could do to refrain from throwing herself down on the bed with her legs flung wide and demanding he fuck her. She would not, of course.

Unfortunately, his work and fundraising commitments regarding NBAF, combined with Rusty's obligations, which included late training sessions due to the lighter evenings, meant they did not share as much time together as he had hoped.

Excited by the proposition of catching a glimpse of the celebrities who would also be at the evening's do, Rusty had naturally obeyed him when Charles told her to wear whatever he provided for the swanky, fundraising event at which he was to preside. She followed to the letter the instructions that he texted her during the day. On arrival at the apartment, as soon as she had donned her collar, rather than finding out whether or not her Master was also home, she went straight up to her room, where she found a dress, underwear, shoes and handbag laid out neatly for her on the bed. Attached to the panties was a note instructing her on everything from how to wear her hair to which items to carry in the handbag he provided. When she was ready she was to join him downstairs in the lounge.

She fell in love with the strapless dress from Monsoon in an intense shade of purple. Feminine and knee length, it had a fully boned bodice, and a skirt that had rows of deep ruffles and with a ruffled hem. There was a black belt with a lavish, silk satin black bow at the front. Although she admitted it was gorgeous, it was not the kind of thing that, had she been allowed a choice, she would wear without leggings underneath. In fact, back at her own flat she had a similar version in black that she did just that with, though her black dress was a less well-made copy that she had picked up cheaply at a street market. But in spite of not having matching leggings to go with it and which would be more in keeping with her usual style, she was touched by his thoughtful generosity as well as impressed by his expert eye. After taking a shower, washing and styling her hair piled in a sophisticated, upward sweep, she reapplied her make-up again following his instructions she wore a claret lipstick rather than her usual shade. Then she changed into the clothes provided.

Firstly, there was a suspender belt and sheer American tan stockings. Next came the panties that matched the suspender belt and bra. They were the same shade as the dress and, looking in the mirror, she thought it seemed a pity to wear anything over the top! Still, she could hardly waltz into the place dressed in just her underwear, and so slipped on the dress. She transferred only the permitted contents of her shoulder bag into the neat, purple clutch handbag that he had also provided, ruing the fact that it was not big enough to fit in the other items she habitually carried, and then set off for the lounge, where Charles was waiting.

"You look stunning," he told her, kissing her gently on the top of her head and admiring the smudged-smoke look of her eye make-up. "Now, just one more thing. Pull your knickers down and bend over."

Wide eyed with surprise, and mildly irritated now that she was ready to leave, she did as he asked anyway. She felt his hand cool against her labia. Then his fingers were inside her, turning her insides into molten lava.

"That's it. Pull your knickers up. Come on, quickly!" It was not until they were in the lift that he told her, "I've inserted a device in your vagina, just a little something for my amusement." As the doors swished open and they stepped out into the lobby where the concierge greeted them smilingly, he added, "Don't make me angry by removing it, bitch."

Rusty laid her hand in Charles' proffered palm and allowed herself to be helped from the backseat of the car, and with her hair up, she was surprised to feel the warm evening breeze on the back of her neck. When Charles had informed Stratton of the time he wanted to be picked up again, she folded her hand neatly into the crook of his arm and allowed him to escort her up the steps to the front entrance of one of London's most glamorous hotels. More used to wearing chunkier high heels, wedges or motorcycle boots than the elegant stilettos Charles had bought her especially for the occasion, she wondered as she listened to their click click click on the steps whether everyone else would realise how unaccustomed she was to wearing them. Mentally crossing her fingers that she would not let herself down – or more importantly let him down – by wobbling, she clung on to his arm with one hand and the clutch bag at her side with the other.

Bolstering her confidence with a silent but with heartfelt, Come on, you can do it, girl! she smiled politely at the uniformed doorman.

Acknowledging her smile with one of his own, the doorman declared himself "charmed" then addressing Charles he asked, "Will Sir be requiring the usual services?"

"Not this time. I'm on official Charity business."

"Very good, Sir. Just call if you need anything."

Still on Charles' arm, Rusty found herself swept inside. For a moment she could almost believe that she had been transported to a different planet; for someone more at home among flyers, engineers and old planes, or bikers like Jake, and more accustomed to craggy cliff tops and windswept hillsides than swanky hotels, opulence took some getting used to. Wealth radiated from every angle of the spacious reception area, from which you could follow the signs to the various function rooms, restaurant or bar, take one of several lifts up to the gym and sauna, go to your room or suite, or simply relax in one of the comfortable chairs to wait for a taxi. And if none of that appealed, you could simply watch the other guests. And what a glittering bunch they were, she thought as movie stars and wealthy businessmen and their wives made their elegant entrances.

Although the staff treated everyone with old fashioned courtesy, to Rusty it was obvious from the start by the way they greeted Charles that he was no stranger to the establishment. And the doorman's veiled offer …..of what? A whore for the evening? Whatever the "usual services" were, she was pretty sure they involved the sating of his basest desires – the very services she now provided.

Two function rooms had been booked for the annual fund raising event and charity dinner. It was a black tie affair, and Rusty thought that Charles looked sexier than she had ever seen him before as he wore his black evening dress with an ease that spoke of his familiarity with formal occasions and high living. He obviously felt completely at home, she thought as her dress rustled with every step.

For her part, Rusty felt overdressed, despite her lack of leggings! And never in her life had she worn such an elegant hairstyle. Until she had met Charles and he had taken her in hand, she had rarely worn anything overtly feminine, mostly just make-up and jeans, her only real concessions to her gender's liking for silk, lace and satin being her skimpy tops, and her bed sheets.

As she walked beside him, she could not possibly know how proud he was of his achievements regarding her training. That he thought more of his success in subjugating her than he did of her pain-racked contribution did not seem at all immoral.

And as he nodded to acquaintances and shared pleasantries as the invited guests arrived and made their way through to the one of the rooms at their disposal for the evening, he hoped he could eventually turn the bitch who walked so elegantly at his side into the full-time slave he craved. And once again he told himself that he needed a slut who would be there, at his beck and call, twenty-four hours a day, every day, not someone he had to share with aeroplanes! He slipped his hand in his pocket and felt for the little plastic disc with a button in the middle. As he used one hand to wave to someone he recognised, he depressed the button once, and immediately he felt Rusty's hand tighten on his arm as she visibly jumped at his side and drew in a pained hiss of breath.

Smiling at the thought of the current that had just passed through her cunt, he was tempted to do it again. Instead, he inclined his head toward her ear and gave a harsh whisper.

"You must learn not to react, my dear," he said with fallacious smile to a well known footballer, " You'll only attract the wrong sort of attention." He depressed the button a second time, and this time her reaction caused heads to turn. "I'll be doing it again throughout the evening. But another reaction like that and people will think you're suffering from some kind of affliction. Bear it! Do try not to soak your panties. They were rather expensive."

She pressed her thighs together, for the tiny shock of electricity had set her cunt quivering and seeping its sap just as he had known it would. It would not be wise to sit down for some time yet, she told herself fearfully as she imagined the patch of wet she was sure would appear on the back of her dress once she was seated.

Feeling completely at his mercy was something she was beginning to grow accustomed to. Except he had never done anything quite as bad in public before, and she was swamped with the fear of humiliation, because to be disgraced in front of so many noteworthy people would be more than she could stand. And with her hair piled on top of her head, she felt strangely exposed. She only hoped the flutters of arousal he had woken would soon abate, or else she would have to find a man to drag her into a cupboard and fuck her! For she doubted that Charles would oblige while on official business. Her nerves were juddering and she felt sicker with nervous tension

..... and more vulnerable.... than she had done since her first flight in a Tigermoth when she was a youngster.

Someone took her wrap and, now that most of the guests had arrived and gone through, Charles led her toward the first of the two function rooms. Feeling way out of her league as they stood in the doorway of a room full of the great and the good who milled around laughing, clinking champagne glasses and talking too loudly, all Rusty wanted was for Charles to take her home. She would rather do a dozen bungee jumps for charity than enter that room of refined, elegant or simply famous men and women.

As if reading her thoughts, he whispered, "Pull yourself together, Caroline. It's only a dinner after all, far less risky than looping the loop."

Suddenly, an eerie silence descended as people noted their arrival. All eyes in the room were turned upon Charles and the unknown staggeringly attractive woman at his side, and for the first time, horribly conscious of her short, stubby nails as she gripped his arm, Rusty wished she had at least taken the time to apply nail enamel. She could have had extensions fitted. She could have found the time in the middle of the week, when she had finished work a couple of hours early. She could have….. her thoughts faded to nothing as she became aware that whispers had broken out. If she could have made out what people were saying, she would have been bolstered by their compliments about her upswept, red hair that showed off her high cheek bones and long, finely chiselled nose, and insulted by their observations regarding her "too-pale" skin.

"She ought to do something about the freckles!"

"Perhaps we should give her the number of a good beauty consultant."

"We could give it, dahhhhling, but would she use it?"

"Beauty Consultant? More like a Harley Street specialist! She'd need a complete new face to get rid of that many freckles."

Rusty realised she was trembling, and caught her fleshy bottom lip with her teeth. She also knew that the fascination with her was exactly what Charles had wanted and that he had brought her along as eye candy, purely as a way of gaining the attention – and large donations – of the distinguished and well-known guests. And he had dressed her accordingly. To complete her outfit, once they were in the car he had produced jewellery that he loaned her for the evening. The drop diamond earrings were the most exquisite items she had ever seen, the stones set into filigree chains of gold. They hung down so long that they actually swung when she walked or moved her head, brushing against her neck and almost reaching her collar bone. He had also loaned her a matching bangle and choker. Having never worn any jewellery save a watch and a pair of tiny studs in her ears, while relishing the chance to wear such stunning pieces she was also nervous about having what amounted to a small fortune about her person.

The heels of the purple stiletto sandals he had provided added four inches to her normal five foot six and brought her up to his height. With her hand still hanging on to his arm, she felt a sudden upsurge of confidence and smiled, but then was embarrassed all over again as Charles gave what she thought was an inappropriate imitation of a royal wave. After all, he was only senior management, the same as some of the other guests, and certainty no more important than anyone else. Although as the Vice Chairman of NBAF he was the speaker and chief fundraiser for that evening's event, Rusty had discovered that he was only sitting in for the top man who was unaccountably delayed on his trip to Africa.

As normality returned to the room and the noise increased to its earlier levels, Charles led her toward one of several waiters. He slipped his hand in his pocket, delivered a charge to Rusty's cunt that made her give a cry of surprised pain, which immediately had heads turning in her direction and left the waiter visibly perplexed. As if he hadn't noticed, Charles helped himself to two flutes of champagne from the waiter's tray. Handing one to Rusty he hissed the command.

"Bear the shock quietly."

She smiled sweetly, released her hold on his arm and lifted the flute to her lips.

He turned his head toward her, smiled, and hissed, "Drink it slowly!"

Wanting to make a bolt for the door, nevertheless she followed him closely as he stopped to make small talk with people she had only ever seen on the TV screen or in movies, and some she had never seen before. He introduced her as Caroline, the name she had become used to again after seldom hearing it for years, and she smiled politely, occasionally sipping her drink, not daring to speak for fear of letting herself down. Realising suddenly that she was adopting completely the wrong attitude, she corrected her thoughts, telling herself if was more important not to let her Master down. And yet it seemed as if that was exactly what he was trying to make her do because even while he chatted and laughed, every so often he would slip his hand into his pocket and deliver another charge.

As he led her from one group to another, behind her the comments continued. And two female TV presenters that she recognised looked her up and down, then as if she were no longer present spoke in scathing undertones as Charles stood chatting to their male companion.

"It looks like Charles goes in for cradle snatching these days."

"At least she's got more class than the fillies he usually brings along!"

As they moved on, the shortness of her dress was the subject of discussion between all three.

"That's the shortest dress in the entire room."

"One can only hope that, unlike the last one he brought along, she's wearing knickers."

"Can you see any lines?"

"I'm not looking for any."

"No, you're just looking at her arse, Reggie!"

And so the evening wore on. Having eaten nothing since lunch time and dreading the moment when her belly would start rumbling, Rusty began to long for the dinner itself. Besides, she was beginning to feel bored. She glanced around in the hopes of catching sight of her favourite celebrities. Instead her gaze took in her surroundings. The glitzy function room that was normally the venue for wedding receptions and dances had been transformed for the charity dinner. Where usually artwork hung on the walls, that evening they had put up posters of gaunt black men and women, some homing in on their faces while others showed small groups standing around outside shabby-looking buildings or in the middle of dusty roads beside huge trucks. And where exuberant flowers arrangements usually stood, carved wooden statues of the same gaunt men and women stood, each one with a plaque beneath it that claimed it was the work of African tribesmen.

Yet Rusty thought there was something bizarre about the grandeur of the glamour and the smell of money that permeated the air as women in ball gowns and men in evening jackets wandered among the posters of shanty towns in Blawanya. There were other pictures too, of bony black men wearing old T-shirts and shorts and who pushed handcarts full of what looked like rock debris, or served food to equally ragged men in some sort of cafeteria. And there were other posters, too, of a low, white building that stood out starkly against the squalor, that had big, bold red letters painted on the side that declared, "CLINIC."

Charles gave her a shock to gain her attention.

"Caroline. Say hello to Judith."

Judith was a tall, attractive brunette who was totally unrecognisable in her jewels and gown from the downtrodden character she played in a popular, afternoon soap. And it was Judith who finally put Rusty at her ease.

"Tell me, my dear, where did you and this old reprobate meet?" she said, balling her fist and giving Charles an affectionate thump in the chest.

Rusty turned to Charles, smiled questioningly, waited for the slight nod of his head. Then without thinking how strange it was that she had sought his permission, she answered, "At work. He came for lessons."

Judith laughed incredulously. "Lessons? I can't imagine Charles needing any kind of lessons!"

Realising that the woman probably thought she was some kind of escort…. or hooker…. Rusty laughed as she told her, "at the flying school. I'm a flying instructor!"

"Really? How interesting. I had no idea that women did that sort of thing!"

Charles smiled. "No? Perhaps you're more used to women doing this sort of thing!" He slipped his hand into his pocket.

"Aaargh!" Beside him, Rusty jumped, then she doubled up as her hand flew to the front of her dress to try and ease the pain that bounced around the walls of her cunt as Charles repeatedly depressed the button in rapid succession. She shot him an accusatory look as he delivered the worst pain of the evening so far.

As a small crowd gathered round to watch and tried to figure out what was wrong with the stranger in their midst, Rusty felt her face burning red.

"Oh, you poor girl!" Judith said in a way that suggested she knew exactly what was going on. She slipped an arm around Rusty's shoulder as Charles withdrew his hand from his pocket. "It's nothing to worry about," Judith explained to the crowd, "just the result of minor surgery. She should be at home resting."

She lied so well! Rusty thought.

"Yes, indeed she should," Charles told them, taking up the story and embellishing it. "But she was determined to come. And as one of our largest donors to our cherished organisation ...." he paused until the startled breaths and comments had died away, "someone who normally prefers to remain in the background....she was hoping to talk to the founder of our organisation and set up a special fund for the clinic. But sadly, Mr Van de Velde has been delayed on his fact-finding trip."

Judith took over again, "Nevertheless, she was determined to come. This poor, unwell woman is, ladies and gentlemen, someone I....we.... feel privileged to know, Charles and I felt it our duty to give into her demands if that's what she really wanted. If only everyone were as generous! And so, despite the obvious pain that seems to strike quite randomly, I asked Charles to do the honours and escort this fine, young woman. So please, ladies and gentlemen," Judith pleaded with such Oscar winning plausibility that Rusty was starting to believe it herself, "stand back and give the poor girl room."

Acknowledging a signal from the head waiter, Charles slipped the disc into Judith's hand, then called everyone to order. "Ahem! Ladies and Gentlemen! May I have your attention please! Thank you." He temporarily relinquished Rusty into the woman's care. "Dinner is served, if you'd be so kind as to go through and take your seats."

With a conspiratorial whisper Judith told him as the crowd parted to allow them a way through to the dining room, "The Dutchman would love her!"

THE MEDITERRANEAN, GUAVENCIA

Darkness settled over the island of Guavencia. Half way up the ragged hillside, on a Moorish terrace lit by lamps and overlooking the sea, two men sat drinking coffee from small, delicate cups. Seated on opposite sides of a round table with a central, cast iron base and a marble top, both men were recovering from the exertions of the discipline sessions they had participated in earlier that evening.

The Spaniard, having spent several hours fucking a delightfully compliant girl who wore her nakedness like a million dollar dress, and whose hands and feet he had tied to the posts of his bed, had carefully inserted eight, six inch long, steel needles into her tits. She was wearing a leather slave collar, and to this he attached a leather leash. Then, leaving the needles in place, for the sheer hell of it Alvaro had taken her down to his wine cellar where he had suspended her by her wrists and flogged her. Afterward he had returned to his room, taken a shower, donned his silk robe and then come out on the terrace where he had fucked the young brunette who currently stood naked at his side.

Van de Velde had also spent much of the evening fucking, though in his case he had chosen the back passage of the Spaniard's wife, who was wearing the costly new collar that he had delivered himself. She was also naked and tied down, though to a low bench running the length of the guest bedroom rather than the bed, because when it came to sleeping, he preferred to actually sleep alone.

Face down with her breasts flattened beneath her, the attractive Spanish woman had been placed in the centre of the long bench, one end being occupied by Pik Van de Velde's empty suitcases and the other by a casket containing a selection of disciplinary equipment, with her hands roped together beneath it. Her position was made even more uncomfortable when he twisted her head to face the wall so that she was resting her cheek against the hard wood, and raised her up until – still with her hands joined beneath it – she was kneeling on the bench with her backside stuck attractively and conveniently in the air. Then standing with his own legs astride the bench, he had buggered the hours away, every once in a while leaning forward to slip his hands between the bench and her breasts in order to further torment her mammaries, or run a pinned roller up and down her back. Especially adapted from commercially available pin wheels, it was gold plated. About four inches long with a diameter of two, the barrel had needle-sharp tines embedded in almost its entire surface area. Producing little indentations or tiny pin-holes depending on the pressure brought to bear, it made rather attractive patterns on a clean canvas of unblemished skin. But it also produced rather fetching results on whip-marked skin.

Then having grown bored of the bench after the third or fourth reaming of her back passage, he had instead restrained her over a whipping bench placed at the foot of the bed, where he had taken great delight in giving her a good forty lashes across her rump with a rather nice stock whip that had been left at his disposal, before emptying his balls into her backside as he buggered her one final time. After that, he had too taken a shower. Once he had dressed again and one of Alvaro's servants had packed his suitcase ready for the morning, he had left Pilar Cortez still restrained over the whipping frame and had joined his host on the terrace for coffee, where he noted the girl had spunk oozing from her cunt and dripping down her thigh.

In his mid forties, Alvaro Cortez was the younger of the two men. The shapely brunette still stood beside her Master with her hands clasped behind her back. Apart from a black leather collar that circled her neck she was naked, with every body hair removed. Across her breasts and her pert behind, her otherwise smooth skin was emblazoned with welts that ranged from the fading lines of a flogging delivered days earlier, to more recent ones. Alvaro slapped her tanned, welted arse and sent her round to the elder man.

With her hands still clasped behind her, she shuffled into a position that offered Pik easy access, then without being told to she opened her legs, and at once he sank his fingers deep into her warm and welcoming cunt.

"It was good of you to bring the collar yourself," Alvaro told his guest in accented English as he lifted his cup to his lips and drained the last of the bitter liquid.

He answered his host in the perfect English spoken by the people of the Low Countries. "I can assure you that the pleasure was all mine. As I had to go down to Blawanya and knew I'd be stopping off at Morocco on the way back, I thought I may as well take a little detour and bring it along as an excuse to drop by to see how my former slave was getting along. I'm glad to say that she's getting along just fine."

"You should know that you don't need an excuse! We're happy to entertain you anytime, and Pilar is always at your disposal." Alvaro took a red and white packet from his top pocket and opened it. Shaking the packet of Fortuna he leaned across the table and offered it up to the girl who, without dislodging Pik's hand from her cunt, obediently leaned forward and dipped her head toward it. Using her teeth she extracted a cigarette which Alvaro snatched from her lips. The cry she gave when she straightened was engendered by the vehement jabbing of Pik's fingers, as unperturbed, Alvaro replaced the packet before lighting the cigarette. He did not offer his companion one for he had been acquainted with him long enough to know that smoking was one of the few pleasures they did not share.

"Still, you value your privacy and I can understand that." With his long, thick finger still poking around inside the girl, holding the small cup in his other huge hand, Pik drank the last of his coffee and replaced the cup in its saucer.

Alvaro blew out smoke. "It's a pity you have to leave us so soon."

"As I believe I mentioned, I have a series of meetings to attend in England. There's one in particular that I don't want to miss, at the weekend as a matter of fact. Though God only knows why it's being held at an airshow." He slid his slick finger from the girl's cunt. "I've already had to cancel the talk I was due to deliver at a charity fundraising function in London this evening, and I had hoped to combine it with a report on the Blawanyan aid project."

"Si," Alvaro acknowledged before adding with a benign smile, "But it's a pity – my wife was just getting used to having you around."

Pik's smile was equally benign, though at the same time and without warning he slid his slick finger into the girl's rectum, making her cry out once more. He eased it in and out, disregarding her whines of protest. "But I know my dear Pilar is in good hands. And the collar suits her so well. It's a nice, snug fit, though I have to say that initially I had some reservations about its design. I believe that a collar should be plain and functional. But after putting it to the test last night, I have to admit that the functionality of Pilar's collar is almost as good as…..." he paused, then just as suddenly as he had inserted his finger he withdrew it, reached up and hooked it beneath the brunette's collar and yanked her down toward him until her face was inches from his own. He smiled, then pulled her down further until her head was touching his knees and wiped his finger in her short curls. Then he pushed her under the table.

Obediently she settled herself between his legs then, again without being told to, she drew down the zip of his trousers. Once she had taken his cock fully into her mouth and begun to suck noisily, he began again.

"Its practicality is as good as any other and, of course, it suits her almost as well as the leather one suits this slut. How long has this one been with you?"

"Less than a month." Alvaro turned his head slightly, took another drag of his cigarette and, blowing out the smoke, called for his maid. "Consuela!"

Wearing her advancing years like a worn out blanket, even at that late hour the once attractive woman appeared on the terrace as if by magic, her wiry grey hair tamed by a black headscarf tied beneath her hair at her nape. Dressed entirely in black with a set of keys and a whippy-looking cane hanging from the waistband of her knee-length skirt, she was a formidable looking woman indeed.

"Si, Sênor?"

Ignoring the slurps that came from beneath the table, in Spanish Alvaro told her to bring more coffee, then as she returned back through the patio doors and inside the house, he reverted to English. "So how are things in Blawanya?"

With both hands on the back of the girl's head, Pik pushed her face into his groin, forcing her to take his cock down her throat. If he noticed that she gagged uncontrollably as she fought the dual battles of performing fellatio to the best of her ability without choking and actually breathing, he made no mention of it but kept his hands firmly in place.

"I have a bit of crisis. Nothing that can't be solved, but it is most inconvenient. Not to mention expensive! It seems my pilot absconded with a cache of diamonds, as well one of the mine's slaves. Luckily, the infrastructure leaves a lot to be desired, and he was picked up at the border. Currently he's languishing in a Blawanyan prison cell. The diamonds have disappeared, of course! The slave was returned to the mine. I may have to abandon the place altogether and relocate the operation, perhaps to one of the new mines over the border, if I don't find another pilot soon. Either that, or find another form of transport and a series of mules! Perhaps I should look up our old friend in Sambiya, and see if he has any slaves that he could sell me for the purpose. The only thing wrong with that is, the slaves would cost me more than the diamonds I'm bringing out!" He paused while Alvaro laughed sympathetically, noting that the girl had finally recovered herself once more and was slurping again in a most satisfactory manner.

"No hope of finding a replacement at this airshow?" Alvaro suggested.

"Perhaps. I have a contact. In the meantime, I've left my man in place. Doctor Dowling's something of a Godsend." He smiled, slid one hand from the youngster's head and reached down to take a long, rubbery nipple between his finger and thumb. He pinched it so hard that she drew in a shocked breath. Yet not once did he so much glance beneath the table or show any genuine interest, and when he spoke in a matter-of-fact tone, his question was prompted merely by curiosity. "Where did you say you found this slut?"

Alvaro gestured vaguely up and behind him as Consuela returned with a fresh pot of coffee and topped up their cups. "One of the guards found her, on the other side of the hill, over by the old settlement."

"She was alone?"

"No. There was a young lad with her – another student – but I paid him off and he went off happily to Morocco, relieved to be dropping his studies and having the wherewithal to bum around for awhile! When – I should say 'if' he decides to either be found or return home, his story will be that they were kidnapped by bandits and only he managed to escape, leaving the girl with the cut-throats!"

Pik nodded approvingly. Removing his other hand from the girl's head to grab the other nipple and torment that also, he was pleased to note that she did not take the opportunity to expel even the slightest amount of his cock but kept her face buried deep in his groin. "And there was no hint of a submissive nature when you found her?"

"None at all," Alvaro confirmed as Consuela stepped back and awaited further orders.

"I must say that you've done a grand job on her!" he congratulated as he twisted both nipples sharply. "I made no allowances when I used her yesterday afternoon, and I was most impressed. Rarely have I come across such obedience in such a short time with a non-submissive."

"That, my friend, is thanks to Consuela." He dismissed the elderly woman with a wave of his hand. "Consuela's an excellent maid, of course, and with a callousness toward the girls that I can only admire. I understand that in her youth she was an exceptional slave herself. She knew how to take the whip and, I'm glad to say, she knows how to apply it."

"So I've noticed." Below the table, the girl's ministrations finally paid off. Pik grunted, then emptied himself into her pretty little mouth. Still without looking beneath the table as she struggled to swallow copious amounts of hot, masculine liquor, he gave her nipples another sharp twist, then let his hands drop away. He placed the heel of his palm against her forehead and pushed her away dismissively.

Leaving the girl to her own devices as spunk dribbled from the corners of her pretty, skilful mouth, both men drank coffee until they had exhausted conversation and the pot was empty.

And all the while, the girl stayed where she was, kneeling with her hands behind her back, her long nipples throbbing and her quim quivering with the need to be filled. She did not dare to wipe her mouth since she hadn't been given permission. Then suddenly, a command to move was given in the form of a prod from Alvaro's shoe on her backside, and obediently she crawled out from beneath the table, just as the men rose from their seats. Uncertain exactly what was required of her, she stopped midway between the table and the patio doors as the men pushed back their chairs, the sound of metal scraping on stones jarring her nerves as well as the stillness of the air.

"What shall I do with your wife when I've finished with her?"

"I shan't be needing her myself, so keep her as long as you wish. But when she ceases to amuse, just send her back to our room. She has a rug beside the bed."

"Very well, then. I'll say goodnight my friend." With that, he returned to the guest room, where Pilar was still tightly secured over the whipping frame.

The first thing he did was to untie her and help her to her feet. The second thing he did was to bend her over it again, this time backwards. Once she was secured back-breakingly in position with her legs wide and her head hanging down so that her short hair was almost in contact with the marble floor and the weight of her new collar made it shift toward her chin, he gave the roller a couple of turns across her pubic mound. Paying no mind to whether her lack of screams were due to her obedience and control or having simply cried herself hoarse in his absence, he set the roller aside and took up a small, narrow-tailed flogger. He delivered twenty stinging strikes across the same sensitive, pin-dented flesh, making her count off each one in English, before changing his aim and striking along the slit of her red, exposed cunt a dozen times.

He hadn't spoken once to her since bringing her into the room shortly after the evening meal, and did not speak to her again until he had set her free once more. Now, having helped her to feet, he planted a kiss on her lips and told her, "away now to your husband, Pilar."

CHAPTER EIGHT

LONDON

The function room that usually served as a glitzy restaurant had also been transformed. Some of one of walls were adorned with more of the posters, and giant screens had been erected so that every one of the round, elaborately laid tables had a good view. And a small rostrum with a lectern had been set up at the front of the room, slightly to the side of one of the screens.

Despite the lavish food for which the guests had paid handsomely since the majority were keen to be associated with the event whose proceeds were in aid of charity and hoped the media would pick up on their generosity, Rusty was unable to do anything more than pick at her plate. For one thing, she found it too rich for her palate. Also, unlike many of the celebrities present, she found it difficult to eat with the posters of gaunt black men ……fewer women she noticed…..receiving meagre meals at some African cafeteria style eating place in a dusty shantytown. Thirdly, she had been placed at the top table between Judith and Charles, who discreetly passed the disc from one to the other and took turns giving her shocks of varying degrees throughout the meal so that she was either in a state of fearful anticipation or in the thrall of electrifying pain. And all the time there was the terrible desire to climax.

However, she was allowed another glass of champagne and to some extent that seemed to help. Again there was the instruction not to drink it too fast. As the evening wore on, she found it easier to cope with the shocks and even looked forward to them with happy expectation, each harmless jolt filling her quim with high-voltage need, and a thrilling warmth that spread deep into her belly.

At the end of the meal and while the dishes were cleared away, drinks were once again provided as Charles left the table and climbed the rostrum. Standing behind the lectern, he called for quiet.

Judith leaned closer and in a conspiratorial whisper she told Rusty, "Charles and I go way back, we're old friends. He usually brings a whore, or a fully trained slave to these events, but I gather you haven't been with him long. You really must control your reflexes in public, no matter how great the surprise or painful the shock. Has he put it over your clitoris yet?"

Rusty shook her head.

"Then you've got that pleasure to come. Instead of being a little electrode that clips invisibly to the inner wall of your cunt…. incidentally, my dear, you're to be commended for not removing it before you arrived tonight… the clit clamp that Charles uses just that, a painful clamp with an electrode fitted that nestles against your clitoris while the jaws of the clamp hold it in place. It works the same way but delivers a slightly more powerful shock, and is certainly visible under tight clothing. Of course, not everyone realises what they're looking at! Now, while I have you in my care, I may as well get some entertainment out of you!"

At the lectern, Charles was addressing the audience. "As you know, our esteemed founder Mr Van de Velde could not be with us tonight. So I'm afraid you'll have to make do with me." He paused for polite titters. "A poor substitute I know, but when you see for yourselves where our founder…..no, our friend….has been for the last few days…..where he still is as I speak, I'm sure you'll understand." The room was dimmed and the real business of the evening got underway with a video whose narrative was provided by Charles himself.

It started with a tall, grey-haired man walking along the narrow, dusty road, followed by a large truck piled high with bulging sacks. As the man and truck made their way closer and closer, Charles narration informed the guests that "at this very moment he is Blawanya, helping with the delivery of the aid that has been provided by the funds you have so kindly donated."

Rusty started as she felt soft fingers tugging at her panties. As they negotiated the fabric and explored her denuded vulva in search of the way in, Rusty kept her gaze on the screen, watching as the man was lovingly greeted by a ragtag group of black men. Few women, she noticed.

"Unsurprisingly, given Mr Van de Velde's nature, the people have come to love him and look forward to his regular visits….."

Judith leaned closer and whispered, "Open your legs wider, dear."

Stunned by what she had heard, and not wanting the woman to give a bad report on her conduct, Rusty obediently opened them.

"Wider, dear."

On screen, the man was shaking hands with a handsome white man who was wearing a white clinician's coat. They were standing outside the clinic Rusty had seen in the posters. "Dr Dowling was overjoyed with his new clinic, built with the funds you…….."

Judith's fingers slipped into her tight channel and began to move rapidly inside her. Working quickly, she removed the device that Rusty had obediently kept in place all night, and without removing her fingers managed to manipulate it from the fingers inside to her other hand outside. Realising how vulnerable she was to the actress' surprisingly predatory inclinations, the lovely redhead knew she had no choice but sit it out. It was either that or make a fuss by getting to her feet, accusing the woman of taking advantage and then fleeing. But she could never do that, of course, not while her Master's commanding, husky voice kept up its narration. Trembling, she tensed as Judith continued to probe her insides. Then Judith, without moving from her chair, found Rusty's hand and slipped the device into her open palm. The girl was immediately struck by the warmth of it, and the shameful knowledge that it was her own body that had produced the heat, and that it had been inside her for hours.

"As you can see, ladies and gentlemen, he was there this very afternoon, inspecting its facilities on your behalf……"

Still Judith's fingers agitated her until all she could think of was that it was woman's fingers that were inside her, not a man's! Even as her pussy quivered and juiced as freely as it ever had, the thought of a woman's fingers bringing her to that state seemed outrageous....disgusting.... and the poor girl had to stifle a sob of humiliation and misery. She would die of shame if anyone were to discover the shameful secret as Judith innocently watched the screen while at the same time she had her long and elegant fingers buried deep inside Rusty's vagina. With her emotions stretched to breaking point, in desperation Rusty turned her head toward the screen again.

Now the two men had been joined by a group of smiling white nurses in surprisingly clean and starched uniforms given their location. "Never before has the diamond mine of Blawanya had its own clinic! But now Dr Dowling and his dedicated team are able to treat the sick at the diamond mine......" on cue, a straggly queue of black women moved forward, all wearing what were obviously donated blouses, skirts and dresses which were ill-fitting and made the women seem smaller, "and those who come from miles around to receive the medicines your funds have provided and which are regularly flown in on a special plane. The expertise of Dr Dowling and his nurses......"

And so the mendacity of the video continued. And all the way through, Rusty bit her lip to contain her cries as Judith worked her into a frenzy. And it was with horror that she realised that the most terrifying part of her ordeal was that she was actually beginning to enjoy it.....not just the furtiveness because up until tonight, the danger of being caught had always given her a thrill, though she was having to get used to Charles pushing her boundaries. But if she were to get caught tonight..... "oh......oh......." then it was just too bad. "Oh...." She tensed. Just as the video faded with the tall man smiling benignly into the camera, the lights came up.....and Rusty orgasmed at last, with her head lowered, eyes screwed up and her balled fist shoved into her mouth to stifle her cry of release.

"And so, my friends, it falls to me to beg, on behalf of the Netherlands Blawanya Aid Fund, but more importantly, the poor men and women in Africa..... and in particular those who work tirelessly in the Blawanyan mine to extract the little baubles that you have dangling from your ears, around your necks or cufflinks and tie pins.....I beg you to dig deep in your pockets this evening and......"

GUAVENCIA

Dawn came early and brightly to the island.

"Goodbye, my friend. Perhaps next time, you'll be able to stay a while longer," Alvaro said with a genuine smile in his voice. "You're a very welcome guest."

"Thank you for your hospitality. Say goodbye to your charming wife for me."

"I will. I know she'll miss you! I could hear her snivelling and groaning in her sleep. And thank you again for delivering the new collar."

After a brief farewell, he went back inside the house to collect his belongings from where, to save him the bother of returning to his room, the servants had put them in readiness for his departure.

Alvaro Cortez resumed his seat once more. Watching the girl, still on all fours, waiting uncertainly for instruction, he called for his maid again.

"Consuela!"

She appeared almost immediately, wiping her hands down the front of her black skirt.

With the departure of his guest, Alvaro reverted to his mother tongue, telling her in Spanish, "Secure this bitch, clamp her, then fetch my wife!" English would be banned from use except in exceptional circumstances or until another guest arrived, which could be months – or years – away.

And so, once the girl had been chained and clamped as directed, Consuela went to release her mistress from the chains that had bound her to a wooden frame for the past three hours.

At the foot of the bed in the room Pilar shared with her husband, while he slept she had suffered from the unpadded, horizontal cross beam biting into her flat belly. While joyously suffering the after-effects of

Pik's debauched discipline, she had thought fondly of her husband's love for her as, positioned toward him with her hands fastened to the bottom of the frame's front legs and her ankles secured in the same way to the back, she had listened to him breathing. Unable to see him, she had wondered throughout the long hours which of the three other slavegirls was actually in bed with him.

"Stand still, stupid slut!" Consuela told her now as, having released her from the frame at last, the maid bound Pilar's hands behind her back. Then she hitched a long chain to Pilar's new and costly collar that adorned her elegant neck, took the cane from her waist and swished it viciously, depositing lashes across her breasts that had Pilar screaming.

Laughing as she replaced her cane, Consuela talked rapidly. "They should be nicely developed by the time we reach your husband. Now come, filthy slut." Consuela gave the chain a jerk and Pilar found herself led from the room.

Once outside the airy chamber, Pilar stumbled on a step, then slipped on the marble floor. Unable to save herself, she fell awkwardly. The maid merely swore and gave a tug on the chain to encourage the woman, who was technically her mistress and who paid her wages, to gain her feet, then without speaking to her again or slowing her pace she marched Pilar through the house to join her husband on the terrace.

"Ah, there you are!

As Pilar fell to her knees to greet her husband in the required manner, taking his cock into her mouth to show him the reverence due, at the same time Pik was climbing out of the buggy that had driven him from the house to the foot of Draco Cueto.

The air was scented with orange and lemon. The murmuring of the wind in the trees and the almost musical quality of the sea had its usual calming affect on Pilar as she stood beside a spreading almond tree. She turned and, with one hand resting on a branch as she stood against the balustrade and looked along the coastline, her eyes were drawn to the cabin cruiser just off the coast where people relaxing on deck might well be looking across in her direction. If any one of them were able to observe her they would have found it hard to believe that only moments earlier the choppy-haired woman in the diaphanous robe had been a seething kernel of pleasure and pain, her essence entirely sensual.

From where she stood, Pilar could see the upper half of Draco Cueto, and the small car of the funicular railway as it travelled to where the helipad, just past the half way mark, had been constructed on one of the terraces which had been cut into the side of the dormant volcano centuries earlier. Up above, at the very top and almost on the edge of the crater, were two, stone built shacks that had once been used by the early explorers and later, the intrepid tourists on the Grand Tour who had come to look into the crater itself, but were now used as lookout posts by the island's guards. What she could not see was the lower half of the craggy hillside, where the golf buggy that one used to travel between the house and the foot of the volcano had been left beneath the Dragon Tree which, according to legend, was over 400 years old.

She threw a furtive glance back over her shoulder to where her husband, the man she looked up to as a paragon of domination with coal black hair and even darker eyes, was seated. A mature cherry tree and luxuriant bougainvillaea cast welcome shade across the side of the sunny, Moorish terrace where Alvaro Cortez was enjoying a breakfast of croissants and coffee. Kneeling naked at his feet with her distended nipples clamped and blue-tinged, the young blonde slavegirl who had shared his bed begged charmingly for titbits from his plate. Choosing to ignore her in favour of the new, American blockbuster on the table before him, Alvaro lifted his cup of bitter coffee to his lips and read on.

Pilar turned back to look at the top of the volcano. There was a sadness in her heart as she watched the chopper take off from the helipad, carrying their house guest to whom her husband had played the perfect host. At first she had considered taking up his offer of going along with him, just for the pleasure of the journey and change of scenery, and to see to his needs of course. But because the pilot was paid to follow Alvaro's instructions and always sought clarification before following hers, she had thought better of telling him that she was taking the place of the girl who had been assigned the task, though she would dearly have loved to accompany their guest, for old time's sake if for nothing else.

A feeling of pride swelled inside her and set her cunt clutching hungrily at emptiness as she slipped her hand inside her white, transparent robe and ran her fingers over her breasts. She flinched, for the welts that criss-crossed them and were clearly visible through the gauzy material were still tender beneath her fingertips, and she knew the flogging that had erupted across her breasts was a goodbye gift she would long remember..... the flogging and the fucking afterward. Yes, she thought, her husband had been the perfect host and had offered her on a plate to the rich Dutchman in exactly the same way as he had offered the other three sluts, one of which was probably even now sucking him off or bouncing up and down on his impressive cock.

Of its own accord, her other hand slid downward and inside the robe, only stopping when it alighted on her shaven quim. Using her forefinger she began to masturbate madly, using a rapid rubbing motion to torment her clitoris, all the while keeping her gaze locked onto her husband as she contemplated their life on the island.

Back in January and February, the cherry's blooms had been magnificent, and now its fruits dangled in tempting abundance from its branches above Alvaro's head, though it was more than even Pilar herself would dare do to pick them without permission. The tree, like Pilar's family, had its roots here on Guavencia and had been a part of the island's history for generations as it passed down through the female line, though neither the tree nor Pilar herself could ever rely on being truly safe for both were subject to Alvaro's whims; the tree could be replaced by a parasol as easily as Pilar herself could be supplanted by another woman whose carnal tastes matched her own.

Her considerable wealth, however, could not be so easily replaced and she was all too well aware that that was probably the main thing holding her marriage together. For though she had signed her life and self-determination over to Alvaro, she had kept control of her fortune, trusting in her family's Spanish law firm – a firm that had been practising on the Spanish mainland for over three hundred years – and her bankers to keep her millions safely away from her husband's clutches. He had carte blanche when it came to her body – he could whip her until she could no longer stand, suspend her naked from the Dragon Tree or hand her over to the guards to fuck and whip, and she would love him all the more for it – but he would never gain control of her fortune.

The thought of all the things he would do to her now that their guest had gone set her cunt aquiver and she began to rub her clit faster. Even though she had done everything at his command, she knew he would punish her for being so filthy because it was just the way things were......the way they were supposed to be.

"Stop it, Pilar." Alvaro spoke to her firmly in Spanish, though he had still not looked up from his book.

With immediate obedience she withdrew both hands and concentrated on the view. That was the thing about Alvaro, she thought, he always seemed to know what she was doing. She swung her gaze skyward. The helicopter was just a speck in the distance. And it was with mixed feelings that she realised it was unlikely she would ever see Pik again, for his various business interests and sexual pursuits left him less free time than when she had first met him all those years earlier in Monaco's casinos, when they had been drawn together by their love for diamonds as much as their lasciviousness. She had no idea, of course, which of his interests was taking him to England this time, though she doubted he would give her another thought as he arrived on time and refreshed.

"It's always been one of his strengths," Alvaro told her, still without taking his eyes from his book as he turned the page, "he's always been an expert at exploiting one weakness to fuel another."

Alvaro's uncanny knack of reading her thoughts still took her breath away, even after their years of marriage. And what he had said was true, for Pik had exploited them both, which is how she came to be married to Alvaro in the first place, for it was Pik who had introduced them when his own weakness for Pilar's attractions had began to pale. Then one night in Amsterdam he had met Alvaro, an avaricious man several years his junior but with the same brutal way of using women, as well as with a lust for wealth with no feasible means of acquiring it! And so Pilar, whose need for discipline had always ruled her head, had found herself being handed over as if she were just another piece of unwanted property, the irony being that it was her own wealth that was used to buy not only her unwanted freedom from Pik but also her subjugation to Alvaro.

As both recipient and donor, Pilar was as much a slave in this cruel paradise as she was its sadistic owner.

The diamonds around her throat glittered as brightly as the sea which lapped against sand that was as warm to the touch as her perpetually bronzed skin. While it was indeed an extravagant item of jewellery, it was nevertheless as much of a slave collar as the stark black leather that encircled the slavegirl's throat. Another thing the pieces had in common was that they both possessed a ring to which all manner of things could be fastened, like the rope which was currently clipped to the slavegirl's collar and whose other end was tied to the Moorish-style fountain at the other end of the patio, allowing her enough leeway to move around when directed while still denying her freedom. Like the collars themselves, the rings were made of vastly different materials. In the case of the leather, the large ring was set in the centre of the two and a half inch high collar and was made of shiny, silver-coloured metal. But the stunning diamond collar was half the width of the leather one and hanging centrally from the bottom was a diamond-studded platinum pendant to which a platinum ring – smaller than the slave's but just as effective – was attached and nestled snugly against her collar bone. Pilar had designed the piece herself, though it had been Alvaro who had ordered her to do so and then had it made for her. She was fortunate in that she had several different pieces to choose from, and it was essential to Alvaro that Pilar did not appear without one of them around her pretty neck. The slave was less fortunate; her only collar had been fitted on her arrival and hadn't been removed since.

Pilar smiled dreamily as she focussed her attention on the glittering seascape, then the beach where a muscular, off duty guard from the lookout post on top of the brooding and dormant Draco Cueto, was swimming naked, his clothes piled neatly at the water's edge.

At this time of the year the sun's heat was considerable, and before long she would either have to retreat inside, or find a shady spot in the garden below her, where Moorish water fountains were set among the geraniums, palm trees, myrtle and cypresses, and all manner of colourful plants. As she looked down from the patio she caught sight of a bobbing blonde head among the subtropical vegetation, and recognised it at once as one of the slavegirl gardeners responsible for the gardens' upkeep. The island must seem a paradise indeed from the decks of the vessels that toured the Canary Islands. The low-rise building which sprawled across the terraced hillside, a former monastery built on the ruins of a Moorish stronghold, was graced with fountains, arched cloisters with roses and other lush vegetation climbing over its ancient walls and could easily be mistaken for a hotel. And the clusters of tiny, stone houses on the rugged, volcanic hillside and other side of the island could just as easily be mistaken for picturesque villages.

The nearest towns were Agadir in Morocco, just one hundred miles away, or one of the closer but hyper-active, over-developed tourist destinations on the neighbouring island of Lanzarote. Yet Guavencia was not the ideal tourist destination it seemed, and the few, favoured guests who visited its year-round hot and sunny shores were a very different kind of traveller indeed. The perpetual sense of calm that hung over the island was far from being a fair indication of the lives of its inhabitants.

Being in private hands since 1890, Guavencia was closer to North Africa than Spain, and although the Canary Islands were owned by Spain, Guavencia was named after some of the island's early inhabitants known as the Guanches. Later, the island had been appropriated by the Crown of Castille, which had allowed the Hispanic culture and tradition to flourish, until Guavencia was handed over to a religious order during the late seventeenth century. But that had come to an abrupt end when Pilar's rich and powerful ancestors had seized the island for themselves. Since then, successive generations had equipped the island with every modern amenity and convenience, though it still remained charmingly undeveloped.

Over the centuries there had been many changes and catastrophes to befall the island, including volcanic eruption and conquests. The evidence of Guavencia's long and turbulent history – both geological and archaeological – was everywhere and was an archaeologist's dream. But Pilar and Alvaro could not take the risk of the place being invaded, dug up and logged! And so the island was heavily guarded and any intruder was seen as a threat.

Pilar turned suddenly and flung the slavegirl a derisive look......the youngster had been an archaeology student who dared to come ashore. But she hadn't been allowed to leave with her note books, photographs and finds. They, along with her clothes and other belongings, were safely under lock and key.

CHAPTER NINE

KENT

It was Saturday and the first day of the Saxon Hill Airshow and Rusty set off early from the apartment, at her Master's insistence naked beneath her leathers. She was thrilled at the thought of openly displaying her welts, but at the same time she wished he had allowed her a T-shirt at least. It was just that she was not always this marked, and she usually had somewhere private to change. But for some reason, Sir had chosen this day for her condition to become public knowledge.

The city traffic was as horrendous as usual, and she was thankful when she reached the motorway.

She made good progress along the M20, swapping from lane to lane and weaving in and out of the traffic heading for Folkestone. But unable to really open the bike up and give full rein to the Fireblade's awesome power, and suffering the soreness of a flogged vulva, beneath her helmet she was beginning to grow irritable. Virtually lying along the bike's length rather than sitting on it, she turned off at the junction.

The traffic was already building up as she rode through the Kent countryside. By the time she reached the turning for Saxon Hill, her entire nether regions felt as though they had been rubbed over with an electric sander. To make matters worse, the long queue of traffic for the airshow was at a virtual standstill. The show this year was bigger, thanks largely to the fact that although the teams were sponsored by Charles' cosmetics company, the two day event itself was sponsored by Charisma's associate company Galandway Chemicals.

She turned the bend and at last the airfield was in sight. Now that she was this close, her mood began to lighten at the thought of being airborne once more.

A dribble of vehicles was being directed through the main gate by the uniformed security team and the men who were drafted in for the weekend event to monitor traffic and take care of the parking arrangements, which turned the grass into a car park. As she tried to continue straight on past the gate to the flying school's entrance, she was halted by a more solid member of the security team who showed no fear as he stood in the road, blocking the progress of anyone who dared even to attempt to drive past. Fighting to keep her excitement at bay for just a while longer she showed her pass and then accepted his apologetic, mock salute with grace as he waved her on up the road toward the private car park. It was unusually crowded due to the vehicles of the other four women without whom there would not be a wingwalking team, and the male flyers of the aerobatics team.

She slotted her motorbike in-between Tim's gutsy, low-slung convertible and her brother's old van. Allowing herself to relax, she let the adrenaline build. With her heart pounding so much that she barely noticed her juddering nerves, she killed the engine and swung her long, shapely legs to dismount. She loved this feeling of being alive, she thought as she lifted her black visor. To her relief they had a good day for it, with the skies clear and blue, and the wind little more than a whisper that fluttered a paper napkin through the air, and wafted the tempting aromas of hot dogs and burgers. As her stomach rumbled in response, she wondered if there was time to wander off to the spectators' area to find a van. No, too early for a burger! she told herself resolutely, wishing she had taken McBain's advice and stopped for a bite of something before she had left Charles' apartment.

She peeled off her gloves and placed them on the seat before removing her helmet and pulling her long ponytail free. With all thoughts of her Master temporarily banished from her thoughts, she concentrated her mind on the thrilling business of the day ahead. Or rather two days, for it was a weekend event and to her delight she was booked for both. The weather forecast for tomorrow promised much of the same, which meant two perfect flying days! Her heart doubled its efforts at the thought, and for a moment she held her hand against her chest as if she were trying to stop it leaping right out of her chest. She grabbed up her things and, with her special soft, calf-high boots that she wore for wingwalking slung over her shoulder by their laces and her special, lightweight apparel packed into her fashionable hold-all, she raced from the flying school's car park.

With her pert and naked backside swaying as it was sheathed tightly in leather, she ran through what was still considered a male-dominated area, despite there being one part-time female engineer as well as the other Angels members. The design of her new leathers that Charles had bought for her emphasised her femininity by clinging to her considerable curves and seemed to be drawn deep into her crotch so that the outline of her pubis was clearly defined.

She arrived breathless, dashing into the hangar as if her life depended on it. Immediately engulfed in a world that smelled of oil, aviation fuel and masculine sweat, as always she was aware of other lingering smells........bravery, and fear too.......of the young men who had been ready to scramble at a moment's notice. There were no squadrons based at Saxon Hill these days, of course. Apart from the flying lessons and parcel delivery, they were all just a bunch of dedicated enthusiasts, the individuals who cared enough to rescue and restore the planes from both World Wars so they could be flown once more, this time simply for pleasure or to raise cash for charity.

And once a year the airfield played host to thousands of supporters, aircraft buffs and well-wishers, some drawn simply by the thought of a day out, or nostalgia for the old planes, while others came specifically to watch the aerobatics and wingwalking. Of course, the biggest draw was probably the guest appearance of the RAF's elite with their own aerobatics team.

Rusty loved these shows! Once, when she was sitting in the cockpit of a visiting Spit, she had actually frigged herself to climax. And another time when she had been sitting in a simulator, she had shot down a Messerschmitt. She had come out with wet knickers that time too, though she could not say with any certainty whether it was from fear or orgasm that time.

Trying to catch her breath, she stood a moment and watched Diane, the only female member of the ground crew, scoot beneath a wheel of a plane to effect a last minute repair. Once recovered, she hurried down the hangar, the men all turning their heads to watch her. She stopped at far end, where a fair haired, bespectacled man in grimy overalls was working on the Pitts Special, giving it one last check.

"Hi, Danny!" she said breezily.

"I was beginning to think you weren't coming," he said without concern or turning his attention away from the plane.

Tossing the hold-all to the floor beside an upturned beer crate nearby, followed by her show boots, Rusty did not acknowledge the other four women who stood by the tea and coffee urns on a table in the corner, but instead threw herself down to sit on crate and took a few moments to catch her breath.

One of the radio engineers whom they had only recently taken on, wandered over and was blatantly watching her heaving breasts. He was about to speak when one of the group of women sauntered over to them.

Addressing Rusty through taut, peony glossed lips, she asked, "You okay, Rusty?"

Wouldn't you just love it if I wasn't! Rusty thought as she glared up at Stella who, like the other women, was togged up already. Although there were five Saxon Angels, including herself, only four actually walked the wing, making Stella the stand-in. She was willing to bet that the bitch had been hoping that her lateness was due to her having gone down with some ailment or other...... something..... anything.... that caused her absence this weekend. Because only then would Stella get her chance to displace her. But the trouble with that scenario was that while Stella had recently completed her training and was a fair-to-middling wingwalker once in the air – if one overlooked her aversion to waving to the crowds – she could not actually fly a plane. Rusty, on the other hand was proficient at both; not only was she able to walk the wing – both with the group display and a solo stint – and acknowledge the crowd, but could also put on a good show flying in the stunt plane later! She disliked the woman intensely, and it was comforting to know that Stella would never be good enough to replace her.

Yet her uneasiness did not abate; there was the added tension about her marks; as soon as she began to change into her other clothes, her secret would be exposed for good. Because last night, Charles had given her a good going over with the suede flogger. But when she opened her mouth to speak, Rusty's level tone gave no hint of the passions which raged within her.

"There were roadworks on the motorway."

"We've all had to cope with that!" The serrated edge of Stella's voice caused more than one head to turn in her direction.

The two women had never really hit it off and only tolerated each other for the sake of the team. But Rusty refused to show how rattled she was by the slightly older woman's argumentative tone and merely took off her motor cycling boots. Then taking a breath to steady herself for the onslaught that she knew was heading her way, she stood up and unzipped her leathers, peeling off like an outgrown skin the one-piece leather garment that Charles had bought her. Seemingly without a hint of embarrassment she ignored the winks and nudges, horrified gasps and sniggering from most of the men on the premises, including the entire aerobatics team, who were now gathering round to watch the impromptu striptease. And deciding it was probably best to get it over with, she stood up and turned around so they would all see her back first.

Wriggling the garment off her shoulders, she pulled it down to her waist.

As the men ogled her welted back, she hooked her fingers in the sides and eased it down, revealing an equally welted backside.

"Christ!"

"What's happened to you, Rusty?"

"Who did that?"

"Want me to sort him out for you, Rust?"

Having grown used to what she saw as the beautification of her body, she resented the rancour. Feeling no need to defend either herself or Charles' harsh treatment of her, she said simply, "my Master."

"What's all this 'master' stuff?"

"Nothing to worry about guys!"

She waggled her arse provocatively as she bent from the waist, and was gratified by the cheers. She swept up her leathers which she folded neatly and placed beside the crate.

Staring lasciviously, the new man hissed, "I wish the bitch would turn around!" He nudged the man beside him. "Hey, Jack. Are her pubes as red as her hair?"

"Yeah, a fucking raging-red thatch of pubes like you've never seen between her legs!" Doing their best to stifle their laughter, they watched as she continued to tease.

"You mean you've seen……"

"We've all seen it, mate, at some time or other! She's put it about a bit has our Rusty." Then as she turned, with a wink Jack caught her eye and told the new man, "Don't worry, your turn will come round soon enough. You ask Gibbo."

Behind him, Gibbo smiled wryly. As she turned, he was the first to notice the absence of pubic hair.

"But you're too late. Look, the pubes are gone, mate!"

But it was the sight of her maliciously marked breasts that really attracted their attention, though few could ignore the splendour of her naked genitals for long.

She bent over and pulled her gear from the bag and tucking her leathers in their place, before straightening up. Stark naked, she plonked herself down again, and the energy generated when her bottom came in sudden contact with the crate set her juicy breasts bouncing in such a tantalising way that several men reached for the front of their trousers.

Seeing that she now had the attention of Tim and Tony as well, she smiled feebly and, without relating the real reason for her late arrival since knowing she had actually spent the night with the Managing Director of their new sponsors might not be such a smart move, she wound up her excuse by telling them, "Then when I turned off the motorway I hit the bloody traffic coming here!"

"Don't knock it, Rusty," Tony laughed, his eyes wide at the sight of her beautifully marred nakedness, "we need the crowds this weekend to stay afloat!"

Something caught Rusty's eye and she glanced up. Her breath snagged in her throat when she saw Charles approaching. She'd had no idea that he was expected and her heart almost crashed to a stop with joy. But there were other feeling too, like horror and humiliation that he should see her flaunting herself like this. But their sponsor did not acknowledge her or even glance in her direction. Instead, she just looked away as Tony and Tim took him aside into the cubicle of an office to talk business.

"Well, at least you're here now," Stella said caustically as she turned her back and headed off in the direction of the other, brightly painted biplane at the side of the hangar.

As the little crowd reluctantly dispersed and went about their jobs once more, her brother wandered over. She dropped her gear on the floor and accepted his proffered mug of coffee with the beginnings of a smile. "Sorry I was late, Bro. I hope you weren't too worried."

Ignoring her nakedness, he told her, "I stopped worrying about you a long time ago, Rusty. It's none of my business where you were or what kept you.....has to be either a man or a machine. Judging by the state of you, I'd hazard a guess that it was a man. In any case, I was beginning to think that Stella was going to get her chance at last. I'm just going into the office. We'll talk later."

Damn it! She just knew that now Danny was going to be asking a whole lot of awkward questions. She also knew that she had to put it from her mind because, today of all days, she needed the full adrenaline rush of a good show. She guarded her position within the Saxon Angels jealously, and even though she had overheard suggestions between her brother and the other two brothers lately, she was not prepared to take it in turns with Stella. The bitch would just have to wait for Rusty to drop out, which she had no intention of doing. Despite the sponsorship deal for the entire season from Charisma whose logo they now carried on their headgear and overalls as well as on all the planes, they could not afford to buy additional planes and take on extra pilots.

Although the flying school operated Cessnas and Pipers, the airfield also had two other single wing aircraft for their fast growing delivery service. Then there were the five Harvards; single wing for the formation flying, and the one Stearman biplane for the wingwalking displays. As the day went on there would be Rusty's solo wingwalk, plus she would join the others when they went up together, in the morning and repeating in the afternoon. But for Rusty's solo aerobatics display, she would fly the only other biplane, the Pitts Special, which belonged exclusively to her brother. She hadn't objected to the use of her share of her parents' money to purchase it since she knew she would be the only pilot apart from himself that Danny trusted to fly it. But she knew that in his heart, what Danny really wanted was a Hurricane to restore. That, of course, would never happen.

By mid afternoon, Rusty was already feeling the pressure. And now it was time to go up again, this time for her solo walk. Attached to her special harness, she was sheathed in a slinky, made-to-measure, turquoise flying suit that was designed to be glamorous and sexy as well as durable, and underneath which she was still stark naked. She sat in the centre of the wing with her legs open scissors-fashion, mentally preparing herself. With her cunt pressed against the fabric-covered balsa wood of the top wing of the biplane and her arms stretched out as a counterbalance, she waited while Gibbo checked the strapping of the special safety rig one last time. Her hair was piled beneath the special, equally tight fitting hood that carried the all-important logo, and her feet were laced into her lightweight boots.

In the cockpit below her, the pilot turned the ignition while another member of the ground crew spun the prop. As the engine spluttered into life, she welcomed the pounding in her pussy as the vibrations travelled through the structure of the aircraft and hoped that any sap that leaked from her quim would dry in the air before she landed again. Added to that was the sensation of her heart pounding in anticipation and pumping the blood wildly around her hyper-excited system as the seconds ticked by.

As they waited at the end of the short runway for the instruction to proceed, she practised her breathing techniques. Once they were airborne, as always adrenaline would overcome any unpleasantness from the G-forces as they soared into the air in a steep climb. First her body would feel exceptionally heavy, and then unbelievably light and her feelings would be of profound joy when they went over the top of a loop and dropped away again. Then there was the painful whipping of the wind against her face at such speeds. And somehow the whole intense experience would transmute into another expression of supreme enjoyment and freedom. She loved the feeling of being at one with the elements and lamented the fact that it was never quite long enough. Because it was moments like these that she lived for! And she knew for a fact that for once her Master was here to witness the event and that made the whole thing extra special.

Unfolding himself from the backseat of the car, Van de Velde's diamond-studded cufflinks caught the light as he smoothed a stray lock of his steel grey hair back from his forehead. Having left instructions with his driver, he made his way across the airfield's VIP car park, followed closely by a mini-skirted young woman whose leather choker was studded with diamonds that flashed as she walked. Having acquired her from Alvaro and Pilar, he knew he need not worry about her as with her head bowed, she hurried to keep up with him as he strode on.

Dressed in a sharp suit that was his trademark and with a diamond punctuating his tie like a pretentious full stop, Pik was urbane, vigorous and handsome. With penetrating blue eyes, he was as much at home in the boardroom as he was in the bedroom.... or playroom. As respected by men as he was certainly adored by women, he did not look a day over sixty, despite his greater age, and was as comfortable with the latest bit of essential electronic kit in his hand as he was with a rattan cane or flogger.

The distant cheering reached a crescendo and he raised his eyes skyward to see a tiny dot some hundred or so feet above the airfield. As he drew nearer to the crowd around the main arena and the plane dipped lower, he saw that the tiny figure standing on the wing of the biplane was waving to the crowd. Driven by some bizarre instinct, they shouted and waved back.

"Thanks then to Rusty!" a disembodied voice informed him over the public address system.

So, he thought dismissively as he turned and strode head and shoulders above the throng, that's the wingwalking over and done with. Throwing a glance over his shoulder, he told the girl, "if you don't behave yourself, I'll have you strapped to the wings of one of those things and get them to loop the loop." Smirking at the thought, he turned to look where he was going and heard the disembodied voice again.

"That's our girl! Give her a big hand."

Another pointless exercise, he thought, sure the airborne party could not hear the crowd's applause. To him there was no point in allowing oneself to be strapped to some flimsy aircraft while the pilot put it through a series of aerobatics. Nevertheless, he knew it took courage. And while he pondered on the futility of it all, he missed the fact that the wingwalker was female.

Turning, he stopped so suddenly that the girl almost walked into him. With a mumbled "Sorry, Master," she put her hands behind her back.

He gave one simple word of command. "Down!"

Ignoring the fact it would give anyone behind her a tantalising view of her naked backside and sex lips, at once she obeyed. And despite the crowds who, on the whole, would not understand, when he set off again without another word she dutifully crawled like a dog behind him. And even though people constantly bumped into her, sneered and tripped over her, knowing she would face the severest punishment later if she did not keep up, she kept as close to his heels as possible as he strode through the swarm. Giving no thought to girl's cries as people trod on her fingers, and without paying attention to anything that happened behind him, he walked on. Mentally he disconnected himself from his surroundings as purposefully he strode past the hamburger stalls and memorabilia stands, weaving between the hordes as if he were born to it.

It was not the kind of venue he usually honoured with his presence. He simply had no interest in aircraft, except, of course, for the old, refitted Mustang which currently stood in a hangar on a strip of land in Blawanya, awaiting its latest cargo and a pilot to fly it. And the private jet and helicopter that were at his disposal and which periodically transported him around the world to his various meetings. The jet in particular was popular with the sluts he often took with him. There was something extra special about putting a girl in bondage and thrashing the daylights out of her at 25,000 feet. Pilar certainly had relished the experience when she had been his to command. It had been good to see her again, he thought as he recalled her suffering. He knew she was happy with Alvaro, but only a fool would miss her, and that made him the biggest fool of all! This slut would never live up to Pilar. But he doubted he would ever find one who did. His recent visit to Guavencia had brought it home to him that it had been a mistake to part with her. She was not only the most obedient, pain-loving slave that one could wish to own, she was also an excellent companion.

But what was done was done! he told himself as he brought his mind back to the present. As chief sponsors of the airshow his hosts, Galandway Chemicals – the manufacturers of some of the leading brands of household cleaners – had their own corporate marquees, as did its cosmetics and toiletries company in the shape of Charisma. In fact it was his dear friend and a director of both companies who had, for reasons best known to Charles Hilton himself, chosen the venue at which to entertain their most important clients and associates. And Pik Van de Velde of Pikaken Pharmaceuticals and VeldePik Diamonds was possibly the most important of all. Far and wide he was looked upon as a living legend.

Resolutely ignoring the aerobatics of the RAF flying overhead, he shrugged aside one of the mini-skirted girls who was distributing leaflets about the flying school. It seemed everyone wanted to fly these days! So why the hell was it so difficult to find a suitable pilot for the Mustang? Perhaps Charles would know one.

He came at last to the two Galandway marquees. It was easy enough to identify them among the others due to bunting in their corporate colours. The entire frontage of one was rolled up. On the remaining three sides, poster-sized photographs were set up which showed the company headquarters, its two British factories and its most popular brands. More discreetly at the back were photographs of their more intimate products such as massage oils, lubricants and erection gels, and a table on which a selection of the actual products were stacked for sale. He accepted a free sample of lubricant from a prettily posing and sexy girl distributing samples, wearing mile-high shoes and dressed in a sky blue pleated skirt that barely covered her crotch, and a matching bustier with a heart-shaped neckline. He thought her outfit was greatly enhanced by a rather nice and undisguised bruise just above the bustier and situated between the top of her left breast and her collar bone. Surmising correctly it was the result of a bite by someone who had chosen a non-fleshy part of her body, he accepted the little black plastic carrier bag she offered him to put the sample in, and made her mouth fall open in shock when he bent down to place the handle in his slave's mouth. Straightening up once more, with a knowing smile that made her blush, he left her wondering if he had meant what he said about coming back and giving her a matching bruise on the other side.

A display set up in the centre of the marquee was dedicated to the popular Charisma brand, and pretty girls were on hand once more, extolling its virtues and claiming that the event's wingwalkers used their cream to protect their skin from the one hundred and fifty mph winds. Accepting a free sample for his slave, he bent down again and placed it in the bag.

Other pretty girls outside who were more modestly dressed handed out leaflets and free samples of familiar, less "offensive" products in sachets – perfumes or foundation creams for the women and cologne or facial cleaner for the men. Accepting a sample of perfume in a tiny bottle as well as cologne for himself, he heard several sharp gasps as once again he placed them in the bag that was growing heavier by the minute.

"Come!"

Dutifully his new slave followed. As the men watched with lascivious and envious eyes, the women looked on with disgust, some calling out after them. Except for the odd one or two women who were rather covetous of the slave's position.

The larger, hangar-sized marquee had been designated for hospitality, and had an oversized flag with the company's logo flying from the mast which sprouted from the marquee's summit. He ducked inside and judged it a pleasant enough distraction from the noise of the wretched aircraft and woefully inadequate PA system which spluttered and blared in machine gun fashion outside. He made his way through the unexpectedly imposing surroundings to the well stocked and presented bar which took up the entire length down one side, and a full-sized mock-up of a biplane positioned at the back. With the company's eye-catching logo displayed among the tastefully decorated interior, the hospitality marquee was complete with white painted metal tables and chairs, and a buffet area that offered a lavish selection.

Pik was expected, his reputation going before him, and he took for granted the fact that the barman had poured his favourite champagne before he even reached the counter, handing it over with a smile the moment he arrived.

"A bowl of water for my bitch."

"Yes, Sir. At once Sir."

Within moments, the barman had found a suitable bowl and when it was placed at his feet he took the bag that his slave offered up, and she lapped thirstily.

"Mr Hilton will be with you in a moment, Sir. In the meantime…." the barman gestured toward the blonde who was making her hip-swinging way from one side of the marquee to the other, toward Pik, "Miss Davenport will take care of you."

He appraised the approaching girl. Raising his glass to his lips he noted that, like his own personal assistants, at first glance she appeared every inch the director's amicable and efficient representative, confident enough with the company's affairs to hold the fort in her boss's absence. But a more circumspect assessment took in the shortness of a hem that stretched tightly across the top of her silky, bare skinned thighs, along with the transparency of the unbuttoned blouse which revealed a quarter cup white bra beneath, told him that she could take care of anything at all if the need arose.

Smiling as she stood before him, she bowed her head, standing her ground when a man accidentally elbowed her in the back as he bustled past her, then fell over the slave, and staggered to the bar. The man gave the little group a puzzled look but did not offer an apology. Nor was one expected as the girl merely crossed her hands behind her back and awaited the Dutchman's pleasure.

His gaze travelled in a downward direction and took in her narrow waist, then further down to judge the shapeliness of her long legs.

"I've been directed to take you and your slave through to the back, to amuse yourself until Mr Hilton's arrival," she said in a hoarse and sexy undertone.

Although he was not a man given to following, especially women, there were compensations when an arse wiggled as invitingly as the one he followed through an opening at the back of marquee. And still on all fours, with the bag of samples once again in her mouth, the slave followed him.

By the time Charles arrived to join them in the substantial, US style Winnebago that was parked directly behind the marquee, Pik was working up a sweat as he amused himself, while his half empty champagne glass stood on the table. With both girls stripped and tied, standing breast to breast, he plied the whip that had been thoughtfully provided.

"Good to see you," Charles told him. "A new slave?"

"Yes. This is yours?"

"My PA," he smiled.

"You do have a slave, don't you, Charles? If not, I could pick one up for you when I – "

"No, no, that's quite alright," Charles told him as he picked up an additional whip, "I do indeed have a slave. But I'm afraid she's unavailable at the moment. I wonder, could I borrow yours?"

CHAPTER TEN

Toward the end of the afternoon the men, having conducted their business over the slaves and champagne, went their separate ways. Pik strolled outside, his dressed slave following behind with the bag. It was only when he reached the edge of the arena that he realised he hadn't broached the subject of a pilot with Charles. To his chagrin, it looked as though he would have to go through the tiresome affair of advertising after all.

Everyone around him was watching the sky intently. Stopping for breath and to consider the deals they had discussed. Despite his lack of interest in flying, he nevertheless turned his eyes skyward, where some kind of old plane was performing a solo aerobatics display. And as he watched, the stunts became more daring. For some reason he was reluctant to turn away. He kept his gaze locked onto the old plane. More surprisingly still, he found himself hanging on to every word the announcer said.

"This lovely, plucky little plane is in private hands. It's been lovingly restored by her owner, one of the organisers of this great, yearly event."

The plane went into a steep dive and then, just when it looked as if it were heading for the ice cream van, the pilot pulled it up sharply to cheers from the crowd. The plane waggled its wings, and the announcer began again.

"Today she's being flown by the equally plucky little gal, Rusty. Her Dad booked her first lesson as a means of keeping her out of trouble. She got her licence to fly when she was just sixteen. She's been flying ever since! At the ripe old age of twenty-four, she's an instructor herself, right here at Saxon Hill. If you fancy taking lessons, then.....”

Pik wasn't listening. If it were not for the fact that he needed to rest after his exertions with the slaves, he would have moved on. As it was, he stood his ground, relieving his boredom by kicking the bag to set it swaying as it hung from his slave's mouth. He remembered the way she had relished sucking their cocks, draining them of every drop of spunk. Nodding to himself, he appreciated the effort Alvaro had put in to bring her up to such a level.

Still the infernal commentary went on. He set the bag swinging again, sneering at the girl's glazed expression and was delighted that her painful welts were, thanks to the shortness of her skirt, clearly visible to all.

“When she's not actually flying planes, our gal can be found wingwalking ....” The announcer's words were momentarily lost in the amazed exclamations of the crowd as she performed another stunt, but were loud and clear as he continued. “If you missed it earlier, you can catch our gal wingwalking again tomorrow..............”

Good Heavens no! he shook his head. Whatever made the organisers think people were interested in having a two day event? And still the announcer droned on.

Pik thought again of the refitted Mustang sitting in Blawanya. He had heard and seen enough. Turning quickly he clicked his fingers for the slave to follow, confident that he had the solution to his problem. Heading back toward the VIP car park where his chauffeur was waiting, he considered everything he had just seen and heard. This Rusty character sounded exactly the kind of flyer he needed, he thought as he made his way along the long line of parked cars. He had a plane and he needed a pilot. Not just any pilot, but one who did not get cold feet every time he landed to refuel and found himself faced with an officious, over zealous and greedy customs officer. He had never considered a woman before, but now he laughed at his stupidity. After all, a woman had a built-in hiding place!

He failed to notice he had left his new slave straggling behind. As he reached his car and the driver got out to open the door for him, Pik wondered again why he had never considered a woman before.

"The slave, Sir?"

"It appears I've lost her. Run and fetch her, there's a good fellow."

A few moments later, with the slave safely stowed in the boot once more, the car set off bumping over the broken tarmac toward the entrance. By the time they reached the exit, he had retrieved his mobile.

"In return for that little favour you asked of me Charles.......while you're still at the airshow, I'd like you to pop across to the organiser's booth. I want them to track down a pilot for me......."

Nothing had prepared Pik for the cute, doll-like creature who entered the office of his London headquarters that nestled between the top-end jewellers of Bond Street. His critical gaze swept over her. She was wearing a pair of black leggings with a white top, and was nothing like he had imagined, or had been led to believe. Briefly he wondered what madness had possessed him to come up with such a scheme. As she turned to close the door, he took in the tightness of her leggings over her tantalising bottom. Then when she turned round again and made her way diffidently across the office, his gaze swept over her breasts that were barely contained by the thin cotton top with a deep V. He found himself fascinated by her large, kohl-lined eyes that were the oddest shade of green – no, not green exactly, he thought, perhaps amber with flashes of silver. Another thing that did not match his idea of a pilot was the generosity of flame red hair that tumbled in a lively fashion over her shoulders as if trying to dwarf her figure. He followed the line of her leggings down to her feet, upon which she wore a pair of denim blue wedges. The quirk of his lips foreshadowed his sceptical smile. She hardly looked old enough to be out on her own, let alone fly a plane!

By the same token, nothing had prepared Rusty for the opulence of the office and she found herself holding her breath as she entered. Treading lightly on the claret carpet for fear of her shoes leaving dirty indentations in the thick pile, she wondered if the works of art hanging on dark green walls that necessitated the glittering chandeliers to be ablaze were authentic or copies. Surreptitiously she looked around her as she approached the wide, oak desk behind which sat the man she had seen in the video on the night of the charity dinner. Looking debonair and handsome, sexy too, she was surprised to recall that Pik was almost seventy. He looked bigger somehow. With steel grey hair, the sparkle in his eyes was only outshone by the flashing of the diamonds at his cuffs and in the centre of his black tie. Looking more powerful in person than on screen, she felt intimidated as she stopped in front of his desk, not daring to even touch the chair that was placed in readiness for her.

He subjected her to a cold, hard stare. "So, Miss Paget......is it Rusty or Caroline?"

On the verge of blabbing that she had a master who always called her Caroline, just in time she realised that it was not the kind of admission you made to strangers, and it was one that not everyone would understand.

Inhaling deeply to steady her juddering nerves, she smiled and said with more confidence than she felt, "Rusty." She held out he hand in greeting.

But he did not take her hand to shake it. Instead, he barked, "Sit, Rusty."

Taken aback, she sat, crossing her legs elegantly. Feeling strangely out of her depth, as a kind of talisman, she held the mental image of Charles close. Thinking of him now simply as Sir, she told herself that he was her master and that he was the only man in her life who had ever meant anything. And that prompted her to uncross her legs again, as she remembered that Sir had forbidden it. Even in his absence, she would not wilfully disobey him and, parting her legs in the way he insisted, she sat with her hands clasped in her lap. She was not clear at all why Sir had wanted her to attend the interview in the first place since she had a perfectly good job that she loved dearly, but he had told her to attend and so here she was. She could only assume it had something to do with NBAF.

To her relief, it seemed the man that Charles called Van de Velde, rather than the more personal Pik despite claiming theirs was a longstanding friendship, was not a man to waste time and he came straight to the point.

"I want you to fly my Mustang. It means giving up the flying displays, of course. But it will be on a regular basis."

Excitement flared in her belly. Her eyes widened. She had only flown a Mustang once, when one of Danny's friends had asked if he would do some work on it, and she had taken it up for a test flight. Flying a Mustang! It was a tempting offer. Except she was not at all sure that it was an offer. She excused the fact that it sounded more like a command, and put it down to his abrupt manner and very slight accent. She considered the offer again. But she could not abide the thought of giving up the stunts! The adrenaline rush was everything. She shrugged noncommittally. Despite the command from Sir to treat Pik with the same respect and courtesy that she treated him, and obey any command that he gave her, since Sir hadn't accompanied her and so would not know any different, she flung him a defiant look. After all, she had been obedient, she had turned up when summoned!

"Why would I want to do that?" Something about the man made her shiver. It was as if everything was a front and that she was not seeing the genuine man. Feeling as if his eyes were boring straight through her and deep into her soul, she doubted that anyone ever got to the heart of the man.

Cursorily he looked her over. "Because the offer comes from me."

Something about the way he said it made her feel that it definitely was not an offer but a command after all. A feeling of déjà vu convinced her that she should get up and leave. But despite the uneasiness gnawing at her insides, when she made to stand she discovered she had no real will to get to her feet. What was wrong with her? she asked herself as she stayed seated picking nervously at her short finger nails. Yet even as he outlined her duties, she had the uncomfortable suspicion that he was treating her like a fool and keeping something from her.

"For a girl with your adherence to discipline and who loves flying, it's the perfect opportunity. Working for the charity with which I'm deeply involved, your role would simply be to fly the Mustang from its base to the Netherlands, then fly it back with a few medicines and bandages on board. Your living quarters would be provided and you'd be paid for your efforts.

It's a good offer, Rusty. You'd do well to remember who you're dealing with." He steepled his hands on the desk in front of him and in a way that seemed threatening, he leaned toward her. "Perhaps you need a little persuasion?"

Opening her mouth to speak, her teeth caught on her lower lip. Staring across the table at him, her mouth went dry. Suddenly in the grip of dread, she was cold and tense. "P....per......" God! What was wrong with her? At last she found her voice and putting a great deal of effort into speaking calmly, she said, "Persuasion? What kind of persuasion?"

He summoned his secretary from the outer room. "Come through. Bring your things."

Rusty had already met the bespectacled blonde on arrival, and thought her an abrasive woman, disliking her on sight. But she had been in no doubt that she was efficient, and so when the woman failed to appear for a good few minutes.... minutes when she had to sit under the scrutiny of the austere Dutchman, Rusty was taken aback when she finally did appear.

She hadn't heard the door open and so the first she had known her presence was when she felt, rather than saw, her standing beside the chair. Rusty turned her head and inclining it upward, her first thought was that it was a different woman. But it only took seconds to realise that the blonde was not just a secretary, she was also a slave. The spectacles were gone as were the clothes, and in their place was a leather collar around her neck, like the one she sometimes wore herself. Also gone was the abrasiveness, replaced by a willingness to serve that Rusty recognised all too well. She smiled slowly, sure that she understood the relationship between her and her boss. She was still smiling as she turned back to face him. But he was not smiling.

"You've brought the items I requested, slut?"

"Yes, Master," the girl passed over a silk duffel bag.

He placed it on the desk, then told her to attend to his other guest in the adjoining room. And she could only admire her obedience as the blonde obeyed immediately, leaving the office through a door on Rusty's left. And with blinding clarity she knew what working for him meant. When they were alone again, he addressed her imperiously.

"I'm sure you've had orders to do as I command."

As she heard herself answer, it was a feeling of disloyalty to Charles that troubled her and not the way she allowed her defiance to fade. "Yes, Master." Why had she called him that? Although Charles was her master, she did not even address him by the title. What was wrong with her?

"Stand, bitch."

She stood, casting a glance toward the door by which the girl had left, and from behind which squeals were emanating. And the cracking of a whip!

"Eyes front!"

She did as she was bid, then went one step further and bowed her head. Without thinking about it, she stood with her legs apart and her hands on her head.

"You're no good with your clothes on. Strip! Put your things over there." He snapped his fingers and pointed toward a couch against the wall.

To the accompaniment of squeals from the next room that were fast turning to screams, and the regular Crack! Crack! Crack! of a whip, she undressed quickly. Once her clothes were piled neatly on the couch, she began the journey back across the office, thinking it seemed further on the return, to where he now stood beside the chair that she had just vacated. She turned around when he told her, and stood with her back toward him. He grabbed her arms and tied her hands behind her.

"You wanted persuasion," he said, then ordered her to turn face him again.

She turned around. He produced a kind of gag with which she was still unfamiliar, although Charles gagged her often. She opened her mouth to allow him to place the pink rubber bung between her lips. Shaped like a squat dildo with a flared base like a butt plug, he positioned it on her tongue with the end pointing toward the back of her throat, then had her bite down on it to keep it in position, with the base on the outside of her teeth. He tore off a strip of tape from a reel he took from the bag and stuck it to the skin on one side of her mouth, over the base and then to the skin on the other side.

And still she heard the flogging in the next room continue.

He held what at first she mistook for a piece of black cloth. It was not until he shook it out that she realised how wrong she had been. Trembling as the full horror was brought home to her, she looked up at him with her big eyes pleading as she was so frightened of having her head completely covered that Sir had never made her wear a hood! Terror inched its way into her being. Sir had only covered her eyes, of course, she had worn all kind of helmets and tight-fitting hoods for her other activities, but never had her face been completely covered. But whether or not Pik understood made no difference because he slipped the fabric hood over her head anyway and fastened the Velcro at her neck. Sobbing as she tried to come to terms with having her eyes, nose and mouth covered, she nevertheless realised that she was able to breathe quite normally. She felt him grab her arm. And then he spun her around.

"Keep turning until I tell you otherwise."

She turned round and round on the spot, just as Charles had made her do in her own hallway. Unable to see, she was completely disorientated, and was swaying dizzily when, after a few minutes had passed, he finally commanded her to stop. Swaying giddily and reaching out her hands to save herself if she fell, once again she felt his fingers pressing into her shivering flesh as he again grabbed her arm. He half marched and half dragged her across the room.

It was only the fact that the sounds of the flogging had grown louder that made her realise that he had taken her into the other room. The flogging that had been delivered with a short split-end whip ceased the moment they entered the room, and she heard male laughter, followed by scuffling noises. There was a little cry as, unseen by her, the girl was released from the bonds which had held her down over a table, and seized by the neck. Then his guest tied her hands behind her, and with his hand gripping the back of her neck once more, walked her across to a corner where she was made to sit on the floor.

But Rusty knew nothing of this as, directly the girl was released from bondage, Rusty was made to take her place. Within moments she found herself spread-eagled with her breasts flattened against the highly polished wood beneath her as her head was turned to one side and her cheek also flattened. Although she could not have raised herself even had she wanted to since she knew she had no choice but to undergo whatever torment was decided for her, she felt a hand in the small of her back pushing her down, while other hands worked quickly to tie her hands and legs in place.

Although there was at least one woman and two men in the room, Rusty felt terribly alone and vulnerable with her senses denied her. Unaware that the other man was her own Master, she quivered with alarm, and vehemently denied the throbbing of her clitoris and the lava flow of sweet, arousing warmth that spread through her as she waited. Silently and unseen, the two men raised a glass of Krug over the prone body stretched tautly across the boardroom table.

And as the secretary sat quietly in the corner, nursing her bruises and welts, Rusty was treated to her first two-man usage.

Crack! Crack!

Unable to scream due to the bung in her mouth, Rusty managed only muffled sounds as she jerked under the two blazing lashes that felt as if they had stripped the flesh from her bones fell simultaneously, one across her shoulders and delivered right to left, and the other across her backside and delivered left to right. Unbeknownst to the shivering, writhing girl, both men were in possession of long, single-tailed whips that delivered a caustic bite.

And then they struck again with the hellish implements.

Once more her body jerked and if it hadn't been for the bonds her body would have leapt several feet in the air before crashing back down. And then again, each lash producing muffled noises. Having no understanding of the incongruous sensations that blitzed her flesh as surely as the whips lashed it, he drew his own conclusions regarding her moans. And for the first time since entering the room, he spoke.

"I can assure you she feels nothing but pain, my friend. If I thought there was the slightest possibility that the bitch was enjoying it, I would stop immediately and advise you to do likewise. I only know of one woman who can extract even a tiny amount of pleasure from such a ferocious lashing, and that woman is a

Spaniard." For a moment he thought fondly of Pilar, then continued. "Of course, if it did turn out to be a kind of pleasure that makes this whore groan, then we'd have to find some way to punish her for her sin. Make no mistake that it is a sin for a slut to enjoy herself when the pleasure should belong only to the Dominant.....or in this case both of us."

The shattering arrogance of his words left her breathless.

The terrible lashings went on, until each man had delivered a dozen lashes that, timed to perfection, fell across her prettily trembling flesh at exactly the same moment.

Although there was much scornful laughter from the two Dominants, to keep their victim in total ignorance of Charles identity the men communicated by gestures alone. Circling the table they changed places, then together they struck, one across her thighs and the other below her shoulders. Laughing, they delivered another dozen, blisteringly painful strikes each, then stopped for more champagne which Charles had provided and lavished on his friend and mentor. Paying no attention to Rusty's snivels, once again they circled the table, so that Charles stood at the head of the long table with Pik at the other end. Again the gesture and, having decided on twenty, they struck together, Charles lashing her brutally from shoulders to feet along one side of her prone body, and his guest reversing the brutality. Then, moving around the table once more, they began again, until they had repeated the whole procedure twice, hardly noticing the snuffling sounds emanating from inside the hood.

Laying the whips aside, they indulged in more champagne before Pik made use of his favoured hole. With the agility of a much younger man he climbed up onto the boardroom table and settled himself for the best possible entry…… best for himself and the worst for her, he thought hopefully. For unlike his protégé, Pik's pleasure came from knowing that once a woman had been used by him, she would never be able to confuse him with another; even if he were to have a slave prepared for him in his absence, using a hood that was so effective it cut out every sound, the slave would be in no doubt who it was that had delivered the most painful flogging or arse-fuck because once they had experienced his treatment, it would be engraved on their senses forever.

Unable to do anything but endure it as the full length of Pik's thick and powerful weapon plundered her rectum, yes , indeed she acknowledged with a stifled cry he did indeed use it like a weapon. Rusty sobbed and fought to control the agony that she thought would never abate. There really was no pleasure in this, and beneath the hood, she was a mess; her tears left muddy mascara trails, the hood was wet from her dribbling, and she was only too well aware that snot bubbled around her nostrils And all the while, she wept at the thought of her betrayal to her beloved Master, who would surely be expecting her home from work at any moment.

At last her ordeal was over and she was freed from the table. With one of the men gripping her arm, she was escorted to the other side of the room. Horror boiled in her senses as she recognised his voice when at last he spoke.

"Sit, Caroline."

It was Charles! Sir! Her beloved……….

"I said 'Sit!' I warn you, don't humiliate me by defying me. Just do as you're told and everything will be all right."

Slowly, she sank down, lower and lower until she realised there was no chair and she was expected to sit on the floor. As soon as her naked and rawly welted bottom made contact with the carpet she screamed against the thing in her mouth. Then Charles kicked her legs open. Once she was settled in the corner, bound and hooded so that she was still unable to speak or see, Pik freed his secretary to return to her normal duties. She closed the door gently behind her.

The two men sat together on one side of the table, drinking and discussing Rusty as if she were no longer there. She had no choice but listen as they decided her future.

"We have to find some way to obtain her services without alarming her previous lovers. And her friends." Pik insisted.

"No problem. She's always flitted around from one lover to another, in and out of their beds without compunction. And there are few people she would consider close friends. They're more like acquaintances who know her through her flying and other exploits. They would just naturally assume that she'd moved on to try something new."

"Family? She has a brother, I believe, a man who's involved with the airfield. Anyone else I should know about?"

"No one else. Luckily, my bitch girl is more attached to aeroplanes than people! There's only her brother, and he can probably be bought for the price of a few spare parts."

"What kind of parts? I need to know what sort of money we're talking here."

"Danny Paget is an old plane enthusiast. Likes to repair them, do them up and get them flying again. I know he's rather keen to get his hand's on a Hurricane."

"That's costly!"

"So is the suspension.....or worse, the cancellation of the operation, I would think."

Pik looked thoughtfully across to the hooded and bound creature in the corner.

"You really think she's that good?"

"You've seen her flying!"

"But is she obedient?"

"I thought she'd done well enough this afternoon to prove it."

"Yes, I see you have her under control, Charles. But I wonder, will that authority still govern her.... hold her..... when you are parted? After all, it's a long way from Blawanya to Europe. Can we trust her?"

"I don't see why not. It's thrills she's after. She just keeps coming back for more. If your man at the mine....the doctor....can find some way of making her non-flying time exciting and keep her in line...."

"You're right, of course. Dowling will take care of her."

Unable to find his voice as he took in the contents of the attaché case, Danny's head swam; there was more money than he had ever seen in his life, piles and piles of it, all neatly packaged with the pristine bands still in place. It was not merely a fortune, he told himself, it was the representation of an exciting new project ....and all that was evil.

"Enough," Charles told him with polite persuasion, "to buy a Hurricane. Not a bad deal, really, for a plane with such historic significance. Enough to get her airworthy."

"No...." Danny said simply as he closed the case that snapped shut with a very satisfying click, "no."

Apparently unfazed, Charles smiled, his surprise and disappointment betrayed only by the marginal twitching of his slightly raised eyebrows as he looked at the case and considered Pik's money one last time. "No? Are you sure, my friend? Such an offer isn't likely to come your way again."

"I said 'no'...." he looked directly into Charles' face. "No, it's not a bad deal. I shall be happy to accept. Just don't Rusty ever find out....."

"That her brother sold her? Of course not. I know you won't regret your decision."

Danny pulled a face. "But she'll miss flying. Planes have been her life...."

"I promise you that Caroline will be more than happy with the life I can give her. There'll be some flying, too." His smile was sincere as the two men shook hands and Charles told him, "I know of a nice little Mustang that would benefit from an outing now and again."

CHAPTER ELEVEN

Travelling in the back of the car with Charles, Rusty wallowed in misery at leaving the world she loved behind. And Charles too, of course. But on the other hand, there was such excitement in her belly at the possibilities that her new life would open up for her that, by the time she reached the North London airfield, she was a mishmash of nervous tension.

It was easy to spot the charity's own modern aircraft, its high visibility yellow livery emblazoned with the NBAF logo along the fuselage.

Once Stratton had parked the car, Charles escorted her to one of the hangars, where he introduced her to the Charity plane's pilot, and then the four male passengers – three English and one Dutch – who were charity workers travelling with her.

The man who seemed to be in charge introduced himself as Braam, then told her, "We're just finishing loading,"

With her insides a maelstrom of emotion as she turned to face her Master, she said bleakly, "So it's goodbye then, Sir."

"For now, yes. Maybe I'll come and visit you some time." He had every intention of doing so, though he rather doubted he could be bothered to travel to Africa. Besides, once she boarded the plane, he would be done with her, because she belonged to the Dutchman now. Maybe he would pop across to Holland sometime and see if he couldn't borrow her for a day or two. But then, after taking a shine to Pik's secretary, he was collecting her to be his new, live-in slut when she finished work for the last time this afternoon. Apparently Pik would not be needing her any longer since he had acquired a new slave on his recent trip who would do the job adequately enough when they were in London. And then there would be Rusty, of course, bringing him the diamonds every few weeks and who he would enjoy breaking in to his own standards. Fixing his lecherous gaze on the girl who had served him well, he removed her collar and gave her a final warning.

"Obey your new master, the good Dr Dowling." Her watched as her hand flew to her elegant neck as already she felt the vulnerability of being without a collar. "Remember, Caroline, you belong to Van de Velde now, and he's a ruthless man. Whatever else you do, don't cross him. If you do, I promise that wherever you go, he'll find you. And when he catches you, the results won't be pretty! Don't let me down, Caroline."

"Sorry Sir," one of the charity's two crew members, a tall, no-nonsense blonde man, bustled between them and caught Rusty by the arm, "we have to go now."

Staying her by holding her arm, Charles just had time to kiss the top of her head before she was torn from his grasp. Ushered to her seat, she was strapped in beside Braam and they were in the air within moments.

Whether it was simply that they were unaware up until then, that she was a sex slave and been told to keep their hands to themselves, or that they simply had no interest in her sexually, she was not utilised in any way throughout the long flight. In fact, apart from the crew members serving her with drinks and food, no-one took much notice of her at all; the three English charity workers hardly spoke, and Braam himself was the only one who struck up any kind of conversation. Keeping talk centred around the normal things like movies, it was not until they neared their destination that he laid bare the shocking truth.

"They all know that you're the Dutchman's bitch, and that he put you in my care until we reach Thomassentown, where you'll be handed over to Dr

Dowling. They won't touch you unless I give the say-so. So you see, it's up to me whether you arrive fully clothed and in one piece, or naked and shagged fucking senseless."

She had no time to dwell on his words for a few moments later they touched down. And having had an uneventful flight during which they were the only other passengers, she was totally unprepared for the dramatic changes that followed.

Under the watchful eye of a black, uniformed man with a gun, they hurried across the tarmac, followed by the pilot and the two crew members. While the airport's scant ground crew unloaded the plane's cargo, they went through to the small, airless airport, where Rusty was quick to assimilate the facts that there were seldom more passengers than the guards and customs officials, and that Blawanya was unbearably hot and dusty. She was a bit miffed to find herself shuffled to the back, behind the men. When she eventually had her passport stamped at a small, rancid smelling booth while the pilot and crew disappeared through a door for their onward journeys, instead of giving it back to Rusty, the customs man handed it to Braam.

"Things are different here," Braam explained, "Blawanyan women don't have rights. There's nothing unusual about slavery here."

"But I'm English! Tell him!"

"This paperwork – " the customs official shook it at her, "says you come to live here. That means you obey laws. And laws say we treat you like one of our own," he smiled toothily.

Braam smiled back. "While our plane's being unloaded, I need to see the man in charge about the woman. Send someone to fetch him."

Rusty stared in disbelief and was about to protest when, on an unseen gesture from Braam, one of the Englishmen took her by the arm and the little party peeled off to the side of the room to sit on a ripped, blue leather couch to wait. Braam shared a joke with a couple of the officials, before joining them and settling himself beside her.

"Get used to it. They think I'm your owner."

"My what?"

"Shut up. You're in a different world now and from now on you do as you're told!"

As soon as someone had been dispatched to find the head man, under the scrutiny of the black men who seemed fascinated by Rusty's hair, shockingly, Braam ordered her to stand up and strip.

"In front of them? You've got to be joking!"

"I'm in command and they expect me to keep discipline. So do it, or I'll have to make you," he warned. "Besides, you'll be dealing with these guys regularly, so it's best to start how you'll have to go on."

Was this really what Charles had trained her for? she thought with self-disgust as she got to her feet to comply. Surely he had never envisaged this! Hesitating just a moment, she shrugged off her red cotton top to stand in lacy pink, with her blue leggings tucked into trainers. She hardly had time to stand up before the Englishman sitting behind her alerted the others to her welts.

"Fuck me! Look at her lads! She's had a right pasting and no mistake."

She knew she was being ridiculous, but without the protection of her collar, she felt more naked than she ever had before. Afraid they would jump her, knock her to the ground and shag her, she was frozen to the spot.

"Take it all off, or we'll do it for you," Braam threatened.

Realising she had no choice, she bent to unlace the trainers and removed them quickly. Then half straightening, she stripped off the leggings, following them with her the fine, lacy underwear that had been a parting gift from Charles. In some corner of her mind she admitted that it was a relief to get her clothes off for her skin was already beaded with perspiration. Standing barefoot on the dirty, cracked floor, she coloured up under what felt like hundreds of pairs of ravenous eyes as the black officials gathered round.

And quite suddenly it seemed, Rusty felt a great swell of pride as she listened to her travelling companions' conversation.

"You should have told us, Braam, what kind of filthy whore we had on board."

"Yeah, we could have used her ourselves."

"I've always fancied flogging one of our own."

"Yeah, I know what you mean. I get a bit fed up with the black bitches and I've even tried beating the wife. But she's having none of it!"

But it was not the charity workers who took advantage, but the black men who had swooped by the time the head customs official arrived, and she was already being poked and manhandled by the group.

He said something she could not understand, and immediately they stopped, stepping back to allow the man access. One of the Englishmen shooed them away as the man ran his hyena gaze over the fire-haired English girl whose pale, white skin bore the marks of a recent beating, with livid lines criss-crossed lines over older, fading ones.

Braam stood up and went to stand beside him. "Get to know her intimately, because she's the bitch you'll be dealing with regarding the medicines when they come in from Europe."

"And then," another man took over, "on her return flights from your wonderful country to Europe, she'll most likely have 'a little something hidden' away for you."

One of the men behind her stood up and hissed in her ear as the official began probing and mauling her charms, "that's diamonds up your arse for him to buy his silence and clear the Mustang for take off."

He was used to beating his own wives, of course, and other Blawanyan women, but to have the opportunity to beat a white girl was not something he would pass up lightly. Nor was the chance to fuck her. Summoning one of his men, he demanded, "Take her to my office!" Then to the four Englishmen he said, "you wait here. I get someone to find you beers. You take her when I've finished."

True to his word, he had beers provided. And while they sat back on the couch whose stuffing was bursting through the rips, the official used a stick that he kept in his office for keeping order to brutally beat her. Originally obtained from the tree outside the airport, it was long and whippy and had been stripped of its bark. He swished it deftly, beating her bare bottom with gusto as she leant over his desk, and delighted him with screams that echoed around the entire building. And then she screamed again as he took her from behind and filled her cunt with Blawanyan spunk.

Only when he was completely satisfied and his knowledge of her body was indeed intimate did he march her back, sobbing with shame, to her travelling companions. While his men gathered around once more and enjoyed a last grope, tearing at her breasts, her welts and quim, he gave the charity workers permission to take away their freight.

"And your bitch! Teach that because she's white don't make her special. If you want her to fly her plane in and out like Roy did, she's got to bring special gifts in her arse!"

Once outside, she saw for the first time the old truck that was loaded with the sacks of aid, and the white driver. The driver helped her up into the back and propped her up on one of the hard seats. While one of the men went to join the driver up front, Braam and the other two joined her in the back with sacks. It was then she was finally reunited with her blue leggings and red cotton top, though her underwear had disappeared en route. Dressing hurriedly while the men watched, she discovered that her leggings had been chopped off above the knee. Her top had received the same treatment and now barely covered her breasts, leaving her with a bare midriff. Only her trainers remained intact.

"Remember," she said feebly, "that whatever happened in there, I'm a pilot and I'm only here to fly the bloody plane!"

"You're here because Van de Velde sent you, and everything you do is for him," Braam reminded her.

"You won't tell h…."

"Tell him what happened in there? Of course I will. He'll be delighted!"

Yet after it seemed that she was not to be trusted after her ordeal and, despite the importance of the vacancy she had come to fill, Braam's attitude toward her, and that of his colleagues, changed, and they treated her with the contempt that by now she knew she deserved. Leaning toward her across the sacks between them, Braam tied her hands to rest in her lap for the duration of the long, dusty drive from the airport to the distribution centre.

At last they arrived but she was not allowed to leave the truck. Besides, she had nowhere else to go but to their final destination, and so she sat tight while she watched while men rummaged through the sacks. She noticed they were setting some of the goods aside. Once these were loaded onto the truck again where Rusty still sat, they set off again, this time heading for the Thomassentown mine.

On the way, they stopped at a village where the charity's men set up an impromptu market in the centre of the village. Rusty was mortified to see such blatant re-selling of the donated goods, and knew that Charles would be horrified if he knew. But, of course, she realised with a jolt, he probably did know. The Dutchman too. After all, it was his organisation. And, as she had eventually been informed, his smuggling operation, and Sir was his right hand man. And with a sick feeling in her stomach she realised that Sir probably also knew the kind of indignities she was being forced to suffer.

It was an hour before dark when they arrived at the mine. Rusty found herself forgotten as the few remaining goods – the ones that villagers on the way had rejected – were unloaded and the charity men left them in the care of the mine's guards. And it was here, on her very first day that she discovered the soul destroying truth about the NBAF. For everyone connected with the charity who passed through Thomassentown was aware that while the men strutted around proudly in the Westerner's cast-offs – which they paid for out of their meagre earnings rather than receiving as free aid – and eagerly awaited the next delivery, the slaves themselves never set eyes on the women's clothing which, in truth was never intended for slaves in the first place, since the outside world knew nothing of their existence. In any case, only the most basic of garments, the shifts made locally, were permitted for the slaves. Nor were they permitted anything on their feet. The whole thing was a shameful scam!

It was only when she jumped down from the truck that she was even noticed. Then her hands were untied by one of the men, and she too was given over to one of the guards. Threatening her with all kinds of calamities if she tried to escape, he escorted her to the clinic that she recognised at once from the video at the charity's dinner. A white nurse into whose care she was entrusted welcomed her.

"You're filthy!" the nurse informed her. "You need a good scrubbing down before the doctor sees you. I'll have one of the other nurses do it in a few moments."

Feeling more exhausted than she had felt in her entire life she did not object when she was taken through to a cubicle where the nurse subjected her to a quick and intimate examination.

"I've never seen evidence of so much sexual activity in a white woman! I wasn't expecting a whore," the nurse told her nastily.

Afterward, she called for another nurse to bring a large enamel bowl, a big block of foul-smelling soap, a scrubbing brush and a towel. And then, leaving her in the hands of the second nurse, Rusty was made to stand in the bowl. Having no strength left to object let alone take flight, she did as she was told, and for half an hour suffered the agonies of a literal scrubbing down as the harsh bristles ignited the pain of old welts and bruises, as well as making painful scratches of its own.

Provided with a bed with clean sheets, Rusty was kept at the clinic overnight. It was not until Dr

Dowling arrived around mid morning that Rusty met the man who was to watch over her and provide accommodation. In fact, it was Adair Dowling who had been instructed to see to all of her needs. And seeing her now for the first time as she slept soundly in one of the clinic's isolation rooms, he was well satisfied with the deal he had struck with Pik.

Swiftly, he pulled back the single sheet. "Wake up, slut!"

Alerted to sudden danger, Rusty woke instantly. Opening her mouth to speak, she made to move. But Adair's hand shot out to stop her and he splayed his fingers against her neck.

"Nurse!"

At once the nurse appeared, with a white towel draped across her arm and carrying a kidney shaped dish that contained a syringe.

"Never mind that. Why isn't the bitch tied and chained?"

"Sorry, doctor, but I wasn't sure …."

"Fetch a collar and rope. Now! And a chain!"

The nurse set her things down and hurried away. Not daring to move a muscle, Rusty slewed her eyes right and left, taking in the bleakness of the room. There was not even a proper bedside cabinet, just a rickety and chipped table beside the bed. And Rusty noted that along with the things the nurse had left there, a small flogger with twelve thongs rested. Surely the patients were not beaten? she thought with horror.

"You'll be in my care until it's time for you to deliver the goods. And then you'll report directly to me on your return. To a certain extent, you'll be allowed to come and go as you please around the shanty town, but you may not leave other than to fly your mission. In return for watching over you and providing your clothing, food and a bed, there are two things I want from you. One is ……" he broke off as the nurse returned with the items he requested. Slipping his hand from her neck to her hair, he pulled her into a sitting position and, grabbing her hands, he used the rope to tie them behind her back, then continued as if there had never been a break. "Your complete co-operation since I need to perform a quick and painless procedure." He laughed at her shocked expression and held up his hand to retain her silence. "I don't need your co-operation and am quite prepared to do it without since the procedure has been sanctioned by the Dutchman anyway. Secondly, I want your total subjugation to my will. And this I will have, by force if necessary. Do I make myself clear?"

Her reply was instantaneous and servile. "Yes, Sir."

As he held up a wide, black collar made of stiff leather for her to see, pointing out that in Blawanya the colour denoted that a slave belonged to an individual and not the mine.

"As your guardian I'm simply your master by proxy. Your real Master is Van de Velde."

She just had time to notice that the ring embedded at the front was larger than the one Charles made her wear and there was another one on each side, before he scooped up the length of her fiery copper hair and signalled the nurse to hold it out of the way so that he could fit the collar around her neck.

"He had this one sent especially. Unlike the ones you've been used to, this one doesn't come off!"

She tensed as she heard the ominous Click! when two prongs that formed half of the latch at the back married with two holes to permanently fasten it. The nurse let her hair fall back in place, and Adair pushed her back against the wall. He snatched up the chain and fastened it to the ring.

Holding the chain firmly, he advised as the nurse retrieved the syringe, "make it easy on yourself. Do I have your co-operation or shall I operate without it?"

Her skin was blanched with terror. Without any idea of what he intended to do to her, how could she possibly make any kind of judgement? Besides, she thought woefully, what was the point if he was going to do it anyway? And then again, what was the point in making things more difficult than they need be? Visibly trembling, and still with her hands tied, as he held the chain she looked up at him hopelessly. "Y…y…you have m…..my…..co-op…." Unable to continue, she let out a loud sob that shook her shoulders.

"Good girl. Nurse, continue."

With no appreciable bedside manner, the nurse tapped her upper arm, held up the syringe, and then simply jabbed.

"Aaaarghh!"

Adair tugged on the chain. "Come on, hurry you stupid bitch. We've just got time to reach the theatre before the injection works."

As she slipped groggily from the bed and followed where he led on legs of jelly, she had no way of knowing how basic the theatre was. Nor did she know that she would not make it the short distance. Falling unconscious as the small party passed through the isolation room door, Rusty was scooped into his arms and carried the rest of the way to the tiny shack at the back that served as the rarely-used theatre.

The first thing Rusty was aware of after the procedure was a soreness in her back passage. Assuming that the doctor had taken the opportunity to fuck her up there while she had been out for the count, she manoeuvred her still bound hands into a position whereby by stretching, she could finger around her own hole to discover whether or not there was the flared base of a butt plug. Finding nothing, she lay back and tried to work out where the earthy, woody smell was coming from. But her eyes were heavy and within moments she was asleep again.

She awoke to find herself still breathing in the strange smell. She discovered that she was lying in a similar bed as in the clinic, except this time she chained was by her collar to the wall above her. Except it was not a wall......
not a real one in any case but something else entirely, something rough and an odd shade of light brown.

Nor was she alone. Sitting on a squat stool beside her was a black girl, who introduced herself as Freedom.

"I'm Master Dowling's slave, and we're going to be sisters! Master said you're going to live with me here," Freedom told her excitedly and spread her arm in a gesture that took in the oddly shaped, sparsely furnished chamber. Without stopping for breath, she went on to explain that "here" was actually the inside of the great baobab tree at the bottom of the doctor's garden.

"My bed's over there. I'm chained every night, unless Master wants me to attend to him, and you will be to. And we'll be beaten together too, side by side."

"Oh….." feeling weak, the last thing Rusty wanted just then was to be beaten. But seeing how excited her new 'sister' was….. a sister who wore a brown collar, she noticed….. she managed a smile and, realising her hands were still tied behind her she said, "that's nice. Listen, Freedom….I've had some kind of operation….."

"Oh, that's nothing!" she laughed. "It's so Master can find you if you wander off, that's all."

Turning suddenly as something caught her eye, Rusty saw a black man standing in the giant fissure that was the entrance to the tree's hollowed-out interior.

Then without asking he strode in and stopped beside the bed.

"He's Jacob," Freedom told her as the servant unfastened the chain from its ring above her head in the tree's bark.

"The doctor Sir, he wants you. He says 'hurry.'" Pulling the chain roughly to encourage her from the bed, without waiting for her to find her feet, he jerked the chain again and set off, dragging the poor girl behind him.

Naked, barefoot and with her hands tied, she had no choice but to follow, crying out as her soles made painful contact with unfamiliar, spiky plantlets and leaves.

At last she found herself in an airy, surprisingly well furnished and whitewashed room at the back of the adobe bungalow. One bookcase was filled with an impressed collection of erotic literature as well as medical tomes, and a second one contained several dozens of paperbacks. Occasional tables and colourful rugs were dotted throughout the sizeable room, and tribal art hung on the walls. There were three sumptuous-looking leather sofas, as well a wing chair. And it was in this chair that Adair Dowling was sprawled, with a glass of beer in his hand.

"Jacob. Good man. Put her over there. You can untie her hands and unclip the chain."

When Jacob had deposited her on the floor in front of one of the couches directly opposite Adair's chair, he was dismissed with a wave of the hand.

"You're very trusting," she told him as her treatment so far rekindled her old defiance. "Aren't you afraid I'll run off?"

"Doesn't matter if you do. You see, on your master's orders, I've sewn a little device.....GPS to be precise.....into the wall of your anus. It doesn't matter where you go, I'll find you."

For the first time, her duties were fully explained. First and foremost, she was employed – yes, there would be payment just as her master had promised – to transport diamonds from the mine to Holland, where she would hand them over to him. However, it was not straightforward because there would be no duty paid on them. To this end, she was to bribe the customs officials – both here in Blawanya and in the Netherlands – with a few stones that she would secrete especially. He assured her it would be easier for her than her predecessor because, as a female she could hide them up her cunt as well as her arse!

"Arse for the Africans, who will also refuel you each time, and cunt for the Dutch. Of course, you'll have to slip them into your cunt after you've been cleared by the Africans because they've been promised sexual favours from you too." He laughed. "Of course, you're already acquainted with the customs officials. According to Braam, you had quite a time of it, and I'm sure the 'gentlemen' will be happy to see you again. Whether or not you offer yourself to the Dutch is up to you, but I'd advise against it."

She pulled a face that suggested she was already bored by the subject. "So where do I get these diamonds?"

"I'll supply them. But where I obtain them is no concern of yours." He drained his beer glass, called for Freedom to fetch him more, then continued. "You'll spend a few days in Holland each trip, during which time your master will utilise you in your role as sex slave, whoring you to his associates as well as using you for his own pleasure. He'll then supply you with medicines and bandages donated legitimately by the

Netherlands Blawanya Aid Fund, so the only bribery needed will be sexual."

Freedom arrived with his beer. When he had taken it from the tray, he told her to show the new slave her cunt, which the girl seemed surprisingly happy to do, Rusty thought. Standing directly in front of her, the girl pulled up her shift and thrust her hips toward the sitting redhead.

Rusty gasped in horror. But at the same time she was almost overwhelmed by the flames of arousal that licked the insides of her belly as she focussed her attention on the savage-looking stainless steel clamps which seized and crushed her dark and swollen pussy lips. Chains attached to the ends of the clamps and fixed at the other end to a restricted steel band around her waist drew the lips apart, revealing the soft, coral interior that glistened with honeydew.

"That's enough, you black bitch. You can let her smell it later! And take that fucking shift off. And you," he pointed to Rusty as Freedom pulled the shift off over her head, "I told the Dutchman I didn't want you here, not a filthy tramp like you. I told him you'd be trouble and that he should find another male pilot, but he's not a man to take advice. So just remember what I said, if you want feeding and a roof over your head, I want you subjugated to me. If that's what it takes to get the job done, then so be it. I won't make allowances – as far as I'm concerned, you're just a whore. So, let's start as we mean to go on. All fours, now!"

Rusty was quick to obey and waited on hands and knees for the next command which she knew would not be long in coming.

He took a swig of beer then, addressing Freedom again, he sent her across to one of the tables to fetch a flogger. Then he made her put it in Rusty's mouth before dismissing the black girl. He had another swig of beer before making Rusty crawl across the room to bring it to him.

With his gaze zooming in on her wobbling breasts as she crawled toward him, he unzipped his trousers, pulled them down his legs and removed them. He stood up as Rusty approached and offered up the flogger. He snatched it violently from her soft lips. Then after lashing her thirty times across her rump and then another thirty across her breasts, he had Freedom bring the trolley, and he clamped her delightfully long nipples with the square clamps he used on his black slave. Then he had Jacob remove her to the garden, where she was mounted on the frame while he staked Freedom face down on the ground. When his slave had taken thirty lashes with a single tailed whip without uttering a sound, he turned his attention to the mounted English girl.

"Let's see what you're made of. I'll give you the lashing of your life, just to find out if you've got the blood of a white woman or a black slave-whore." He slapped the undersides of each breast to see them wobble again, then tightened the clamps. Then he stood back, braced himself, and struck.

Crack!

"Aaaarghh!"

Crack!

"Aaaarghh!"

And to Adair's surprise, the sixty, spirited lashes he delivered, spread evenly – apart from those he lavished on her tortured tits – down her front from neck to feet, brought him such pleasure that he felt he was a man in paradise. With her pale skin welted, her nipples clamped so harshly they were made amusingly purple appendages to her inflamed tits, and her ridiculously, fiery hair plastered with sweat to her face, she was quite the most beautiful creature he had ever set eyes on.

And he could not deny that he was greatly amused by the prospect of shoving the metal canister shoved up her arse, and even more excited by the thought of the customs officer removing it when next they met.

The days and months passed. With no thought now to her brother, to Charles or the life she had once led, Rusty accepted everything that came her way with grace and obedience.

The rhythm of her life was a restricted one, though that did nothing to downgrade her lust, which grew rather than abated. Although she was humiliated regularly, she felt no remorse and somehow extracted a small amount of pleasure for herself from almost every dishonour she encountered. Her real, glowing pleasure came from knowing she was doing the Pik's will, for she was always mindful that he was her true master, and everyone else – even Adair – merely his representative.

Sometimes Adair wouldn't touch her for days, and she was never quite sure whether it was because he was punishing her for some unknown act of disobedience, or that he simply preferred black girls to white. But when he did utilise her body, either with Freedom or on her own, it was always an occasion to be relished, for the cruelties he inflicted were agonisingly sweet, and the "medical" disciplinary proceedings undignified and sweetly, divinely humiliating.

Within a few days of her arrival, the whipping post was relocated and another put in its place, a similar but sturdier post with the addition of a crossbeam and two bracing struts at the bottom, so that he could mount the two girls upon it at the same time. Some days he ccopied the Baobab tree's furry-coated seed-pods that looked like rats hanging from their tails. Using rope that Jacob wove from the tree's bark, Adair suspended the girls by their feet. With their hands tied behind them, Rusty knew he found them an amusing sight. And he told them that it made whipping them an absolute joy.

Because of the tracking device, within certain time frames set by Adair, she could come and go around the shanty town pretty much as she pleased without the fear of being molested. The mine workers themselves viewed the white woman as some kind of ethereal beauty who, as the property of the doctor, was off limits. And so although the guards searched her simply for the sheer hell of it, it seemed they too were in some way afraid of overstepping the mark with the doctor.

And so she relished the indignities imposed upon her by the African authorities at the airport, and the men who refuelled the plane, all of whom treated her as some kind of hybrid by subjecting her to contempt as if she were one of their own women, and at the same time seeing her as some kind of Goddess that they were privileged to defile. From Blawanya to Holland and then back again, the whole operation went smoothly, the bribes being paid in occasional, low-grade stones or rolls of US bank notes. But whichever it contained, the canister's contents were always gratefully received, as were her ever hungry cunt and unprotesting rectum.

And then, at the end of each flight, there was either the refined sadism of her master and his friends who wined and dined her before abusing her and presenting her with expensive gifts – all of which he kept for her in his safe – or the efficient cruelty she and Freedom shared. Either way, every aspect of her life was dictated, processed and deliciously perverted. The only time she experienced anything like freedom was when she was in the air, just her and the Mustang.

CHAPTER TWELVE

AFRICA, SIX MONTHS LATER

Having located the middle of the bundle of rope that was coiled at her feet, the Customs official draped it loosely around her neck as she stood barefoot and naked on the floor of his office. He glanced at the generous, coral-tipped breastmeat that was spattered with colourful bruises and tiny amounts of scabbing. Tempting as always, they were readily available for his use.

Taking the rope in each hand, he proceeded to bind her breasts in a figure of eight. He used that configuration twice before binding each delicious, bouncing globe separately, first one as he noticed that its usually pale, freckled flesh was taking on a pink tinge, then the other, also pinkening, building up the layers until the rope was coiled attractively and tightly.

He pulled the ends of the rope up between them then tied them behind her neck. And never had he seen a neck that was so charmingly graced by her a collar. It was not just that it was black, stark against her white flesh, it was more aesthetic than that.

He took a couple of steps backward. For a few seconds he just stood and admired the work he had done on this unusual white bitch that he had the good fortune to sexually maltreat on a regular basis. Sometimes he found her already carrying the livid evidence of another man's beating, and at other times he had a beautiful expanse on which to inscribe his own marks.

The blossoming breasts were turning a very deep pink indeed and stuck out even further than normal!

He always enjoyed the restriction of her tits, the way their flush grew deeper the longer and tighter they were tied, burgeoning like.......he laughed.

"Now they look like a baboon's arse!" he told her unkindly, and watched her own gaze drop to take in the grotesque swelling and discoloration of what he had no doubt were agonised breasts. He walked to the corner and returned with his stick. "Now they're ready!"

Her scream curdled the air itself as the stick crashed down across the tight drums that were her breasts. Laughing, he beat the wildly, then he glanced down and noted the wet patch on the floor between her feet. Either the whore had wet herself, or she as soaked and fuck-ready. But first, there was something more important to attend to.

"It's time you paid me!"

Without being told to, she turned around and bent over. At once she felt his fingers at her bottom hole. Prising it open, he stuck his fingers inside as he rooted around for his prize. Then, as they always did on such occasions, he extracted the metal canister the size of a lipstick that contained his bribe.

Once he had released her and she was given clearance, she returned to the Mustang trusting that it had been refuelled. Wriggling about in the small confines of the cockpit she buckled herself in. She slid the canopy into its closed position. With flutters of excitement at the prospect of being airborne again, she checked the dials. As always the flight would not be logged. How could it be, since it was illegal to smuggle diamonds? If she were to be discovered, the Customs official would deny she had ever been there in accordance with the long-standing deal he had with the Dutchman – a reward for the contents of the canister.

It would be several hours into the long flight before she would have to place an identical one in her quim for the Dutch officials. And it was a long, long way from Blawanya in southern Africa to Europe.

Pulling back on the stick, she eased down the short runway, readying herself for takeoff. Her excitement was mounting in a way that was almost sexual. She relished being in the air again, and took advantage of the all-round vision offered by the canopy, levelling off at a below-legal altitude, to take in the sights of Africa and its wildlife. She was on an incredible high, even more so than usual, and somehow in her brain everything merged, from the erotic binding of her breasts to the indignity of having her rectum searched to the spectacular views unfolding below her to the freedom of flight........ she gave a little giggle...... it all melded into one almighty high that she would not change for the world. Nothing compared with the eroticism of being alone with your thoughts in the sky!

She gained height, though she probably would not take it to its maximum altitude because she was having so much fun. Still climbing. There was something special about today. She didn't know what it was, but there was such a throbbing in her cunt and a giddy happiness spreading throughout her being that she just knew that something wonderful was going to happen today. She felt so emotional that she took full advantage of her situation and began a series of stunts. It felt like she was playing with the clouds, wrapping them around her as if she were wearing them. God, this was great! she thought as she dipped and dived, spinning and weaving ......

She giggled. Half-heartedly she told herself that there was no time for this fun. She was already well behind schedule. If she didn't arrive on time, Pik would get anxious. She wished there were some way to let him know that everything was okay and that she was on her way. But she could not, of course. Still, if he got really bothered, he could always get Adair to check her progress on his computer, thanks to the tracking device he had implanted in the wall of her back passage! Even though her flights rarely followed the normal flight path to Holland it would be easy enough to track her down.

So why not just enjoy herself?

And with this thought at the forefront of her senses, the sky worked its charms and she bathed in the glory of real freedom. Up here, with Africa spread out like a relief map below, almost behind her now. The wrinkled sea stretched before her beyond the coast, everything was fine and anything was possible. And time, like the plane itself, flew so that she lost all track of it and rarely looked at the instruments. There was no need. Everything was fine. Leaving her worries behind her as she climbed, she smiled, and was so engrossed in the beauty of the emptiness, the expanse of sky and the land below that she hardly noticed as her hand strayed to the front of her jeans. Sliding the zip down, within moments she had frigged herself to the stage where orgasm was imminent. Her cunt muscles clutched at her finger…

A noise caught her attention. She frowned as her climax evaporated. She would have to try again. There was the noise again. Something was most definitely amiss. Rusty looked down at the old instruments. The fuel warning light came on; she was almost out of fuel. No, she couldn't be. She had been re-fuelled at the airport. With the addition of the droptanks there was easily enough. She tapped the glass on the gauge. She remembered mentioning that the instruments needed servicing.

"Switch to reserve tank," she told herself aloud.

There was a phutt phutt sort of sound. So she was short on fuel! Those bastards hadn't filled her properly! She was losing altitude. Phutt phutt. Panic gripped her, making anus clench as the plane began to splutter. Now she was in real trouble. Shit! She didn't dare put out an emergency call because of the clandestine nature of the flight. Phutt......there was nothing for it; she would have to land. She looked down, she was over the sea now. There was no way back.

Below, an island. The mountains reared up. She began to circle, looking for a spot to bring the plane down. She had flown over these mountains many times. Just watch out for the big one. There had to be a place to bring it down. She over flew a sprawling, low-rise building, probably one of those places that had been turned into a hotel for wealthy tourists. There was nothing for it; she would have to land and then go up to the house on foot for help.

No time to plan it – she had to land......now!

God, there were trees!

Dazed, Rusty pulled herself free of the wreckage. Not too bad, only torn clothes and a few cuts and bruises. But the plane – ah, that was a different matter. Luckily it hadn't gone up in smoke that would have been visible for miles, but the undercarriage had been torn off, it would not be going anywhere soon! She needed help. Food. Water. But most importantly some way to get the diamonds to her master!

She stood and looked around. It was a miracle that she had missed the trees! She was in a small clearing of a wooded area. She picked bits of twig and other vegetation out of her hair as she gazed about her in wonder. Yes, it was a bloody miracle!

It had also been the most exhilarating ride of her life.

In a daze she stumbled some distance before she came out of the trees, to find herself on a scrubby plain. It was only then she realised the full extent of the miracle, for she could have gone crashing into the mountains that loomed ahead of her.

In the shadow of the brooding Draco Cueto, the sun was setting. She thought of going back to the wreckage. But no! There was no time to retrieve the diamonds now. She would have to come back later. But first she must get help. She made her way through the scrub, every now and again flicking her gaze upwards, at the mountain. Squinting to try and see better, she spotted what looked like – even from this distance – some kind of funicular railway, and some kind of terrace about half way up. She had no idea where she was and even if she had known, it would have made little difference, because until she landed on the island that seemed to rear up out of the sea and was pretty much all mountains, Rusty hadn't paid much attention to what appeared as little more than a smudge on her charts off the African coast, just North East of the archipelago that formed the Canary Islands.

At last she came to a dirt track that wound its way upward toward the plateau, and the sprawling place she had seen from the air. Below her was a beach that looked so inviting that had she not been feeling like absolute shit….. but she did not have time to take the thought any further because she heard footsteps behind her. Turning, she saw a man dressed in a blue short sleeved shirt with some Spanish word across the pocket, and dark blue trousers. His whole appearance shouted "guard".

His tone was brusque as he challenged her in Spanish.

"Hi. Is this the way to the house?" she said in English, and wishing she could speak Spanish. She could then at least explain that she was holding her ripped trousers together and not just clutching her crotch

"You're from the plane?"

"Oh good, you speak English."

"What's your business here, miles from anywhere?"

"I had......that is my......" of course he had seen the plane! But she could not simply tell him the truth for fear of the guard calling in the authorities or, worse still, stealing the diamonds. But then again, judging by his uniform, he was the authority in these parts. Thinking quickly, she said, "I had a row with my boyfriend. He threw me out of the car and abandoned me."

"When? No car has passed me. You're from the plane."

"Plane? What plane? No, I told you, my boyfriend threw me from the car. Oh, it must have been hours ago. I had a lie down in the grass I was a bit upset.... you know how it is.....I must have fallen asleep. Look, are you going to the house up there?"

He answered her question with one of his own. "What's the matter with your cunt?"

Straight to business then! Rusty thought as she glanced down to where her hands were clutching her crotch. Her leg was hurting now and looking down at her leg she saw a dark red, wet patch where blood from her scraped knee oozed through her trousers.

"I fell over."

"And your face?"

What about her face? She put her hand to her cheek. Blood. It was not much, but obvious enough to be noticed.

"I must have done it when I landed."

"Landed? In your plane."

Once again, she had to think quickly. "I landed heavily when I fell from the car." Realising how implausible her story was, she grew irritable. "Look, are you going to the house or not? I need to get to a phone.....I've lost my mobile. And I could do with something to eat. Is there a hotel or something?"

The man began to rummage in his pockets. He took out his mobile and made a quick call, talking in rapid Spanish. When he had finished, he put the mobile back in his pocket.

"Strangers not welcome here. Tell your story to Mr Cortez and Pilar, see what they think."

He produced a pair of handcuffs and before she could react, he dragged her hands from her crotch and fastened her wrists behind her. At once and quite inappropriately given her precarious predicament, all she could think of was her time with Charles. And she wondered how she had failed him, for she knew she must have done something to offend him, or else he would never have given her to the Dutchman and she wouldn't have gone to Africa and then ended up in this mess. She thought again of Adair, and wondered how long it would be before he and her master realised......realised what? That she had absconded with the diamonds! Would they even consider that she was in trouble? Of course, she would be in even more trouble if they found her! If only Charles were here. He would know what to do. As her ripped jeans flapped in the breeze and revealed her tiny panties, she thought longingly of her times with him, and all the wonderful times she'd had at Saxon Hill. She would give anything..... anything..... to be back there. But as the guard reached for her pussy, she already had the feeling that that life was lost to her forever.

"Don't you dare touch me! Let me go!"

"I thought you wanted help?"

"I do, but......"

"Then shut the fuck up." He slipped his hand inside her panties and at once his brutal fingers entered her.

Within moments she was swaying on her feet as exhaustion and delayed shock took their toll. And arousal too. God help her! How could she get aroused at a time like this? she berated herself.

The guard pulled out his finger that was slick with her juices. He looked at it, laughed, lifted it to his lips to suck it clean, then walked around behind her and with his hand between her shoulders gave her a shove, not in the direction of the plateau and the comforts of the building she had seen but in the direction of the Draco Cueto.

"Start walking!"

Half an hour later she was seated in the back of a little motorised buggy.

The handsome Spaniard sat behind his desk and feasted his eyes on the sexy, white lace panties that stretched across Rusty's mons, as still cuffed, she stood in bra and panties before him. He raised his gaze to the bare flesh of her midriff above them. Next he turned his attention to the matching bra, its lacy half cups barely containing breasts whose upper swells rose and fell enticingly with each breath she took.

"What's your name?"

There was something compelling about his Mediterranean looks that caught at Rusty's concentration. She felt as if his dark, unfathomable eyes were peering into her very soul. Her mouth was dry and, trying to find moisture, it was a few seconds before she licked her lips and replied. "Rusty. Rusty Paget."

"Turn around, Rusty Paget." He waited as she obediently began to circle on the spot, all the while watching her. He adjusted his position to sit more comfortably and used a long, tanned finger to flick stray lock of coal black hair from his face. After she had made three revolutions he asked, "Does your master flog you?"

Taken aback, Rusty stared in amazement. She realised, of course, that the collar was a bit of a give-away, but who, exactly did he mean? Charles, Adair or Pik? Even she was confused. Her head ached. She had to concentrate. He was talking about her master…. she was being stupid, he could not possibly know any of them! It was nothing but a wild guess on his part. Still, if they did manage to track her down, it would be better for her if she had told the truth.

"Yes….." what was the question? Why couldn't she concentrate? Those big, dark eyes, looking at her….. "he flogs me."

Noting the lack of marks on her skin and the absence of even the faintest bruises, he demanded, "when was the last time?"

"Last week…..the week before…..I don't recall exactly."

"I don't recall exactly, Sēnor!" he corrected. Then as if losing patience he told the guard, "Take her to the sick room."

"Si, Sēnor."

"See that her injuries are attended to. Then have her cleaned up. Give her something to eat and drink. And for God's sake get her something to wear. She can sleep in one of the guest rooms tonight. Bring her back to me first thing in the morning and remove the cuffs!"

As the guard moved to release her, Rusty felt the room swaying. A hand shot out to grab her.

Rusty blinked. The light was coming from the side, where a large window had its shutters flung back. She blinked again. Her head ached. She must have fainted. She felt for her collar…..yes, it was still there.

Comforted, she fiddled with the three rings, then felt around for a chain – even Pik put her on a chain at night, she thought as she realised there wasn't one – and she thanked her stars that she was safe. For the time being. She had to get in touch with Pik, let him know she was safe. And the diamonds.

She rubbed her eyes as she began the process of waking fully. Thankful of a good night's sleep in a comfortable bed with lots of pillows and clean, white bed linen, she realised there was a beautiful Spanish woman sitting on the edge of her bed. Dressed in a short, red, diaphanous robe that was cinched by a sash at her waist and fell open over her shapely thigh, she had a small fortune in glittering diamonds that formed a choker around her Mediterranean-shaded, swan-like neck.

"Buenos dias ….." the woman smiled a warm greeting. She leaned forward and with feather softness, she ran the back of her fingers up the side of Rusty's face.

"Good morning. You slept well?" she said in attractive but heavily accented English.

The back of her hand was still at Rusty's temple and, in a moment directed by instinct alone, Rusty raised her hand to hold it. "Yes, thank you. Shall I…?"

"Shhh. No, lie still and relax," she smiled.

As the woman slid her hand free and moved it to her own head instead to smooth her short hair behind her ear, Rusty noticed the glint of gold and could not help but admire the wide wedding ring that graced the woman's elegant finger. Then wondering how she could have missed them, she noticed that on her arms, midway between shoulder and elbow, she wore beautifully crafted gold bands, with chamfered edges, that were an inch or more wide.

Smiling, with a feeling that everything was going to be alright after all, she settled back against the stack of fluffy pillows.

There was a creaking noise as the door opened and they both turned in the direction of the old oak door that admitted a pretty girl with long, black hair tidied into a loose coil at the back. She was carrying a tray on which a coffee pot took pride of place, with sugar bowl, small milk jug, cup and saucer. And given Rusty's recent past, it should not have struck her as odd that the girl was naked, except for a little white, frilly apron that did a bad job of covering her sex. But Rusty could not help wondering what kind of hotel, if hotel it was, she had stumbled across.

"Gracias, Isabella," the woman said as the girl set the tray down on the bedside table. The woman turned to Rusty. "Milk?" Noting Rusty's nod of confirmation, she told girl, "Café con leche." While the girl poured the coffee, the woman introduced herself. "I'm Pilar. Yesterday you met my husband, Alvaro." She paused to give the girl an instruction in Spanish. The girl gave a little curtsey and left the room. Once Rusty had taken the cup and began sipping, she continued. "He said you had trouble remembering what happened. So let me help you. Yesterday, some of our guards witnessed a plane coming down."

Now it Rusty's turn to smile. And the smile was genuine. "You knew all the time!" She laughed, and although she could not put her finger on why, exactly, but she had the strangest feeling of warmth toward her. And she found herself wanting to confide. But she could not tell her everything, not yet. Instead she confessed, "I was flying from Blawanya. But I hadn't been refuelled properly and, as you say, I came down. In the trees"

"Luckily, you weren't hurt too badly. But I'm afraid you fainted…."

"What day is this?"

"Jueves – Thursday."

What happened to Tuesday and Wednesday? she wondered.

"We had to have you brought straight here instead of to the sick room. But my maid, Consuela, cleaned you up and tended to your wounds. Here," still sitting on the bed, she turned to reach behind, then offered Rusty a robe. "Borrow this until we get you sorted out."

"Thank you," Rusty said, then in an attempt to extend a hand of friendship she smiled and said, "Gracias."

Pilar nodded graciously. "De nada, you're welcome." There was something almost conspiratorial, Rusty thought, about Pilar's' smile when she said, "We have a special way of life here, we like to share things. We are very private people."

Rusty nodded wisely.

"What was your cargo?"

She bit her lip. "Cargo?" she said, stalling for time. "It's only a small plane, no room for cargo!"

"Yes, there was cargo. It doesn't matter anyway. Our men have located the wreckage in the woods. We'll find the cargo soon enough." Pilar stood up to leave. Again, the conspiratorial smile. "You must be hungry. My husband invites you to join him for breakfast on the terrace."

BLAWANYA

It was National Day and declared a public holiday. Across the landlocked country the celebrations were raucous and wild. While in the desert the day passed almost unnoticed by the nomadic tribesmen and their enslaved womenfolk, in the scattered kraals of the savannahs the men feasted and drank to excess. Meanwhile their enslaved women tended to their every need, and fed every greedy male belly with their own meagre share. Then with legs flung wide they had no choice but to accept every cock that demanded entry, or accept beatings with sticks from the elders, all the while plying the men with yet more drink in the hope of just a few hours' liberty.

In Thomassentown, the black slave who stood in front of the isolation cage was one of a recent consignment whose period had rendered her "unclean." Now she was fit for work, but before he handed her over to one of the guards, Adair taught her how things were done around here. Making her lie on her back in the dirt, in full view of the other isolated slaves, he kicked her legs apart. Terrified, and not daring to move, she stared up at him as he used the toe of his shoe to hook up her short shift. With his foot resting on her naked, black-frothed pussy to keep her in place, he took his vibrating mobile from the pocket of his white clinician's coat and took a call from an anxious and angry Pik.

"She hasn't arrived in the Netherlands?"

According to Pik who, concerned by Rusty's uncharacteristic lateness had already contacted the Blawanyan officials, her only scheduled stop on her uncharted flight had gone without a hitch; the head man had received his bribe and she had been refuelled for the rest of her flight.

"That means she's somewhere between Blawanya and the Netherlands," Adair told him coolly.

"The old plane may have come down." Pik sounded uncharacteristically anxious as he pointed out that the area was too vast for his men to search, adding, "we can hardly report her disappearance and call in the professional agencies to search because that would jeopardise the whole operation! In that case we have no choice but to take the loss."

Chuckling as he considered that it was the loss of the diamonds and not the girl that concerned the man most, with deliberate mischief Adair voiced the other possibility. "Or she's done a bunk with the goods." At the same time he remained unperturbed as he removed his foot from the slave's vulva and crouched down. Jabbing his fingers up inside her, he was already looking forward to Rusty's punishment when she was finally tracked down, he told him, "the bitch won't be hard to find. No worries. I took the precaution of sewing a GPS tracking device into her anal wall."

"Good man!"

"When we find her, it'll be my privilege to discipline her with a beating like she's never had before." He drew a furled whip from beneath his white coat and shook it out, stepping back to allow himself room to swing it.

"I'm head of the operation. Besides which, she's actually my bitch! I'll administer her discipline. You find her."

"I'll report back within the hour." As Dowling broke the connection, he brought the whip down across the slave's thighs.

CHAPTER THIRTEEN

Having freshened up in the ceramic-tiled en suite whose white porcelain utilities were encased in dark oak, Rusty cast her gaze around the bedroom. As she donned the short, floaty, black chiffon robe on loan from Pilar, Rusty realised that what was now a comfortable guest room with pastel walls and old oak furniture – and something that looked remarkably like a clumsy, older version of a whipping bench that Charles had in his playroom – was in fact three rooms that at some time had been knocked into one. It was obviously part of an old building, and she realised that the individual rooms would have been quite small.

She went to the window and looked out onto lush, flowering vegetation, with the sea beyond. It was impossible to see the beach from here and she realised she was on the steep side of the plateau. Directly outside the window, between the vegetation and herself, was a covered walkway and, once outside, she realised it could once have been something like a cloister. That would make the rooms cells, possibly for monks or nuns.

She stepped outside and closed the door behind her. She was just wondering whether to turn left or right to go in search of the terrace when she heard someone shouting rapidly in Spanish. It was coming from an austere-looking woman who rounded the corner. Dressed entirely in black, the Spanish woman whose grey hair was sticking out from beneath a black headscarf, continued shouting. She seemed to be looking for someone who Rusty, hazarding a guess, thought was probably the individual whose big, straw hat showed an inch or two above the vegetation. Rusty ducked behind the vegetation and met the gaze of a naked girl. Smiling to show her good intent, Rusty gestured at her to remove her hat and keep down. The girl muttered her thanks, and then Rusty sauntered out straight into the path of the shouting woman.

"Excuse me," she began, pushing her fiery, unkempt hair from her face.

The woman stopped in her tracks.

Adding a note of question to her statement, Rusty said hopefully, "I'm looking for the terrace."

The woman gabbled in Spanish, before giving directions in rapid but just understandable English.

"Gracias," she smiled, then dodged out of the way as the woman marched off, still shouting. As she walked through the garden with Pilar's black robe fluttering in the breeze and tickling the back of her thighs, she could not help wondering how she would react to her sharing an intimate breakfast with her husband. She wondered also how she felt about all the naked young girls flitting around. Apart from the girl in the bushes, she had seen two others, both with similar hats, on her way to the terrace.

But she needn't have worried. As soon as she rounded the corner and stepped onto the sunny terrace, where Alvaro was drinking his second cup of coffee, she realised it was not going to be so intimate after all. For beneath the table was another naked girl, on her knees with her head bobbing as she fellated him while he sat with an open paperback before him. Smiling as she took in what for anyone else would probably come as a shock, Rusty also noticed that the girl's hands were tied behind her.

"Good of you to join us," Alvaro said, looking more handsome now than he had done before. The smoothness of his voice concealed his brutal nature. "What would you like, juice or coffee?"

"Juice, please," she smiled nervously, eyeing the jug of freshly squeezed orange. She stood for a moment but when he did not offer a seat she sat down anyway. When he made no comment, she reached for the jug.

"No."

His voice was enough to stay her hand.

"Consuela will do that. Now, take off the robe, you won't be needing it."

Oh, what the hell! she thought, realising that enough people had seen her naked by now as to make no difference. Slowly, she untied the belt and slipped it off the shoulders, letting it flutter to a delicate heap on the floor.

"Come. I want to examine your cunt."

She swallowed the shock that caught in her throat. She was a whore, after all, so why should she be surprised to be treated like one? she asked herself as she got to her feet and walked around the table, beneath which the girl's head bobbed enthusiastically. Without being told, Rusty took up the open-legged stance with her hands on her head. Proud of her own obedience she did not move a muscle or make even the slightest sound as, without preamble, two fingers shot up inside her and stirred her juices which, she realised with a start, were already shamefully collecting in her hot well of desire.

"Let's be clear. I prefer hands behind backs. Makes the tits stick out more."

At once, she moved her hands to comply, crossing them behind her.

"This is a place of slaves," he told her unnecessarily as he continued to probe with his hard digits, showing no mercy as they dug and twirled inside her. As her pussy squelched noisily, he went on, waving a hand in a gesture that took in the whole island. "Would you believe, the island didn't even appear on European maps until the thirteen hundreds? As my wife – or any historian – will tell you, Guavencia has a long history of slavery."

His voice was sexily hypnotic and she found herself hanging on to his every word. "It was African slaves who dug all the terraces on the hillside. Later, when the slave trade was at its height, it was from here that slavers took them to the New World." He withdrew his fingers and seized her hip. Then turning her round, he pressed her forward so that she squashed her breasts against his paperback on the table, and her head shoved the coffee pot aside, knocking it over. She turned her head on her side and laid her cheek in a little puddle of cold coffee. While someone unseen hurried forward and tidied the mess, and the girl beneath the table sucked louder, his fingers drove into her once more and he continued his shockingly-hard molestation, so matter-of-factly as he continued his account that she felt the indignity like the turning of a knife in her chest.

"So you see, nothing has really changed, except that now we don't export slaves, we keep them. There are slavegirls who do the gardening, slavegirls to do the chores and slavegirls to keep me…..and my wife…." he gave a little chuckle as he added, "amused. So now I find I have another one to replace the one I gave to the Dutchman."

The realisation hit her like a ten ton lorry. He knew Van de Velde!

"So the first thing you must learn is your place. And that is not sitting at my table!"

" Sorry, Sẽnor, I thought……"

"Don't think, it's not your place to think!"

He withdrew his fingers suddenly and, standing up so abruptly that the girl beneath the table had no option but to expel his cock, he wound Rusty's hair around his hand to pull her to her feet. At the same time, with his other hand he flipped the catch and threw back the hinged lid of an ornate, jewelled casket that sat in the centre of the table. About six inches long, three wide and six inches deep, she saw that it contained a bundle of sturdy, silver chains which he now withdrew. Still with his fingers scrunched in her hair, he used clips on the ends of two of the chains to attach to the sides of her collar. Then releasing his hold on her hair and holding her by the chains instead, he turned her around to face him. He drew the chains forward and crossed them between her breasts before taking them round behind her, where he crossed them again and brought them back to the front by way of her hips, then threaded them back between her legs, taking care to nestle them on either side of her nether lips. Then he clipped the two ends together. That completed, he took four more items from the bottom of the casket.

"Restraints," he told her as he held up the silver slave bangles to show her, each one a simple band about two inches wide with a ring embedded. He fitted them first to her upper arms, and then to her ankles, and as the metal bands snapped closed she realised that the interlocking halves ensured they could not be removed. She knew she had seen something similar recently, but for the life of her could not remember where.

She was just beginning to glory in his apparent oversight in not securing her hands, when he drew a further chain of no more than six inches long with a clip at each end from his pocket. Telling her to put her hands behind her back and her arms as far back as possible, he used the chain to clip the two arm bands together.

"Consuela!" he called and almost at once, the shouting woman she had seen earlier appeared, almost as if she had been hovering close by, Rusty thought. And she knew it was for her benefit and not the woman's that he addressed her in English when he said, "The new bitch wants juice. See to it."

"Si, Sẽnor."

As Alvaro returned to his seat, opened his legs and drew the girl back to his crotch, the woman she now realised was the maid gripped the chains where they joined between her breasts and led her a short way across the terrace to stand beside the house. And she understood also that the maid's duties coincided pretty neatly with those of McBain. Then, hissing harshly in Spanish, Consuela pulled her down to her knees. Using the chain between her arms, she fastened her to the end of an old, rusty chain that was already in place. That done, she fetched a stoneware dog bowl which she filled with juice from the jug and then placed it on the ground in front of where Rusty knelt.

After a couple of words to Alvaro in Spanish, they both laughed, and she reached under the table to drag the girl away by her collar. Staying on her knees, the girl just had time to place her hands on the ground before the maid hauled her across to a similar chain in the wall, where she was secured by her collar and given a similar bowl.

"If you'd be so good as to fetch my wife, Consuela," he said in English, before adding something in Spanish.

It was a very different Pilar who appeared with the maid on the terrace a short while later. Gone was the elegant woman who had sat on Rusty's bed, and in her place was a docile beauty. Naked, she was led by the maid on a golden dog leash that was attached to a ring at the front of her diamond choker, subjugated to her husband to the extent that she crawled along the terrace on hands and knees just as the girl had done.

With a jolt, Rusty realised that the exquisite choker of diamonds around Pilar's throat was as much of a slave collar as the black leather one adorning her own neck. But there was one other thing Rusty noticed and which made her breath catch in her throat and her heart flip over in the most curious way; Pilar carried a flogger between her teeth, just as the she herself had done for Adair. Consuela brought her to a halt on Alvaro's left hand side where both the girl and Rusty could see the leash wound round the table leg and secured with a clip.

Alvaro looked at her coolly, then dismissing the maid curtly, he ripped the multi-stranded flogger from Pilar's mouth so roughly that Rusty knew it must have hurt her. Then after berating her in their own language, causing Pilar's shoulders to shake as she tried to contain her anguish, he switched to English so that Rusty could understand. And in her turn she trembled.

"You failed me, bitch. I wanted answers and still I have none. What I do have is a little metal canister that contains a few rough diamonds. Hardly enough to warrant a plane!" He shoved it under Pilar's nose. "This is all I get for sending a slut instead of doing the job myself! Find some answers, I said. Find out if it's Van de Velde's plane! For God's sake, stop your fucking snivelling! You know how much I hate that noise. Quiet! Now you're going to pay for your failure."

Scraping back his chair, he began to count the lashes as the flogger fell hard. Having been ordered not to make a sound, she remained silent as they fell across her rump, spreading its plethora of leather thongs in what was clearly a punishment beating and not, as Rusty had soon learned to distinguish, a pleasure beating….. neither would gain from this!

"Forty-two, forty-three….."

By the time he reached fifty, there was already a fine scattering of bruises beginning to develop, and pinpoints of blood were clearly visible though the skin was not yet broken. And still he was still poised to hammer them home before the lovely woman made so much as a whimper. And such was her control that without the assistance of any restraint other than the chain which secured her to the table, she kept her pose on her hands and knees.

She watched as Alvaro took a few seconds to wipe his brow and swig a drop of orange juice. Suddenly, he swivelled round and faced Rusty, addressing his words to her rather than his wife.

"That's the level of obedience I expect from you." Jerking his head toward the girl, he went on, "she'll never be any good! But I can't let her leave the island because she'll tell her archaeology colleagues about the wonders she unearthed before she was captured and I got my hands on her. So I'm stuck with a bitch I don't care for. But since you're here......I have high hopes for you!" With that, he positioned himself once more and continued with Pilar's flogging as his wife retained her pose.

"Seventy. Seventy-one....."

As she watched with horror, Rusty's emotions began to tangle. She had seen many women beaten before, yet never had she felt such a wild sense of arousal as she was feeling now.

"Eighty five......"

"Aaaarghh!"

For the first time Pilar screamed. And to Rusty's shame, she licked her lips, her gaze and thoughts centred entirely on Pilar's discipline. And she felt her own arousal like a fire in her belly that was so hot and consuming that she wondered why she had never felt it so acutely before. And bizarrely, she wished with all her heart that she and Pilar could swap places, and that the lovely Spanish woman would feel as aroused as Rusty herself was now.

"Aaaarghh!"

But there was still the problem of the diamonds. If they had the canister intended for the Dutch customs official, then it would not take them long to find the rest. And then when her master found out......she let the thought die, not wanting to dwell too closely on what Pik would do as, unbelievably, she felt orgasm approaching. But that was ridiculous, no one was even touching her!

"Ninety-eight....."

Forgetting all about the diamonds, instead, as she shuddered and moaned her way through an orgasm that was totally the result of another woman's suffering, she made a silent vow that when the opportunity rose, she would live up to this devil-man's expectations and prove herself worthy. And her mind went back to how she had once proved herself worthy to Charles.....so long ago it seemed..... and she with sudden insight she knew that abseiling naked was almost a piece of cake to what Alvaro was asking.

"One hundred."

Crying, shaking and still maintaining her position, Pilar turned her tear-blurred eyes lovingly upward to her husband.

CHAPTER FOURTEEN

It was just hours later that Alvaro gave Rusty her chance. Except it was not quite the way Rusty had imagined it. Without any kind of restraint or – as far Rusty could see, supervision – she and Pilar enjoyed a glass of Spanish wine together. Sitting on a stone seat against a retaining wall which held back the vegetation of the terrace behind, they laughed happily, naked and as comfortable in each other's company as if they had known each other for years they sat close, each with an arm around the other's waist.

"What's going on here, Pilar?" she asked quietly as they sat together in the garden.

It was as if something inside the Spanish woman snapped. Loosening her hold and drawing back, Pilar looked at her as if she were some lower life form that had just invaded her paradise. "Don't speak, just listen. Your Master…."

Playing for time and because she was not sure which of the men in her life Pilar was referring to, the confused girl stood up. Forcing a smile as the thought of the diamonds weighed heavily on her mind, she said too innocently to be convincing, "I don't know who you mean."

"I said be quiet! This is your only warning, next time I'll slap you."

"But really, I don't ……"

Pilar was on her feet in and instant and her hand shot out and dealt a stinging, open-handed blow to Rusty's face.

Rusty jumped, shocked more than hurt. It was just the same as Charles had done all those months ago and in the same way her hand shot to her cradle her cheek. She sat down heavily on the stone seat again. Uncertain of the woman's temper, she thought it best to co-operate when Pilar told her, "just do as you're told. Sit quietly and don't move."

Pilar reached behind a gorgeous exotic, flowering bush and withdrew two spreader bars that had not been put away after a previous use. She grabbed one of Rusty's wrists and, knowing what was required of her, Rusty responded by placing the other one behind her back also. Using the leather restraints fixed to the bar, Pilar fastened it between her wrists. And she had a good idea what was coming next as, still standing behind her while she remained seated, Pilar turned her collar round so that the central fastening ring was at the back. But unexpectedly, Pilar shunned the chain already hanging from the wall and instead, clipped one end of the second bar to the hook and the other to the ring on Rusty's collar so that her head was forcibly held in an upright position and was maintained at a set distance from the wall.

"Now I have your full attention, we'll begin. As I was saying, your Master will be wondering where you are. You know we've found the plane, so what were you doing flying over here? Did you run away with Van de Velde's diamonds? Not that it matters greatly," she said, waving the matter away with an elegant hand. "The important thing is that you're here now and, as it's doubtful you'll be found."

Rusty was doubtful about everything on this island..... except that she would be found....after all, there was the GPS device implanted into her back passage.

Pilar said something in Spanish, then translated. "Don't worry, I'll be back in a moment. I have to fetch something." With that, she gave an elegant twirl and simply left her alone, at the mercy of every guard that came along.

As her head swam, too late she realised that the guard who had first found her and Alvaro were not the only predators on the island. And as memories of Judith came unbidden to her mind, she realised that sweet, submissive Pilar was something of a Dominant herself as far as other women were concerned. Then there was the odd situation between the Consuela and Pilar..... who was really in control of this island? All kinds of possibilities presented themselves, and not all of them were desirable to a grounded pilot who realised that all that stood between her and the wrath of the Dutchman and possibly even a prison sentence was the strange set-up on this strange island.

How long she was alone or where Pilar went she had no idea. Nor did she know what the woman had gone to fetch. But she was pretty sure that whatever it was, it would bring pain with it.

Familiar feelings that had no place here, especially in the hands of a woman whose own position was far from clear, began to resurface. There was an excited pounding of her pulses as blood rushed through her veins when she saw Pilar almost quick-stepping toward her.

There was no fumbling as Pilar went about her business, she knew exactly what she was doing as she fitted the clamps in place and forced Rusty's long nipples through the narrow openings. And she wondered if the cruelty was perhaps greater, for another woman knew exactly how the clamps would feel, they were circular contraptions with openings in the centre, that at first glance could easily be mistaken for some new design of hair slides or ponytail clips because there were certainly teeth around the opening that could grip the hair to hold it firmly in place.

The fear of pain started directly they were fitted over her nipples. The actual pain began a millisecond later.

Pilar fitted them as far back as possible, right to the root of her nipples so that they rested against the breasts themselves, she knew they were not harmless teeth but tiny, spiteful and surprisingly flexible tines whose pin-sharp points nestled against the thin and tender skin of her nipples as they closed around them. With both devices in place, with a slightly evil grin Pilar used her thumbs to simultaneously operate what appeared to be tiny fastening catches underneath, but were in fact the means of driving the tines into the nubs themselves. As they punctured the flesh, the excruciating pain was almost too much and she screwed up her face as if that could somehow help her cope. She would not give her beautiful tormentor the satisfaction of a scream and so she held her breath, biting bite into her lip so hard that she tasted blood. Her nipples responded to the cruelty as they blossomed through the opening by turning from their normal coral to scarlet.

Still she remained stubbornly mute. She absorbed everything and just kept her gaze locked onto Pilar's. But she became uncomfortably aware of Pilar's womanly scent. And a frisson of need clutched at the very root of her as, acting instinctively, she opened her legs.

"Don't be in such a hurry," Pilar purred, her accent growing even thicker with lust. Leaning toward her, she placed a hand on each side of Rusty's head she moved her own closer.

Rusty tingled as she felt Pilar's breath on her face, then her stomach muscles clenched, partly in revulsion and partly in excitement as Pilar's pinkly feminine tongue entered her mouth. Unable to pull away because of the rod attached to the back of her collar that kept her a set distance from the wall, or push her away because of the similar spreader bar between her hands behind her, she endured the violation of her mouth. Consumed by pain and passion, her breathing matched Pilar's as it grew louder. But the tongue became more voracious as it rapidly explored and penetrated the warm cavity. This isn't a man, Rusty reminded herself as her eyes closed in response, this is wrong….. I shouldn't feel like this…..no woman should kiss this way….. so sensuous…….sublime…… Her eyelids fluttered and she just had time to see that Pilar was responding by closing her own, before Rusty's closed too. Her tongue tangled deliciously with Pilar's with a desire she would not have believed possible. This is a woman! she told herself again, except she really didn't care.

When Pilar finally pulled away, both women were breathless.

"Are you hurting?" Pilar asked, gesturing toward Rusty's nipples with such a look of concern that she believed she was about to release them.

Glancing down she saw they were already taking on that familiar bluey-purple tinge.

"Yes," she said truthfully.

Pilar's laugh was so utterly feminine that it made Rusty's stomach clench again. She watched Pilar's beautiful mouth as, still breathless, she talked.

"I'm my husband's bitch, his slave. I love him more than I love my own life. As you'll have already discovered, when young women unwittingly come to Guavencia, we seldom allow them to leave but put them to use working, or if they are desirable, then they join me as one of my husband's sex slaves. If you stay with us, then you'll become his slave too. But you have to be truthful with us because, if your master is who we think he is, then the decision may be out of our hands. But if you do stay, I'll be your lover. But I'll always be your Mistress first. Understand?"

"I think so, Mistress," Rusty smiled, according her the title willingly.

"Now I must go and attend my husband. I'll send Consuela to fetch you and take you to your room." Leaning close, she kissed her on the lips, then stood straight once more and after promising that Rusty would be happy with them, she left her alone once more.

And there she stayed, until Consuela collected her about an hour later. Although she was not chained in her room, she was forbidden to leave it, and a guard was posted outside to prevent it. She was brought a meal of suckling pig and fresh vegetables, and fruit juice to drink.

Then after taking a shower, she fell into bed. Forgetting all about diamonds still hidden in the wreckage, and the master to whom she still belonged, she slept right through until morning.

Rusty woke early the next morning, to find a hand-written note on her bedside cabinet. Having showered and brushed her hair, she slipped on another robe that Pilar had lent her, this time a white, gauzy creation. Then she set off to follow the directions she had been given.

Following instructions, after taking a breakfast with the other two sex slaves, that had been laid out ready for them on the terrace, Rusty walked in the garden. She was walking along the narrow terraced pathways in the garden, when two of the guards found her. But when she asked for help, instead of giving her directions on how to get there, with one behind and one in front of her, they marched her along other terraced pathways to a level part of the garden that she hadn't yet seen.

The courtyard was on a plateau and created in the Moorish style, though whether it was original fourteenth century or a later revival Rusty could not tell.

Breathtakingly peaceful, there was a large, sparkling pool with water lilies, and a channel that irrigated the myrtle and orange trees growing alongside, the whole scene dominated by a magnificent fountain of lions heads. Beyond were the ruins of what looked like a monastery.

The guard's roar shattered the peace. "Down!"

Rusty looked from one to the other, then dropped to her knees, close enough to the fountain to feel the water splashing on her face. As the two men began to unfasten their trousers, without being told to she opened her mouth, her eyes wide and her heart beating rapidly with the prospect of giving head as casually as if she had been asked to put out the rubbish or switch the kettle on. She was beginning to think that this was where she belonged, that at last she had found a home where she was appreciated. Licking her lips to wet them, she took the first guard's tumescent penis into her mouth, taking it deeper into her throat than she had ever done before.

"Make sure you swallow every drop!" she was told in English as it was clear he would not last long. And so it proved. After just a couple of minutes he spurted his hot semen into her accommodating mouth, before surrendering his place to his companion. But this time her mouth was shunned in favour of her cunt.

She stretched out on her back when told to and opened her legs. Then without demur she allowed herself to be violated. And when he had used her to his satisfaction, he grabbed a handful of leaves from one of the bushes, wiped himself clean and advised her to do the same, even pulling off the leaves himself.

It turned out that she still had a short way to go, and the men took her the rest of the way to the ruins she had seen from the courtyard. First they removed the robe, then checking that the necessary equipment was on hand, they positioned her to Alvaro's specifications. After a quick check that everything was in order, they left her alone to wait among the ruins in the early morning sunshine.

Two pillars standing about four feet high were all that remained of a narrow archway that had once opened onto arched cloisters. Like a doll whose owner has stretched the legs almost to breaking point, it was on the top of the pillars that Rusty's feet rested. Her legs were straight, with each ankle shackled, the chains of which were secured to fixings in the ground. Positioned between her thighs was a metal pole with an ancient, large girth dildo fixed to the top. Expertly cast in solid gold with every vein standing proud, it was deeply and painfully inserted into her vagina, with her naked, stretched-to-their-limits pussy lips giving the impression of petals clustered around a stamen. To keep her mouth open, an "O" ring was fitted in place so that although she could not close her mouth or speak, cries were still possible. To complete the picture, a set of Pilar's magnificent, two inch long drop diamond weights dangled from her nipples, flashing and sparkling as they caught the light. And behind her, a spreader bar was employed to keep her hands apart, the ends anchored to the ground by more chains and pegs.

But Alvaro was not an early riser, and so for two hours she was forced to suffer the cramps of being in one agonising position too long, and the burning pain of limbs stretched at a peculiar and unfamiliar angle, and strained muscles. Not to mention the agony of the golden dildo!

When Alvaro finally approached her, strolling along the pathway with all the
time in the world, the sun was already high. It was turning into the kind of day that any normal girl would

spend on a beach, by the time he stood before her, with a furled whip in one hand, and a malevolent glint in his eyes. As panic and relief fought for control inside her, she drew in a breath that caught in her throat and resulted in a short bout of strained coughing.

Alvaro stood directly in front of her, looking up at her as if she were some kind of statuary that had appeared in his garden overnight. Then laughing until her coughing subsided and leaving streamlets of tears on her cheeks, he began his accusations, his accent thick with either lust or anger.

"You haven't been honest with me. You should have told me about the

tracking device in your rectum wall because it's pinpointed your position accurately. Last night I had a phone call. And I can tell you that Dr Dowling is not pleased. He wants you back so that he can show you what happens to runaway slaves."

He turned and disappeared behind a clump of flowering shrubs whose sweet fragrance had been her only comfort during her wretchedness. When he reappeared it was with a wheeled contraption that she soon realised was a set of steps at the top of which was a platform that would bring him up to a height whereby he could wield the whip with ease and accuracy to her raised body, with no risk to himself since the railings around the platform would prevent him from falling. And, she noticed as he wheeled it into position in front and to the side of her, that he locked it in place by pulling a handle. As he mounted the steps he continued.

"You're the second pilot that's let Dowling down, so you can understand why he's upset. On the other hand, someone called Charles Hilton simply wants you back!" He unfurled the nasty-looking whip. And she noticed that his accent was growing stronger.

"He's upset because you've failed him when he had invested so much time and money on your training. But most importantly, the Dutchman is a very unhappy man! He wants his diamonds back! And reparation for his lost plane. I wouldn't want to be in your shoes when he gets here! Yes, he's really coming…. should be arriving some time tomorrow. Don't look so surprised. Did you really think no one would come for you?" Like the conductor of an orchestra, he shifted his stance slightly and raised his arm, except it was the whip rather than a baton he held as he braced himself. "Now the problems all that causes me are these….." An expert in disciplinary whipcraft, without warning he laid down ten, savage lashes across her weighted breasts before he began itemising the list.

"I've been harbouring a known criminal."

Whoosh! Crack!

"Aaaarghh!"

It was a surprisingly well-formed scream given the O in her mouth, he thought, and set-to producing another. And another. Then a flurry.

Having established a pattern, so it continued, Alvaro listing his issues and then striking her breasts repeatedly in-between, each whoosh and crack of the whip being followed by a scream. And then there was another item from his list.

"I've been disciplining another man's slave…"

As she jerked under the blizzard of strikes and her screams grew louder, he began to vary the amount as he struck her, continuing to punctuate the physical cruelty with mental anguish as listed the trouble she had caused.

"Or rather three men's slave and……."

Whizz! Crack!

"Aaaarghh!"

~ 245 ~

"I shall have to face their wrath."

He gave her a few moments respite then began again in earnest, the rhythm of the strikes evenly but rapidly spaced and delivered with greater force so that her cries rang out across the island.

Whizz! Crack!

"Aaaarghh!"

Her breast meat was a mass of red with darker welts already developing over the first. He changed aim and struck across her weighted nipples, and his attention was caught not by the horrific sight of her blue-tinged and cork-like nubs that were dragged downward but by the way the massive diamonds on the ends jerked and danced, flashing their brilliance wildly.

"And it turns out she's a diamond smuggler, trafficking vast amounts of high grade diamonds for months. Now I'd rather like to get hold of the Dutchman's diamonds myself ……."

More screaming.

She could not remember when she had ever felt so alive, so aware of every atom of her body. It felt like her blood was on fire as it rushed through her veins. Exciting whorls of arousal spiralled out of control, turning her insides into a heated cauldron of lust. Her breasts felt as though flames were blazing across them and her weighted nipples grew ever heavier as the unbearable throbbing continued. It was so exciting! And through it all, her aching limbs burned. Each scream proclaimed her agony and tears stung her eyes. Thought had no substance, she was just pure sensation…..that elusive thing she had searched for all her life.

"I need to find them."

More screaming. How did the bitch still have the energy?

He paused a moment and when he began again, he reverted to his earlier, slower pace, not for her benefit but simply because there was little point in exhausting himself when she was so obviously close to insensibility.

Whoosh! Crack!

Even as tears flowed down her face, her cries of pain transmuted into feeble whimpers. Determined that she would stay conscious just long enough for him to reach the end, he raised his voice then aimed a particularly nasty strike that wrapped itself around to her back.

"Pilar's grown fond of you and……."

Whoosh! Crack!

There was no answering scream as she screwed up her eyes. With her mouth open, she looked almost as if she were yelling in orgasm. But that was ridiculous, of course. If it had been Pilar, he could have understood it, but not the copper-headed whore.

"I'd hate to give away one of her valued treasures…"

"Whoosh! Crack!

Still no cry, still the screwed up eyes……

"I'd hoped I could keep you myself."

There! He had said. The delivery of the next few lashes was brutally hard, and had her opening her eyes in horror as her whole body jerked.

Whizz! Crack!

"Aaaarghh!"

That was more like it, he thought with satisfaction as he told her, "I really can't afford to pay all three men their asking price. It's Pilar's money….her fortune," he confided, "she was Van de Velde's whore, but she offered me everything she had to become my slave. He was besotted with her and, luckily for me, though he was a harsh master he couldn't deny her anything. When he realised how determined she was to belong to me, he actually paid me a dowry! In return, I had to promise to leave her fortune untouched. So you see….."

Whizz! Crack!

"Ooooohhh!

"I really can't afford you! So, what shall I do?"

The question was rhetorical, of course, but as he finally laid his whip aside – the final tally being in excess of one hundred – the delicate skin of her breastmeat was rawly welted from the lashes that had left him exhausted and gasping for air.

He took a few moments to recover himself, then moved around behind her and began to work on her back. As her screams were torn from her throat to escape in gargled form from her O shaped mouth, they drowned out the click click of approaching stilettos. He was only a quarter of the way through the hundred lashes he planned to give her shoulders which were already ablaze and criss-crossed with scarlet lines when he was interrupted by Pilar, who came up behind him. Naked, apart from her diamond collar and stiletto heels, with her own breasts welted and sore, she dared to stay his arm before backing off to stand just in his line of vision, with her hands crossed in front of her.

Lowering the whip and chiding her angrily in Spanish, Alvaro reverted to English. Offering the whip to his wife, he commanded, "here, you take it! My arm's already aching and I want to see the bitch's back shredded for the trouble she's caused."

"Yes, my dear husband-master," she answered meekly as they swapped places. "How many shall I give her?"

"Keep going until I tell you to stop. And don't even think of going softly on her just because you want her to love you, make every one count."

Backing off slightly out of the line of a stray strike, he watched as his wife steadied herself, took aim, and then began a barrage of lashes that even he would have been proud to deliver, and left Rusty in need of being carried back to her room.

It was later, while Pilar was tenderly attending to Rusty's raw welts with soothing ointments that Rusty confessed the truth that could land her in even more trouble than she was already in.

"The diamonds," she blinked, her pale eyes sparkling as she smiled, "there are two waterproof pouches. They're hidden in the droptanks."

Having received news that the Dutchman's arrival was imminent, Alvaro had Rusty left on a lead for him outside the building he used as a dungeon. Reached by an impressive archway into a courtyard, it had once been a large hall of some description. But now it housed all kinds of trestles, frames and other delights.

When Alvaro arrived to unhook her from the outside wall, to her surprise he had a laptop under his arm. Once inside, she noted the chains hanging down that, unlike the ones in Charles' playroom had nothing attached to them except restraints. He directed her toward the centre of the room where a sturdy, metal pole, with a circumference of not more than sixteen inches, stretched from floor to ceiling. Still confused by the strange relationship between the man, his wife and the other slaves, and not entirely sure what was and what was not acceptable behaviour, how far she could push him, and refusing to be fazed by the bewildering array of equipment she saw around her, the tone she adopted was glib.

"I'm many things, but I'm no pole dancer, Sěnor!"

"You don't need to be. You just have to stand in front of it. Even a brainless slut can do that!"

Excited by the prospect of fulfilling her purpose, the purpose that Charles had trained her for, it was with a feeling of exhilaration that Rusty did as she was told.

Nothing seemed to matter except pleasing this man, despite the fact that her true master was, even as she smiled at Alvaro, on his way to the island.

He sauntered across to stand beside her and temporarily balanced the laptop on the top of one of the whipping frames. Then he collected some black nylon rope from a wardrobe-like cupboard. Standing before her once more and working quickly, he extracted one length of pre-cut rope from the bundle, dropped the remaining rope on the floor then told her to stand with her back pressed against the pole and her arms above her head.

"Bend your elbows," he said sternly. As soon as she was standing as directed, he made her press her palms together. "Keep them there, don't lower them."

Wrapping the rope around them several times, he passed it between them and finished off with a figure of 8, then repeated it before finally fastening the rope. Then repeating the order not to lower them, he extracted another, longer length of rope which he used to bind her tightly to the pole, above and below her pale, freckled breasts. Tied so tight that it was sure to leave grooves in her skin, she winced as her breasts blossomed – attractively Alvaro thought – between the two bands of black rope that prevented her from moving even a fraction. Next, he made her cry out as he clipped a simple, metal clamp to each long, coral nipple.

"Does that hurt, girl?"

Unsure whether he was as hard-hearted as the other masters in her life or whether the affection she was sure he felt for his wife extended to slavegirls like herself, she didn't know whether it was confirmation or denial that would please him most. As the various ropes bit into her delicate skin, her breasts throbbed and the clamps rapaciously squeezed her nipples, diffidently she settled on the former.

"Y….essss, S….S….Sẽnor."

"Master! How much does it hurt?"

Again, there was a slight hesitation. "Y….yes…..Sẽnor."

"No more Sẽnor. By the end of the day, I intend to have you for mine. From now on you'll call me 'Master.' I think you said something about it hurting?"

"Yes, M….aster. It's…..ver…..very pai….."

"Painful?"

This time she was surer of herself as his dark eyes looked into her watering ghostly ones. "Very painful, Master."

He threw back his head and laughed.

"You see, girl, 'very painful' isn't good enough. I want it to be excruciatingly painful!" He went to the cupboard again and returned with two, elliptical brass weights with clasps at the top, which he fixed to the clamps.

She gave a yell as once her constricted and suddenly heavy breasts were dragged downward. She glanced down to see they were extended…. more cone shaped than round…..and already changing colour.

"You're almost ready," he informed her with a vicious smile, pointing out that there were also clips at the bottom so that he could add more if the fancy took him. But for the time being he seemed satisfied with things as they were. He spread his palm on her belly, and to the quivering, fiery-haired girl it felt as if he were trying to push her into the very heart of the pole. "I want you to rest your hands back against it, without lowering or straightening your arms. That's it."

Keeping his hand on her belly, he crouched down and pulled her right ankle behind the post, telling her to put the left one round too. When he tied them behind the post, it had the effect of making her bend her knees, forcing her to lean forward while the ropes above and below her breasts held her fast. Then he retrieved the laptop and, balancing it in the crook of his arm and using the other hand to open and operate it, he selected a programme and hit a few keys in a seemingly random fashion. But almost immediately there was a whirring noise that spoke of unseen bolts disengaging, operating a previously unnoticed floor-to-ceiling panel in the pole, sliding sideways and opening to reveal an inch wide groove behind her. He pressed another couple of keys and she heard whirring and clicking noises as something unfolded inside the groove and from the floor. It turned out to be a very clever little device in the form of a sturdy hook which extended from the groove and, obeying the laptop's commands, travelled upward until it came to the rope that bound her wrists. Then mechanically hooking the rope, it travelled on further upward, bearing her full weight unaided and, she panicked as her feet broke contact with the floor, it lifting her a good few feet off the ground.

"Aaaghh!"

"Quiet, girl!"

And as the hook still continued its upward journey and she found her arms and legs straightened, his continued use of the word "girl" instead of her name….. any name…..was beginning to make her wonder if it mattered to him who he abused, just as long as he could abuse someone. She was just coming to terms with her painful and stretched predicament, with her legs straight and ankles tied behind the post against which her spine was held fast and hurting between her shoulders and at the base of her spine, when the whirring announced that another panel was sliding back on the opposite side of the post. And once the groove had been revealed, a second hook unfolded and travelled upward until it came to the rope binding her ankles and locked itself in a position whereby raised her feet further upward, causing a concertina effect that bent her knees outward to expose the soft flesh of her inner thighs, and once again bending her arms. With her elbows bent outward her armpits and upper arms were exposed. And the way she was tied that ensured her captivity and total helplessness, and with her arse against the pole and her buttocks virtually separated by it made her feel as if her pussy was being pulled backward also….. in any case her cunt lips were open, exposing her hole! And not only that, but it was placed at just the right height for him to penetrate with his fingers. It was an uncomfortable position and one she hoped she would be able to endure for as long as her current master wanted, because with sudden insight she knew that it was he….. not Charles, Adair or even Van de Velde himself that she wanted to be with, for always.

And she wished with all her heart that he would think of someway to keep her there, hidden from the other men who sought her, because she realised that, for the very first time in her life that she was actually in love. Stupid as it sounded, she knew it had to be love because surely there was no other emotion, not even the adrenaline surge of aerobatics, that could make her know without a doubt that she would endure whatever it took to make him happy. Basically, if it was what Alvaro Cortez wanted, then everything was right with her world. Except even then in her high state of pain-racked arousal she had confused love with willing submission. It was an easy enough mistake to make, but even if she was too blind to recognise the truth, Alvaro knew very well that it had nothing to do with love and that she was on the road to utter subjugation. And with that in mind, he made a few final adjustments to his laptop, snapped it closed, then walked toward her.

She hung her head to look down at him with eyes that were pain-laden and sparkling. And it was then he noticed their odd shade and tagged it as champagne.

"Very pretty, very pretty indeed," he said indolently as he took in her anguish, studying every detail of her restrained, vulnerable body. Homing in on her already juicing cunt, he used his thumb and forefinger to flick her blatantly exposed and engorged clit from side to side, then slid the forefinger of his other hand inside her moist hole. "You're fucking soaked, you filthy bitch! Listen! I've never heard such disgusting noises coming from a cunt!"

He was right, she thought shamefully, it was indeed noisy as he continued slipping his finger in and out, in and out, in and out……he built up speed…..in and out, in and out…….flicking with one hand and plunging with the other……in and out…..until Rusty, watching him with her head bowed as she hung on the post, moaned with delight at the distracting sensations that harassed her tormented clit and incited her quim. Even the pain in her breasts and weighted nipples diminished in comparison. And so overcome was she that she failed to notice Van de Velde and his companion enter the room and take up temporary residence in a corner where a good view was guaranteed.

"I….I….sor……" she tried to speak coherently, to tell him how she felt, as horribly aware of the disgusting sounds emanating from her sweet-drizzling tunnel, she wanted to make amends for…..for what? She didn't know. All she knew was that if she were as disgusting as he said, then she was sorry, even though her heart sang with pride. She tried again. "Forgive……forgive this filthy sl….sl….." Did he think of her as just another slut or one of his slavegirls? She hoped the latter and dared to utter it. "F….forgive this slave! Have pity, Master," she begged, not knowing if she wanted it granted or denied.

Without removing his finger, he gave a quick glance in the newcomer's direction, he acknowledged their presence with a nod of his head before turning his attention back to the slut. Changing tack, he withdrew his shiny finger, wiped it across her belly, stopped his agitation of her clit, and concentrated instead on her breasts. Reaching up, he a gave sharp tug on one of the weights, sending a bullet of pain in a direct hit to her cunt.

"Aaaarghh!"

With a cool smile he noted that her cunt quivered and juice even more. And so he gave a succession of sharp tugs on each weight, listening to her howling in a way that warmed his loins, and made him want to fuck his wife. And such was his cruelty that he could not wait to share the knowledge with her.

"No, no forgiveness! A slut as filthy as you deserves nothing but the very worst kind of punishment. But I can't be bothered with you, not while the sun's shining, my cock's throbbing in my pants, and I've got a wife whose cunt is far superior to your slutty crack! I've done with you! I'm going to seek satisfaction with Pilar, sink my cock deep inside her and give her the spunk that you don't deserve."

Rusty was desperate now. "Please! Master! Fuck me! I love you!"

"Good," he said as he turned his back, trying to suppress his laughter and hide from her the fact that mistreating her had given him more pleasure than he'd had in a while and had made him so horny as hell. As he crossed the room, he called out in strongly accented words, "Then that will make it all the more pleasurable to wring every ounce of agony from your pathetic, dirty body. By the way....." he laughed, you have visitors!"

It was a good few minutes before she could focus on the two figures before her. And when she did, she rather wished she hadn't.

"Gibbo! Master!"

"It rather looks to me as if you have a new Master," the Dutchman told her. "By the end of the day, we hope to have come to an agreement. I get my diamonds back, and use of his whore-wife for the duration of our visit ....."

"Three days," Gibbo leered.

"But of course, I'm being rude! But then, you already know Gibbo. But I suspect that what you are only just beginning to realise is that Gibbo is my new pilot."

"But.....the plane....."

"Your brother is doing me the greatest favour in fitting out a plane for me as we speak. All he wanted in return was that I make guarantee your continued happiness. And it looks to me as if you're quite happy where you are. What would you say, my friend?" he asked Gibbo.

"I'd say so. Or at least, she will be when I've given her a good thrashing."